The Dinosaurs Ball

The Dinosaurs Ball

Cristopher Nash

CARCANET

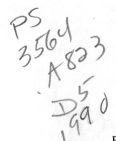

First published in Great Britain 1990 by
Carcanet Press Limited
208-212 Corn Exchange Buildings
Manchester M4 3BQ

British Library Cataloguing in Publication Data

Nash, Cristopher
The dinosaurs ball.
I. Title
823'.54 [F]

ISBN 0-85635-854-1

The publisher acknowledges the financial assistance
of the Arts Council of Great Britain

Typeset in 10½pt Bembo by Bryan Williamson, Darwen
Printed and bound in England by SRP Ltd, Exeter

For my father

Dear   ,

I am overcome by your interest in my little gag-book.
I'm sorry, then, to have to bridle your hopes. In the years since
my manuscript went (so silently?) into the 'predecessor's drawer'
where you say you've uncovered it, the words have evidently grown
indecipherable; as unfathomable in your world as your swift and
splendidly confident signature is to me. Between your interpretation
and mine chasms open that defy our stepping further along the path
you appear to fancy.

There never was any 'dark and elemental truth' – you are wizard
with slogans – about those waggish pages. They were written as light
relief at snatched moments (backstairs, locked lavatory cubicles, turn-
ings of deserted corridors), to make a jolly yarn, full of catchy carica-
tures and topical institutional jibes of a satiric sort, no more than a
dash of dissident graffiti scrawled on the buckling walls. I do gags.

I am advised it has taken me weeks to write to you this many
sentences. But they are complete sentences, I think. Tidy composition
is, under the circumstances, of the essence, and so I go on composing
and recomposing here. Time of course makes no difference.

Where is this 'luminous honesty' you talk of? The American indi-
vidual in whose 'person' my writing claimed to speak was a fabrica-
tion. I never, from when I entered the thicket of his dreary and
astonishing case, found my way beneath his skin as he did under mine
with all his silences. Many – his wife, his brother, the man Hinkle,
others – I never saw but were woven out of the weft of his scattered
daft utterances and the warp of my own ravelled unspeakable imagi-
nation. (O sweet composition, this!) No allegory, no deathless truths.
An impetuous shudder of social protest at its best and fugitive, a
fading negative, a tapestry's mere cartoon.

Who is not smothered under the leaves of voices?
You applaud his 'indestructible ribtickling humour', given his

7

'appalling predicament'. That was never humour in him – not a· jot, not a grain. I gag. I would never have 'loved' him then – or so execrated him now, out of reach as I am of all his petty and monstrous contradictions, beyond even laughter.

Buckling walls? they're as smooth, clean and unchanging as the smile of God.

And what at last can those pages' 'meaning' matter? language exists to put a breathing space, dilating and shimmering, between us and the real thing. Or how should you for one, stood in its presence, survive, whoever you are?

You must of course, for your peace of mind, carry on, yes do with me as I did with them. Out of this scribble cut a paper dolly you can call your own. In fact, I can save you pointless anguish. I never 'regret' but indeed retain many fine practices from my brief time in the healing, the caring profession. I cherish cleanliness and the common sense of things, scrub my hands and arms and hourly change my gauze mask, have discovered for myself the benefits of keeping still, and am thus tolerably treated here, rendered nightless, vowing with every breath not to dream, never aspire to 'take my life into my own hands'. I am gagged. I invented it, do you understand? light-crazed, I invented it all. It is barren and untenanted from beginning to end. Words are dry leaves. I made a bonfire of this man. For pity do not spread it, publish it, while anything – even a whisper of a hair – remains of me.

E.R. Arkwright, M.D.

Incredible as it may seem, I've never made the acquaintance of the Archbishop of Canterbury. What can I say? It never rains but it pours.

Looking back, I should have seen instantly how the situation was deteriorating when I reported home from the doctor's and Teresa started keeping separate sets of dishes.

But first things first.

There's been a rotten misunderstanding from the word Go.

The door had opened and two had come out, one weeping, one pallid, and someone had called 'Next please'.

So what, if you chance to go falling about for a second or two? – the 'queue' had been long, my knees excessively locked perhaps, the head gone a trifle woolly – what's the difference? Did I ask for it? do you *plan* such things to happen in a doctor's waiting-room, to have your whole Condition called into account? Okay, so that's where I made my first mistake.

'Yankee, are we?' cried the doctor eventually. 'I did my pre-intern whatsit in Winetka!'

You didn't, I murmured.

'You aren't just a whistling dickie!'

Dixie, I explained.

'I see. Dixie. Cheers!' he said, clamping open my lower jaw with a tongue stick. 'Mr Wall,' he said with growing warmth, 'let me put you into the picture.'

Why not? I said.

And – while I tried to assess why I'd ever told them (coming-to amongst the assorted shuffling feet on the waiting-room floor) that my name was the name staring down at me from the plaque on the clinic door (him alternately kneeling on my chest to pinch my cheeks and hopping about the anteroom from his crouched position shouting Fancy that! it's my name too!) – he put me into the picture.

'To be quite honest,' he declared, 'on first impressions, between you and me and the gatepost, unless of course it turns out to be the opposite – your days as you know them have a certain number.'

What number, I asked greenly.

'That would be telling, wouldn't it?' said he with a sportive wink.

But you mean – ? I said.

'The eyes of Texas are upon you.'

Ah well!

'Yes.'

There you are.

'Yes.'

I'm not going to pretend I wasn't disappointed with this person's picture of matters. I had come to him, after all, to collect my wife's Valium prescription. I quickly put forward my own interpretation of the thing.

Horseshit, I said.

'One naturally feels somewhat cheesed off in these situations,' he pointed out compassionately, completing a printed form. 'So we'll just have you pop round to Bart's for a quick observation.'

I declined the offer, unconvinced of the immediate benefit of a running commentary on my health, however brief, from the clientele of some local pub.

'To St Bartholomew's,' he amplified, clearing his throat, 'on the off chance I may be right. Or wrong.'

Ditto to St Bartholomew's, I said, feeling the choice of a church equally uncompelling.

'It's a hospital, Mr Wall,' he said; 'just to settle things in your own mind and to see that everything's tickety boo under the circumstances.'

Which are? I said, suddenly wondering at my own sloth of mind. 'Numbered,' you say, my days 'as I know them' – what does that mean, my days *as I know them*? You're saying there'll

10

be certain *restrictions*, is that it? I'm to stop smoking, maybe? stop drinking? diet, is that it? eat less? What?

'It's safe to assume,' he said, and fell silent. He could set forth a thought, this doctor.

Assume what? I said. You're not sure?

'Now who's a Nosey Parker, then?!' he said. 'There's *always* something of a puzzle, Mr Wall, in every sample. An element of doubt. Science begins and ends with a speculation.'

What you're saying is, *you* want to *study* me – I'm some kind of a case, aren't I? Fess up, eh?!

'Now there you have seen us to the very bottom, Mr Wall. Far be it from me to say that you are not some kind of a case.'

And what, I chimed, what if it turns out instead to be – as you say – 'a case of the opposite'?

'Ah!' said he.

Ah? said I.

'In that case you'll be one for the books!'

Well! I said. When you put it that way — !

'Science ever in your debt!'

Well then! I said. I'm only too delighted to help.

'Thanks awfully,' said the doctor leaping forward with spontaneous good will and pressing my hand; he slumped back then into his seat as suddenly, with a mazed and owlish stare.

So I went to Bart's.

I had my own motives, you see.

It could be this character was right. Could be I'd spent long enough anyhow among my fellow men, faithfully pencilling the outlines of paperclips at the tops of agenda and memoranda, listening and not listening and keeping mum in my various glass offices, and no doubt at 35 I'm largely out of the running and some in my place could be fairly invited to call it a day. But that Dr Wall's dreary analysis had to be wrong. And whatever delicious physiological windfall the disclosure of the real truth held in store for me (I've never asked a gift-horse to say Ah), I had personal reason to savour the test itself, as a matter of private fancy.

I'd always had it in the back of my mind, already, let me say, that there was something catchy about being – or becoming – 'British'. With all that that, as I saw it, entailed. We'd never have drifted here in the first place, Teresa and I, otherwise. I was ready to swear that – beside the gushing sentimentalism you and I Americans were prone to, the compulsive sensationalism, the hysterical heroism, you know what I'm talking about – I'd have sworn that these out-of-season limeys (who couldn't build and sell a new toothbrush to the world for a fast nickel but who always quietly had their revolutions and emancipations and got on with it before the rest of us stretched and brushed the baby-sleep from our eyes), these Anglo-Saxons had a cool handhold on the sense and realism and reason that must finally count. I had a taste for that spare kind of spring-toughmindedness; that marrow-deep aversion to persons and situations coming clumping onstage on stilts; that way of living closer to the bone. Imagine the satisfaction of insisting remorselessly on cutting life down to human scale. You can't beat it. Any nation that could stick into its mouth a thermometer on which – as I'd heard – the little red tick spelling Health was etched at '98.4' had got to be two-tenths of a degree closer to sanity. I was prepared to do three choruses of Oy Britannia at the drop of the least audible pin.

That's how we'd come to buy the flat in Kensington, then, Teresa and I – Treeza, as they cunningly utter it here – and started settling in; Treeza to trace her genealogy and me to practise living closer to the bone. I was taking a hard line on the color of the study curtains when that clinical incident occurred. A month was trundling by without our saying a hell of a lot to one another more than Pass the salt; I always took a hard line on the study curtains and so did she. Already, crises of the domestic sort had joined the repertoire of human disorders which the English air had taught us to scotch with barbs of preternatural calm.

Naturally, then, when he presented his hopelessly mad idea, noble Wall (why, lying publicly there across his aseptic linoleum floor, had I taken that name?! feeling otherwise compromised perhaps? exposed?), I went along for his 'quick observation,' pleased to show I was equal to his challenge and his tickety boo. Anything for medical science, after all. Help solve one of those fleeting famous puzzles of randy nature, whatever it might be. One felt oneself of *use*.

'Take off your shirt' said the grey-haired white-capped 'sister'.

12

Prepare yourself, said I, for a new sensation. She remained lukewarm. Pants too? I said. 'It all comes to the same thing,' she said. I have magic dancing feet, I said. Long, wobbly and Christianly firm, the sisters took blood tentatively first, from the thumbs and earlobes. They became interested; they took off my pants; the syringes and pistons grew. They X-rayed and stuck mirrors into orifices never before visited by the eye of civilized man; new faces appeared, female and male; they carried away phials, firkins, stoups of innermost exotic fluids labeled with my pseudonym (too embarrassed was I now to make an issue. 'But the name on your Health card – ?' It's nothing, I said, I keep it for sentiment, it was my father's). They started charts, dossiers, files. 'Symptoms? complaints?' What do I know from symptoms? Silly. Does Dr Wall approve of all this? I've been fine, splendid, a touch of dry skin, perhaps, a little nasal congestion, heartburn maybe in the last month or so, but couldn't be better, worse luck; a slight shortness of breath, a peculiar taste in the mouth, especially metallic, inexplicably – and people behave as though I've bad breath – but nothing – a certain light-headedness, mornings, a trace of lassitude, a nosebleed, once, the week before – but nothing – what are these things? Absurd! Their ears prick, none the less. Relish the attention, I said to myself, while ye may. And what's in a body, besides? (In a spirited moment of dash, between tests, I lose Treeza's tickets to *Die* damned *Fledermaus* down a gutter grate and fire-eatingly splurge on one for boxing at the Empire Pool.) Medicine? I thought Estragen was a character in some incomprehensible modern play; a crown filling was something you did to the Queen. (Cheap cracks? My *grin forced*, you say? If you miss this, ever, the very merit of it all is lost; justice must be seen to be done; entering the cage, the intrepid with his whip and chair must be seen to be skittish, or what's the circus for?)

'Intriguing,' someone said, gazing at an X-ray, pushing back his spectacles; 'the whole thing's gone a bit funny.' What has? I said. 'Jolly good,' he said, and swivelled out of the room on his castored stool.

(I drive home and to work my normal long way round, shifting gears behind rolled-up windows with my wonted orchestral panache, cuffs as always flashing to the rhythm of mute symphonies.)

13

Form-letters arrived. By popular demand I was called for tests at another clinic. 'Confirm presence,' I read over someone's shoulder; 'assess outlet and presentation.' 'Antibodies?' somebody muttered, 'hemoglobin?' Dr Wall? I said, don't I see him sometime? 'Indeed, of course,' they said, 'mais certainement.' They sent me on to other rooms, other clinics, other laboratories, I was clearly doing the circuit, I'd never want for a booking. Students were now foregathering to thump and auscoltate me.

(In Piccadilly I typically squander on one each of every daily tabloid on the stand; newspaper fetishist. Why have I this fervor for others' news? My loft-browed barber drops my as-usual inordinately large tip into his immaculate smock with his customary inordinate indifference; I vent my saps and vapors on the floor of a pricey local gymnasium and exquisitely skin my knee.)

I was held over in a half-dozen venues, they scrutinized my nails and queried my shoe-size, there was talk of my doing Birmingham and Bristol.

(Free hours, I browse at Christie's among the new acquisitions. My parents – long gone, passed-on together in a noteworthy accident involving passion, unusual sex practices, and faulty wiring – they'd have been proud to see how I've come on in this life. Standing poised in the discreet crowd before the displayed restoration-in-progress of a plump lissome Rubens I ponder for future reference the relative forfeits and charms of the receding patina on her half-cleansed buttocks of the cigar-smoke of the Rothschilds. My people would have puffed and clucked; there is no end to my prospects.)

In anteroom after anteroom, there were others come to wait, like me. 'Hodgkins', an old man would say, 'what about you.' Wall. 'Never heard of that one. Inoperable?' In a nutshell, it was everything I cherished in this adopted land, the Principle of National Health. Here in one room, waiting together, were a barrister's clerk, come for the removal of a fishbone, a docker ailing from glue ear, and a marchioness, they say, with the wind up and cursing and praying audibly for her bowel to open before God and everyone; from each according to his ability – I said to the man next to me, lyrically – to each according to his need.

14

'Aye,' said my anonymous fellow, 'this is it, isn't it?'

No one claiming privilege – I said fervently – all for one and one for all.

'That'll be it,' he said.

No American-style trading on each others' egos, I said. None of your endless American emotional barter, your the-world-will-end-if-I-don't-get-my-way-and-if-it-doesn't-there's-a-conspiracy-against-me, your puritanical guilt-built-catastrophism we Yankees cook up to make achievers of ourselves. These people know decency, I doted, by Jove – more material in matters human, more human in matters material – a brotherhood of men giving each other a leg up!

'Aye, well,' he said, 'this is it. It's like anything else, really, isn't it?'

The whole medical affair was immensely convivial and enlightening. I would not soon forget the salutory effect it had had on my life. As to the awful mistake itself – everybody's going to so much trouble on my account, the mix-up, the slippage in the records or whatever it was – I could have kicked myself for enjoying it so. The fact is, it wasn't until the start of the sixth week, with a wistful farewell to the limelight, turning to a white-gowned attendant and not unmoved, that I sheepishly uttered:

What would you say if I told you – I began – that you've got the wrong end of the stick?

They were not to be outdone.

Within instants they had me clapped to one of their tilting tables and experts were debouching from all the doorways. With, in the van, of course, in backward collar, a chaplain. They came prepared.

'Here now, old sock,' said the chaplain, the bottoms of his trousers bloused in bicycle clamps, revealing a smart pair of green soccer boots. 'I know,' he said, 'you want the truth, don't you? Pretending's all a dismal bit of charade, isn't it?' He sat down, lightly swinging a brace of squash rackets, narrowly missing my face with one buttock. 'Well I can tell you, there's nothing to be ashamed of! You're no worse, no different than anybody else, really. Are you hungry? bring this man some teacakes.'

I don't want any teacakes, thanks, I said. I'm going home.

15

'That's the spirit! never a complaint! Going to the bosom of the Lord. "I will keep my mouth as it were with a bridle," wot?'

What?

'I say: "I held my tongue and spake nothing, I kept silence, I became dumb and opened not my mouth," that's it, eh? You know, from the good old last service, folks marching lugubriously to the grave, "I am the resurrection and the life"? Leslie Howard, Ronald Colman, throwing the sod on, "earth to earth, dust to dust", all that. Not bad prose, really. Do have a teacake.'

I can do without teacakes, honestly, Father —

He peered at me with sudden intense interest. 'Why do you say that?'

Beg your pardon?

'You can do without teacakes – why do you say that? Can I take it that, in spite of all, there is something inside you that has found satisfaction and a – and a desire to go on?'

I think you can take it that way, Father – now if you'll just —

'Call me Griffin!' he said.

If you'll just let me be on my way, Griffin.

'You say you can do without teacakes – does this mean that, even during this illness, this awful trial – you feel that others —'

I'm not ill, Griffin —

'– that in Ethiopia perhaps, in Bangladesh and Bolivia, others stand in greater need of teacakes – ? Would you call this *faith*? You are saying that even out of this experience there can come meaning —'

I —

'– that after all, this whole business on earth is pretty much of a snare and a delusion —'

Griffin, I —

'I think that here you are saying that you are stronger now in your faith than ever before – and that —'

Griffin, could you get off my face — ?

Reverend Griffin gazed with a worried species of humility into my eyes. 'Do you know,' he said, 'I'm positive that you'll end up in heaven, and don't worry, I'm not too sure about the details, but —'

If I could just end up home in time for dinner —

'Call me Eustace,' he said.

Fed up, I rose vigorously, and so did he.

'Don't,' he said, bolting, 'don't do anything silly, now —.'
My feet hit the floor. 'I'll look in again —.' With a hearty
heigh-ho as though in backward pursuit of a floating cross-
court lob the chaplain was out the door.

'Hell-lo-ello!'

It was – surprise and at last – Dr Wall standing there in his
place. Extraordinary man, neck so elongated and erect,
Adam's Apple so prominent and full of character and bearing
that at a distance you thought it was a nose, an effect undiminished by the stroke of luck by which what seemed an
elaborate surmounting pinky hairdo turned out in fact to be
his face. 'Well!' said he – 'we shall have you right as a bobbin
in no time!'

I told him I was glad he was satisfied, and began buttoning
things up.

'Just –' he said '– when you've turned yourself round, before
you go, I wonder if you'd give your lady-wife a tinkle and
tell her you'll be home a trifle later. Say Friday?'

Friday!

'It's simply that, on balance, just to be on the safe side – an
interesting concatenation of symptoms – that's to say not
unusual, in no way unusual, mind, but then that's just it, you
see, in your case, a bit of a parson's egg actually, and so our
chappies feel that if a thing's worth doing it's worth doing
well —'

So you want — ?

'Just a little exploratory recky, if you take my meaning, in
amongst your more privy odds and bobs, don't you know,
just to nip in, have a look round, tidy up this and that, get
you right, and off you go, what do you say?

But Friday! I'll miss half of Wimbledon!

'Fair comment, damned inconvenience, that's why I say let
me get on the hooter right now and we can be in and out by
0-nine-thirty tomorrow and you'll be home Friday, what do
you say?'

And if I refuse?

'– It's early days yet.'

Meaning?

17

'It's an if-y question.'

But you've found absolutely nothing!

'Point taken! Full marks for that! Thing is, old cock, you can never be *too* sure, now can you?'

The appropriate calls once made – Treeza's mind proved as yet as innocent of questions as mine – I was bodily shaved, accorded a rectal washout, half-throttled with a large narcotic pill, and told to take a bath; they then sent in a young man wearing a mask who set about me with a felt-tipped pen. The color was orange, I recall, and his job was to prevent errors of a surgical kind due to confusions of identity (eyes with mouths, arms with legs, etc.); he was anxious to do well, and the orange X to mark 'the site' ended up connecting my left ear with my right shin and vice versa. Thus suitably inscribed I was hoisted onto some kind of tottery wheeled bed and left to my own devices in another waiting-room, close up against a coffee machine. It was at this point that I was awarded my first Visitation. Was he to be one of the blessed saviours in my life, I ask myself now, or a holy terror?

The gentleman came and sagged down on the bench on the other side of the coffee machine, so that I hardly saw more of him than an occasionally gesticulating hand, which was missing one thumb from the ordinary place, though whether he might have kept this somewhere else about his person, as I say, I was unable to judge from my current angle. He was not a patient.

'I'm not a patient,' he said. 'I'm waiting for my wife. She's having a beautymark removed.'

I'm sorry to hear it, I said.

'Yes, I've nothing to worry about. My name's Poole.'

Ah! I said understandingly, this seeming the expletive in fashion.

'Matter of fact,' he said, 'I've come to see *you!*'

You have! I said.

'Yes! I have. I've come from you-know-where!'

You haven't!

'Yes indeed. You don't remember me, then – we used to meet occasionally, at the water-fountain? in the outer office? It doesn't matter. I've come from – well, from everybody, really, just to wish you well.'

That's awfully nice, I said; but I'll be back Monday, you know.

'Yes, they thought we ought to send someone along, just to wish you well, and as I had a wife in here anyway —'

You got elected.

'I'm meant to give you this.'

The fingers unaccompanied by thumb extended me a pink envelope.

There was something dreamlike in the whole event.

From the envelope came a lavender greeting card, showing a large rabbit in bed with a baleful expression, a kerchief tied under a peculiarly swollen mandible and the words Get Well Soon arising in a balloon from behind one ear. Inside, the card was more than generously signed with familiar names – 'Anthony Bernard Clive Edward Louis Simon' and continued 'and all the "gals" Alison Beryl Doreen Elizabeth Glenda Sophia' and finished at the bottom with 'and others too numerous to mention!' I noticed that each 'signature' was written in the same unsettlingly legible hand; or was it in fact in any 'hand'? I thanked Mr Poole for delivering this inspiriting message, and asked him how were things down at the office, anyway?

'We have the Frickley case nearly solved,' he said, putting my mind at rest in a word. 'The Grimes problem, the Putney-Carroll affair, the Smedley business are all well under control.'

I'm glad about that, I said.

'And Hinkle....'

Hinkle?

'If anybody knows Hinkle, it's you. What I believe you humorously call the Hinkle wrinkle?'

Yes. What about Hinkle, then?

'Some kind of relation of yours, isn't he?'

Some kind. What about Hinkle?

'...Hinkle's all right.'

So much the better, I said.

'They've given me the Hinkle account.'

...Good, I said.

'For now,' he said.

So much the better, I said.

My teeth unexpectedly chattered.

'Yes,' he said. 'I have everything.'

I'm glad, I said supportively, putting Hinkle from my mind.

He sat looking at an electric plug stuck in the opposite wall.

'Lucky, really. The little lady's just given up her nicest man-friend to stay at home and make the beds, and all. The toddlers are coming into their own, buying and selling, Bangkok and Singapore, dope mostly – completely self-supporting.'

Amen to that, I said.

'The wife's a one,' he said.

I'll bet, I said.

'Loves people, loves kids, loves life. One of these ones that just seem to have an almost born *instinct*, from scratch – this *innate knack* of knowing right away that life's a, well, a desirable commodity? Know what I mean? Constitutionally can't help it – loves life.'

He fished about, and blew his nose.

'Now me,' he said. 'I'm one that can help it. Have brief remissions, of course, once in a long while, very painful, where I can't help loving these things, but generally speaking, I can help it.'

That right? I said.

'I suppose you could say for the sake of argument, Well, if you can't help it, that's the one grounds for carrying on with it. Having kids, the lot. But then, wouldn't you know? that'd be me all over – it'd take a bloke like me to go looking for grounds, eh?...Just don't have a feel for it, I expect.'

I couldn't fault him on that one.

He went silent.

'Looking after you all right then, are they?' he said eventually.

Oh they are, yes, I said.

'Do you know something?' he said. 'When I was a lad, if I fell down, do you know, if I fell down? I knew how to roll. Did you used to roll, if you fell? – sort of instinctively, when you were a lad? I had this natural spirit, I suppose you'd say, to keep myself – what is it? – intact, that's it, to keep myself intact. Then one day – I was about twelve – do you see this?' He held up his hand without a thumb. 'That's right. There was this ice-locker door and the door was closing with an awful howl and I knew I could get this out of the way, it would have taken just a little extra energy – and I didn't. I just let it go. I just – let the thumb go. I don't know why – to this day I don't know. For years, of course, I told myself, Poole, it was a bright thing you did, you sacrificed your thumb to save your life! (Because, you see, there's a way of looking at it – where I was standing, where the door was, where my hand was – that could make it make sense.) But now I don't know.' He blew his nose again. 'If a bloke came up to me and he said, Your money or your life! and if I could hold all my money in one hand and my life in the other – and I don't really care that much for money, mind – would I put out the hand that – well, would I know, without thinking, which hand to put out? If he had a knife to my throat and he said, Give me a reason not to cut your throat, would I at that second be able to find a single reason for saying No? What do you think? It's a puzzle, really.'

He and I each put change into the machine and each had a plastic cup of coffee. The throttle-pill I'd taken was more magic than I'd expected; I was feeling gorgeously dazed.

'Times, you know, when I'm just getting into the bathtub and I think what it would be like if I slipped, how my head might split right open against the side of the tub, like a Spanish melon . . . there are times when I'm as-close-as-not to letting myself fall right over, against the side of the tub, against a wall, into the way of a bus. Funny, that. It's not a matter of depression, or bad thoughts, not at all. What's between me doing it and not doing it is just about as – well – as thin as the difference between turning on the hot water first and turning on the cold water first. Or between stepping off a curb with my right foot and stepping off with my left foot. It's as if, back behind, just below the surface of the Poole that has this line of business and this name for himself amongst his friends and family, down through all the depths there is nothing, just nothing at all between that Poole and an utter – a total – What – ? A hole.' For one instant our eyes met around the coffee machine. 'What do you think?' he said.

Well —, I said. The very clarity of Poole's speech seemed hallucinatory now. Or had the delirium begun the moment I'd swallowed the pill?

'Funny thing,' he said, 'wonder if you've ever heard of it. One of the great medical curiosities. It seems there are certain cases, a fellow'll be running about enjoying life, full of piss and vinegar, and a bucket of laughs one day – and the next

21

day, give him some minor little medical complaint, an allergy, a bad chest cold, something that wouldn't bother a flea – and this chap'll just fold up and pass away. Just like that. Like a straw in the breeze. Gone. One of the great medical curiosities. You've heard of somebody like that, I'll bet. Poor bloke. Just doesn't seem to have the stuff inside him. Nothing to fight with. Never did, all the time, only you never knew it. Till suddenly, puff and he's gone. What do you think?' His eyes were the kind you couldn't help but avoid, like the glommy look of a gent who's been had-up for standing around in a doorway and revealing a bit of pink.

Well —, said I. And slipped ambiguously behind a cloud.

Dimly aware then of being lifted onto a wobbly bed – but hasn't this happened before? – and the whizz of corridors teetering by – 'when you recall your life and contemplate despair' – halls, elevators, the beaming face of the Reverend Chaplain peeping around a door and whispering – 'remember... remember... the precious... behind it all' – and swinging doors – 'if I forget thee, O Jerusalem....'

♦

I came to in a small white room, with a bundle of women's arms around me, hands plugging whirling tape recorders into the walls.

'We would like to interview you in a diagnostic-therapeutic interview,' one said, sitting me up in my stupor and strapping microphones to my throat.

'We want you to be our teacher,' said another warmly. 'Let us introduce ourselves.'

'We are your social helpers —'

'We are learning as *you* are!'

'We want to learn –' said the first with bra-less missionary zeal – could she be speaking American? '– from people in your condition —'

'– How to talk to them as human beings.'

'The importance of one's dignity of the patient.'

I would like to see the doctor, I said.

'Your reactions are very normal.'

I have reason to believe I have just been operated on and I would like to see the doctor.

'How did you take it, this news?'

What news?

'You don't like to think about it. Your pain may stem from all those swallowed feelings of anger and frustration.'

I'm not in pain.

'Get these out of your system without being ashamed and your pains will probably go away.'

There is no pain.

'I'm impressed with your slumped posture.'

This neckstrap is caught around my ankle.

'We can assure you that your reactions are very normal.'

'Last night we had someone who inhaled a pint of carbolic acid. He'd thought it was condensed milk.'

'He had obviously mixed feelings.'

'An ambivalent figure.'

'How does this make you feel?'

It depends –

'So things are *relative*, then?' said one, excitedly. 'Would you say that? that everything is relative?'

'I see,' said the other.

'So to summarize a bit, to clarify the whole thing, what you are really saying is, if you have to go you would like it to be without agony and pain and loneliness.'

'How does this make you feel?' said the other.

'I see,' said the first.

'These things should be brought out. It is important to think about these things and talk about it, and not beat around the bush and say everything is fine.'

I haven't seen my doctor –, I said.

'This makes it excusable, you think. It makes it understandable.'

'You are blaming yourself as a means of alleviating guilt feelings for suppressed hostile wishes toward moribund accident victims.'

'I hope you have had some good experiences too,' said the other, a bit touchily I thought.

'What does death mean to you? I know it's a tricky question, but we are running out of tape.'

I struggled and finally got loose from their harness.

'You don't want to do anything silly,' they said in one breath.

'Well now!'

In the doorway the intern was standing snapping off his rubber gloves in a white cloud of talc, his brow above the mask decked out effectively in sweat beads. The room was suddenly emptied of its tape-recorder ladies, and the deeper meaning of the Medical Mask dawned on me; it wasn't to shield the patient from the wearers' germs – it was to fend the blight from the wearer. So that was it. So this was it. Was he going to say, now, 'Awfully sorry, but I have to tell you, our worst fears are confirmed'? Let him. Ah ha! I would say to him; "Ah ha!" I'll say, "now I feel it only fair to reveal to you that I am actually Burton Smegma, world-famous Medical Investigator and Healthy Person in disguise, and This is Your Test – the symptoms you observe having been assumed by me for the purposes of illustration only; any resemblance between persons living and not is purely —"

'Well now!' he said. 'The operation was a smashing success!'

What did you take? I said with surprisingly bated breath.

'Sorry?'

What did you take, and what's left? I said.

'Hardly took a thing, old son,' he said. 'The odd snapshot here and there. The operation was absolutely spot on.'

Then why've you got your mask on? I ruminated with only slowly diminishing suspicion.

'Fact is,' he said, 'our lads decided on stopping after only the tiniest little incision.'

My squirrel-hunched shoulders settled a little more.

'We'll have you out of here in a matter of hours.'

I heaved an exultantly relieved sigh.

'Super man, our Wall.'

Terrific, I said.

'Eminent brain, lung and derma surgeon,' he said.

Is he! I said, ecstatic.

'Mm. With a taste for obstets and a special line in sweet-breads.'

Really, I said.

'Mm. Pancreas. My grandmother used to get them once a month from the butcher. He had a chronic catarrh.'

Honestly? I said. Nothing better!

'We're getting a bed,' he said, 'all ready for you at St Mary's Peeping.'

I had to sit back.

'Fine hospital, that,' he said, 'Wall's own regular. Looks out on the River Sly.'

What's the hold up? I said inadequately.

'We'll have you sorted out before you can say bob's your uncle.'

25

What seems to be the trouble? I said.

'Or we'll give it a rattling good try.'

I see.

'Otherwise the thing can make awfully brisk progress, you see.'

Progress, I said. Recovery, you mean.

'Well no. The other thing, actually. You see, you've got this, well, not to beat about the – this damned awkward – well – *blob*. In there. D'you see?'

It swiftly, lucidly reconstructed itself in my mind's eye, the scene that had transpired in the operating theater. 'The tiniest incision' made, they'd poked their eye in to get at this or that, and there, 'in there', inside, right and left, everywhere they turned —. Glancing over their shoulders, like convent girls in sudden plain view of a drawerful of rubbers, touching nothing, they'd clapped me slap-bang shut. The devil take the hindmost. Scampering to their rooms.

And off they were packing me to their Peeping-on-the-Sly.

A blob, I said.

He nodded.

Green growing things, I said.

'Mmmm. One corner, anyway. Absolutely stodge full, chockablock. Pity, really.'

Can't blame you, though, I said.

'We-l-ll not re-e-elly,' he said, fetching invisible pebbles a few modest kicks, 'I was only sitting up in the third row rear, actually. Anyhow, must dash!' he said furtively. 'Let's know how you get on!'

So I made ready to go down to St Mary's, Dr Wall's regular, 'the finest place in the Northern Hemisphere for what you've got'. They explained: admission would be a simple affair; they called up Treeza and told her to bring the standard two pints of blood. The incision, in fact, had been just large enough to get a miracle-periscope in, no bigger than a nail's edge and hardly worth a bandaid – I could have jogged the four miles to Peeping and played the awaiting staff a round of ping-pong before sitting down to lunch; I was fit, fit, fit and I'll say no more of that. At their pleasure, I arrived in a ridiculous siren-squalling ambulance.

'I suppose you think you're very clever.'

Treeza was standing at the curb, her upper lip a nasty red from crying, holding the two bottles of blood in her hands.

Yours? I said, giving her a hug.

'Dummy,' she said, 'am I a universal donor?'

I love you, I said, taking the blood.

'I love *you*,' she said.

I love *you*, I said.

On the pavement, attendants were pushing me into an invalid-chair.

Wheee! I said.

'What are you going to do?' she said.

Sit down, I replied.

'*What are you going to do?*' She started crying and thumping the invalid-chair. '*I suppose this is your idea of a joke*,' An attendant fell down. I helped him up and sat down again. '*How did you ever get into this?*'

I'm so sorry, love, I said apologetically; it's stupid, isn't it? I said. Treeza's lashes lowered. They threw a red blanket over me and we started rolling. She trundled beside me up the long ramp toward the hospital entrance.

'What are you going to do?' she said. 'Are you going to die, or what?'

I'm not going to die, silly. I'm not going to die.

'You're not going to die.'

I'm not going to die.

'Tell me and get it over with.'

I'm not going to die.

'You're being flippant. You know I can't take it when you're flippant,' she said. 'Why don't you say what you mean? You came to England to die! I knew it!'

It's Naples, I said.

'What?'

It's Naples and die, dear.

'There, you see! You never say anything straight out. You're worse than ever today, I swear. You're just like my father. Just like my brothers, my uncle, my first-cousin-once-removed – always in a dream-world, never think of us trying to love you.' Fascinated, the attendant tripped in my red blanket. We untangled him. 'Nose in a book, always going off to work – why can't you settle down to anything? You *enjoy* being eccentric!'

27

I don't.

'You do. Moving us to some foreign place, dreaming of even other ones – you *enjoy* it. When will you ever settle down?'

I promise I'll settle down, Treeza.

'Foreign. You *like* it – *a foreign body*, that's you – you say so yourself —' Treeza stopped. 'What do you mean?' she said electrically. 'What do you mean you're going to settle down? *Now*, you mean? What do you mean?'

I only mean —

'You're going to die.'

I'm not going to die.

'This is *your* truth. Look at you.' I looked at myself in my invalid chair. 'You'd think it was all one big holiday or something. What's happening to us?'

I'm not going to die, Treeza darling, I said; I promise. I stopped my chair, dropped my red blanket and stood up. Look! I said. I did a little running-in-place, flexed my muscles, wiggled my ears.

'Why are you doing this? Why?' she said. I sat down. 'Think you're so clever.' We'd reached the entrance. They wrapped the red blanket back around me. 'If this is your idea of fun — I know you. You're running away! It's the mole, isn't it? I know, it's the mole.'

Which mole? I said.

'You know what mole!' They were waiting for me at the entrance to St Mary's. 'You're blaming me for the mole. You brought us to England – to escape from the mole!'

That's your truth.

The plate-glass doors slid open.

'I have to know, don't you see?! A woman has to know!' Attendants were pushing and pulling my wheels, one from behind, one struggling in front, over the bumpy sill through the doorway. 'What am I supposed to do?'

Just wait, Treeza! I shouted. And bring more blood!

She was probably right, it was a thoughtless parting joke, I must have been preoccupied. Looking back, I can still see her red lips pressed in a neat O against the glass.

'What about the curtains?!' she shrilled. By the time I reached Reception she was gone from view. I hopped out of my chair.

28

The admissions desk was sumptuous. I stood chuckling as they made out the questionnaire and insisted on clamping on me a bracelet with my nom-de-guerre 'to prevent mistakes when the patient's unable to speak for himself'. 'Middle name?' No. 'Have you any objection to your body's being used for transplant purposes?' Only when I'm sleeping. (This seemed a sore point; I donned a sober face to match the company's.) 'Have you brought with you a bottle of fruit juice; a nail file and scissors; a cardigan; a supply of ten-penny pieces for the telephone; cosmetics; sanitary towels; two pairs of disposable pants?' No. 'Have you a favorite toy or cuddly blanket?' You've got me there. 'Have you any special words – for going to the lavatory, or for a favorite toy or cuddly blanket?' Who wants to know? 'Have your bowels acted?' (She gave me a shrewd look with this one and put an instant finishing tick with a flourish.) 'Go and lie down.' I did that.

I gave them ten days of my prime of life, sleeping, eating, and rhapsodically, moronically pedalling a stationary bike. On the eleventh, just when I was fed up to the gills with embarrassment at the outlandish near-pleasure I'd been taking from this now obvious April-foolery and was determining to walk out forever after lunch, my system began for the first time to show signs of fulfilling all its initial technical promise. It started with my falling into the unusual habit of swallowing air. I hardly knew what to think. 'Aerophagy,' I overheard an SRN say importantly to an auxiliary; 'associated,' she said, 'with a frequent desire to pass flatus, as sure as shooting.' This was supplemented rapidly that afternoon by 'Hyperemesis, nurse, hyperemesis, bring a mop' and 'Stress incontinence, micturation with laughter and sneezing, how's his BP and where's that mop?' But as you'd expect from what you know of me, I was back on top of things in no time, and by the end of the supper hour had downed my pie and cream with my usual gusto.

And astonishingly, between bouts of sleep, beside the plate on my tray, an envelope. Opening it, I stopped with a jolt. On the coarse paper, in crabbed hand, it said:
'Greetings from Hinkle.'
How did he find me?
What's he think he's doing?

It was the next morning that the funny business of my dropping things got going, and a true wave of spook thrilled through me. I had been reared on enough late-night Bette Davis malignancy movies, it was my first moment of depression; the doctors were right; something was on.

Dr Wall came rushing in, my chart in hand, grinning from ear to ear.

'Dropping things, eh?! Pins and needles, numbness, fingers and palms?' he said.

Yes, I said.

'Carpal tunnel syndrome,' he said.

Which is to say? I said.

'Oedema's begun affecting certain parts of the nervous system,' he said, his famous throat proudly puffing like a bullfrog's. 'Things are moving right along. Didn't I tell you? When you came to me and fell down in my office, *who told you*?!'

You told me.

'Who was a doubting Thomas, hmm?'

I was.

'Who's been a Silly Billy?'

I have.

Something peculiar took place. I suppose it was my expression: he looked at me, and suddenly dashed away.

He was to do this often, don't ask me why.

A minute later he came back as indiscriminately as he'd gone.

'Just want you to know,' he said, 'there's no cause for alarm. These things happen every day.'

To whom?

He commenced haphazardly probing a selection of my parts. 'To us.'

Ah....

I felt the slightest inner twitter, as though there might develop something dishearteningly real about this dream, if one didn't watch out.

Do you want to – would you like to – remove something?

'What?'

... What do you mean, What? I said.

'I mean, what do you think we ought to remove?'

Well, I just thought – I mean, you don't *have* to remove anything if you don't *feel* like it —

30

'I'm easy – if you've an idea —'
No, no, I simply thought —
'You see, it's not merely getting larger – it's getting softer.
This is the way, you see. Making it tricky, for the moment,
to determine precisely the – the exact extent of the thing. Well,
a little time,' he said comfortably, 'and we'll feel it all right.
It'll be unmistakable.'
If I – we could give more blood — ?
'How would this — ?'
I just thought, you might like more blood – I only wanted
to help.
'We have loads of your kind of blood, thank you.'
– I was just unprepared for a minute – a silly fit of the jitters —
'Butterflies, eh?'
Yes. It won't happen again, though.
'We have things for that.'
I'm sure you have.
'And if we just pull our socks up, there's still every chance.'
Yes?
'Unless this – growth – is —'
Is what? Is what?
'Well, we'll know soon enough. The important thing is, I
want to reassure you that this is absolutely common. These
are modern times, this is the twentieth century – we must
wipe out this *stigma*, this unpleasant label that people attach
to – out of sheer ignorance and prejudice, to —'
To?
'To it.'
Of course.... How long?
'How long?'
How long until?
'Oh you mean until you — !'
Yes
'From now?'
Well, starting from now, if you like, I said. Or from tomor-
row?
'Well let's see. Elderly primagravida....'
Sorry? isn't that – I mean – what does that mean?
'I was only thinking of whether it runs the full term....'
That's it – what is the full term?

31

'. . . Some months. . . .'

Months, I said dully.

'Weeks?'

Look – you just said months —

'Now see here,' he said, 'these things are *common*. And anyway, I didn't *have* to come here and tell you they were common, *did* I?' Dr Wall kept from stamping his foot by holding onto it. 'We don't know yet, do we? that's what we don't know. Now we're going to give this thing a right old run for its money, and the rest is in the hands of – the hands of —'

. . . What are we going to do first?

'We're going to see if we can't come to some understanding with these sites of localized sensation.'

Does the blob have those?

'I was speaking of your nervous system, Mr Wall. Your nervous system. Not the thing itself.'

I see.

'I know what you were asking me! I know what you were looking to ask me! You were going to ask me if the thing had a life of its own, I know you, you can't fool me.'

Was I?

'Well it *is* a physical process, isn't it? – and you're asking me if this physical process in this situation has become a sensation! Next thing, you'll be asking me if it's your enemy, evil spirits, heaven paying you back for nasty thoughts, and who knows what else —'

Is that what life is? a situation where a —?

'– There now, you see — ?'

– A place where a physical process becomes a sensation — ?

'Nag nag nag! Righty-ho, now you just go and get your good self into the old kip, and leave the rest to yours truly and the best of British luck.'

So they started me on a course of 'extraordinary treatments', running the gamut; I and this body were giddily exposed to heat, light, cold, dark, radiation, traction, compression, floating, kneading, sinking, baking, basting and chilling, infusions, transfusions and general effusions. They thrived on it.

And again, out of a doze between tests, on my tray an envelope. Inside, the scrap of paper said, Greetings from Hinkle.

What does he mean, doing this? What's going on?

The thought came of that 'Poole', whoever he was, and I cringed. What could he, what can he do about Hinkle?

I was moved into what I came to know and love as the 'we're all mortal' ward.

It was here that I first encountered Messrs Robinson, Austin and Blood.

At our initial meeting, Mr Robinson was lying in a disorderly bundle on the floor beside his bed; a nurse stood over him with her knuckles on her hips irritably explaining that if he'd had the sense to keep his side-rail up he'd not have fallen out. Mine was to be the cot next to his; in some shock at his ghastly pallor (which I learned to regard as a permanent Robinson feature) I gladly helped the nurse get him reinstalled.

'You can't be too careful,' he said apologetically. 'Still, makes a change.'

Mr Robinson settled himself in with ratchety hands, and looked over to give me a slow moist smile.

'Have you had to close up? Shop, I mean?'

I didn't understand; and then a picture swept through my mind of my office, and of the secretaries bustling on about their business, filing their nails.

'For years, I didn't,' he said, musing to himself. 'Then for a while I had a girl answering the telephone. But,' he said, '... what with one thing and another...I had to lock up and let her go.' He opened his hands as though he were letting something precious, a long string of precious things trickle away between his fingers. 'Been having radiation, have you?'

Yes! I said, feeling it was my turn to laugh apologetically.

'They had that in mind for me for a while,' he said, reminiscing. 'They had to have a paper signed. It seems – where they were going to aim it – it was bound to cause sterility and they wouldn't give me the treatment until my wife signed a bit of paper. No good, though. She'd been passed away for eleven years. More. Couldn't make them see, it didn't really matter anymore. What with our Harry grown up and gone and all.'

A cleaning lady passed through, mopping the floor.

Mr Robinson's face brightened.

'Came by ambulance this time, us did!'

Did you really? I said appreciatively.

'Aye. Remember the first time. The missus herself was alive and perky then. I walked in under me own steam. Had a spot on the liver. Later one showed up on the leg. Ate through most of the bone before it were done, that one; had to put a brass pin in. Haven't yet found out where it started, they haven't. That was before this other thing where they can't find my veins anymore. It's a job to manage, this dying business! Well, it's like anything else, really – takes a bit of doing. Still, first our Harry, taken off, hardly grown up, then Molly too, now me going out myself – seems as if there's always something. Well, take the rough with the smooth I often say. How about you, then?'

Oh, I'm all right, I said, ashamed at his attention. I've really got nothing wrong at all, I said.

'That's the ticket! Power of positive thinking, isn't it? Business as usual, eh?!'

It's not that at all, really – I'm just not truly sick —

'Fifty new drugs each year, they say – new treatments – always a chance. The way I reckon,' he said with a nudge-like gesture of the elbow across the space between our beds, 'the main thing is the flaming inconvenience! Well, best cut your coat according to your cloth. Beggars can't be choosers, can they?'

No, I don't suppose they can, I said, agreeing as readily as I could; it was a concept I found easier in the phrasing than in the application.

'We can thank our lucky stars,' he said. 'Why, my old Dad died in a place with no running water, a lump-coal fire, lying on two chairs in the one downstairs room – we're centuries ahead, a different breed of men.'

– Yup, I said.

After a little, he leaned over slightly and said in a lowered voice, 'Sometimes, I pray to get well.' He looked up at me. 'It isn't right, I know....'

Oh –, I said.

'I'll never forget the first time I did that. One night, I had this pain. Of all the discomforts,' he said, 'pain, you know, is the most notorious.'

With a startled reflex, I couldn't help bursting into laughter.

Mr Robinson looked at me curiously, as though I – as if I'd

waved a feather to dispel ranges of mountains I hadn't yet even glimpsed. But he went on.

'One night,' he said again, '– I'd been ailing a long time already, mind – but that night, there I was – crying, like – me crying "I want to go home!" Well, I can tell you, it *was* embarrassing. Mother and Dad were both in the ground, there wasn't any other home to speak of, save what me and Molly had. Well, she couldn't take it. So we decided to put me away. She's always wanted somebody strong, and so'd our Harry, I suppose, come to that. Put me in here, one place or another like this, can't recall which came first – plugged me in, and it's been easier for folks ever since. Have you tried – are they trying you on this cobalt and nitrogen mustard treatment?'

I believe so.

'And the almond-pits one?'

Yes.

'That's it. Anyway,' said Mr Robinson with dignity, 'one's fallen on hard times, but it's no good grumbling; what's the good of dying if you don't make the most of it? you've got to get something out of it for yourself, these days, with things what they are.'

Actually —

'If it's worth doing, it's worth doing well.'

That's it, I said.

'If you want something done right, you've got to do it yourself.'

That's it, I said.

'They hide them, you know,' he said in a tone of suddenly deeper intimacy.

Beg pardon? I said.

'That little door down there, that room is for *the infectious, the septic, the elderly and noisy,* and *for special cases.* You know what the special cases are, don't you? That's where they hide the ones when they're finished. Till they've got room for them, down in the fridge. When they've got room, they come with a special trolley called a concealment trolley, that has a false bottom, and they push anybody who's dead into it and put a lid so when they roll it down the halls it looks like a plain empty trolley and nobody gets upset. That's Captain Blood.'

That is – ? I said, bemused.

'In that bed over there. Captain Blood.'

Captain Blood – actually one Corporal Blood, Retired, but rechristened by some local wag or tender soul finding the 'corporal' too expressive for the setting – Captain Blood lay in the bed across the aisle, an erstwhile unlucky holidaymaker, it turned out, who (on his two-week's package trip to Benidorm two years ago now) had popped a travel-sickness pill which the multinational conglomerate that sold it had failed to remove from the market in time to spare him when he'd gone to the chemist's that day. He didn't travel a lot now, being mostly tangled in the electrical leads from his head, wrists, chest and ankles, the saltwater drip to his inner elbow, and the automatic ventilator with the flap in his windpipe.

'They're keeping a liver fresh for him,' Mr Robinson whispered, 'in America, for when he's ready – it's attached to a baboon out there.'

What, I said, on the National Health?

'The company's keen on some gesture. But he's not so pleased, himself.'

It's nice for the baboon, you mean, but what about him.

'They've got some kind of what-they-call table of compensations, the company, and he's furious that they gave him only nine credit points out of twenty for what the pill did to his lungs, and only six for his kidneys. That gets him only £2,068 and he's suing.'

An ingenious and passionate man, each day for the sole benefit of solicitor Mr Pike, Captain Blood for two priceless minutes would have his respirator tube deflated, to emit a choice handful of earthy Yorkshire phrases while exhaling, in a flood of feelings, before he spluttered and was recapped, and his taciturn legal visitor took his leave. For in-bed entertainment via his own private transistor radio, in a true Tom Swift spirit pinched from no novel but rather distinctively his, he had personally devised a volume- and station-selector which, attached to some private part, responded in the manner of a galvanometric lie-detector to the changing chemistry of his alternately dry and perspiring skin as he lay there, so that we had occasion to hear the news, music and sport in the ward according to Captain Blood's metabolism. When on Sundays the hospital's public address system was opened to broadcast the pious doings from the chapel on the third floor, Captain Blood's volume went hairily up and the stations switched by in a pyrotechnically ear-shattering display.

But – missing from Ward G when I moved in – my slow-rankling personal bugbear was to be Mr Austin. In *all* the wards one heard of everything that they did with Mr Austin. He had a rare disease. They liked to operate on him. They had begun simply, without any fuss. He had first been admitted in an unusual shade of yellow; so they had joined his gall bladder straight to his intestine. His yellow faded almost immediately. The subsequent irritating back-up of bile, however, had led them to remove portions of his intestine, providing for the discharge of feces at various times at various places through the wall of his stomach above and below the pajama string, entitling him as I understand to lifetime membership in both the Colostomy Society and the Royal Ileostomy League. It was at about this time, as Mr Robinson explained it, that Mr Austin had begun to look different – quieter and quieter. At first they'd thought he was afraid of the operations. But he didn't respond to these with anything like the normal kind of fear, so they got started, then, on the really good ones. Ulceration following the intestine-project had obliged them to remove part of the stomach – the unpleasant side-effect being as a rule that now the latter wouldn't have emptied at the right rate, so that at the time they'd also done a pyloroplasty, reaming wider the stomach's outlet – 'or, if you prefer,' they'd said, 'a gastroenterostomy, chopping a whole new extra vent between the stomach and intestine and it'll empty just fine —'

That's when he stopped talking altogether. One day, it seems, as Mr Robinson tells it, somebody said to Mr Austin:

'With this new valve, you've borrowed yourself another whole month!'

And he'd never opened his mouth to speak since. 'A right one, he is!' Mr Robinson would say. To friends' anxious looks and attentions in this phase, Mr Austin would respond first with a fading smile as though they were dumping him endless armfuls of flowers and he had nothing left to put them in, and then as if he were compelled to swallow quantities of some spice-violently seasoned substance that his gut could no longer

37

keep down. Well-wishers would tell him of this new treatment and that, chatter gaily about his homegoing, vow he'd have round-the-clock attention, prattle of all his children and how beautiful the Spring, and swore he'd live forever – and he uttered no answering word. In the third stage Mr Austin's bladder had gone foul and they'd decided to give the urine a new direction by joining ureters and inserting them into a loop of the small intestine, in the process removing one kidney (which was shrivelled, minute, and of no use to anyone and which might lead to high blood-pressure), especially since there was a rather good shortcut to the kidney from where they happened to be working and as long as they were there —. What's he, gone anti-social, then? I said. 'He's the same,' Mr Robinson says, 'with his wife, and all. "You've got to get well!" she tells him. "I won't *allow* you to die!" – it'd make you weep to hear her – "I'll never let you go!" she says. "Come on!" folks rouse him, "courage! be a man!" – but it makes no difference to him, the queer mean fish.' Deeper and deeper inside went Mr Austin, it appears, withdrawing into some other place, as if nothing would ever do but silence. 'A fellow that won't give his own wife and young a sustaining word, if you ask me –' says Mr Robinson, and throws up his pale hands. In due course, Mr Austin had then suffered a prolapse, no doubt owing to the excitement, where the rectum dropped down into the anus – the correct answer being to pass a suture beneath the skin around the anus and – to just the right degree – pull it tight, which they did, followed by daily physiotherapy to encourage the opening to recover its bygone tone by a probing series of local electric shocks just before breakfast. 'He's one of the blessed,' said Mr Robinson; 'his body has a terrific will to survive, he doesn't appreciate it – "all things bright and beautiful" – I don't care who it is – "all creatures great and small".' The by-play of the next event they'd lined up for Mr Austin, a prostatectomy, was that you had to make a choice, and since he wouldn't choose, they went for the specialty of the house and instead of arranging for the sperm to pass now into the bladder, they'd fixed it so he would in future (had he the heart for it) ejaculate his progeny backwards up his digestive tract and out his refurbished Cloaca Maxima. 'It's a crying shame,' said Mr Robinson, 'turning his back on his own, and them leaving no stone unturned for him – I mean it's all right for some, but fair's fair.'

Some response in me to the unseen Mr Austin surged in agreement – 'Man is not an island,' as Mr Robinson so wisely put it; glaring in the direction of the man's waiting bed, we hoped never to be like him; it was a moral nonsense, something hideous. 'Besides,' Mr Robinson added in a somewhat envious footnote, 'it's always them that're the lucky ones – them with the rare conditions.' You mean, I said, they survive the treatments? 'They keep *getting* the treatments.' Because with a rare one — ? 'Well who can tell? it might work.'

The most exciting discovery to emerge was that the rarity behind Mr Austin's case is in fact a disease of the blood – in connection with which there's a persistent difference of opinion as to whether he ought to survive any operations to begin with. The rumor is it's political, some budget crisis looming, and the academic die-hards have made his sort their cause.

Mr Austin wasn't brought to his regular bed until my third week in the ward.

As they stowed him behind his screens I caught only a glimpse of an unexpectedly simple-faced, rather small, round-shouldered man, with an expression, behind the mask of physical anguish and narcosis, of an almost irritatingly quiet and certain nobility.

They've decided to open up his chest and have a bash at things there. 'Well,' as one assisting surgeon put it self-deprecatingly when they were all complimented on their dash, 'one has to push the boat out occasionally.'

It was at this stage in the game that I noticed the staff, doctors and nurses alike, lose interest in me. Even the auxiliary who sat in the ward yawned a lot and became piqued and difficult if I disturbed her reading. They had just put me through a new battery of tests, and by the following afternoon my thundering cavalcade of treatments had come languidly to a halt. As I lay in bed dozily fingering my orifices that morning it bloomed over me like sunburst that all those nettlesome first-days' symptoms – nausea, heartburn, numbness, gas – had been sponged away. I felt beautiful.

They had done it! I was cured! No wonder they were weary and bored with me.

I was on my hands and knees giddily fumbling for my slippers when I saw Dr Wall's feet wriggling and curling in the doorway.

He asked me to sit down.

'We have examined your latest tests,' he said, et cetera; the floor grew chilly as I sat there in my pajamas. 'And I feel I must tell you that the condition is metastatic.'

I realized without a single hitch that this was the word Dr Wall had not managed before to pronounce when he'd begun 'There's every chance, unless it's —.'

'I am sorry to have to say – neoplasm —'

Neoplasm?

'– Unusual cells – anomalous –' he went on '– primitive unconformable tissues –' babbling somewhat '– newfangled – invasive –' he said getting hold of his thread '– proliferating – it is inoperable, there is absolutely no likelihood of remission, and I would advise you to put your affairs in order while you have leisure and strength, as I would have thought it was a matter of weeks if not days.'

I see, I said. I found my other slipper, feeling about.

'I recall that you have shown a particular interest in time,' he said, with an obvious effort toward a businesslike air, '– how much time, and so forth – and I can assure you as I am always assuring people in these situations that it is not a matter of how much but how well, it is not the quantity of life that counts but the quality. These things can be quite fun really.'

This is what you meant by its being common, then – I said – and nothing more. What is common is *dying*. In your line of business.

'Well —'

And you feel this is now my line of business, is that right?

'I hope,' he said, 'that – at the end of the day – you'll be able to say that we'd done everything imaginable to make your stay comfortable.'

* * *

Somewhere along the way Dr Wall's 'opposite case', whatever that might have been (a mere placebo of an idea, perhaps?), had lost itself in the shuffle.

I had come to the wrong palace.

The man in the cape rode up in this gleaming carriage. He ascended the steps and entered with his usual smooth and elegant stride. Down the long gallery he passed into the west library and sleepily stirred the embers in the glowing fire; he sipped a warming cordial as he crossed the anteroom to the damask chamber, dropping his clothing across the deep carpet, and luxuriously mounted milady in the starry canopied bed; he slept a delicious sleep, arose cheerily at dawn to shave himself at the marble basin, and discovered that the blade was a feather's edge duller than it ought. Or was it sharper? And realized suddenly and without question that he had come to the wrong palace.

What place is this?

Don't get me wrong – if I sound upset, I'm not mad at you. You know how it is, I'm a little edgy, that's all. You know, I mean. Don't you?

Mr Pike made an announcement that day; the judge had denied Captain Blood's appeal for more than nine points for his lungs and six for his kidneys. The company was privately offering twelve for his spleen and would throw in the liver free if they could get it away from the baboon. Captain Blood sank back in a rage, his radio switching through all the stations. Mr Pike is going to fight, if he has to go to the highest court in the land.

◆

They keep talking of discharging me. 'For a while,' one says, 'at least.' And then somebody from Wall's office always exclaims: 'Any minute now — !' And they hang my chart back on its hook at the foot of the bed, where I'm ensconced again each night.

The Archbishop of Canterbury's impressive statement was relayed to me by a smiling ward sister this morning. He has told the Royal Society of Medicine, says the blurb in *The Times*, that people have got some matters wrong on the question of health. There is a limit. At a certain point, things become optional. It's a fallacy, declares the Most Reverend Archbishop, to think that Christians are in favor of prolonging life just for the sake of it. Or are in favor of life at any cost. A terminal patient, after all, isn't obliged to accept extraordinary treatment. Any more than a doctor should be obliged to give it. The line has to be drawn, announces the Archbishop of Canterbury. A doctor has a responsibility to his patients, to the Government, and to his fellow taxpayers, and the line must now be drawn, bearing in mind the total resources of the health services, which are not unlimited. We must ask, he concludes, whether the National Health Service isn't neglecting other areas of medical expenditure and spending too much on keeping certain people alive.

Everyone seems pleased. The Editor of *The Times* notes with relief that it's out in the open; he explains that our society is 'tongue-tied and embarrassed by the western way of death', and that there is no cause for shame and little cause for fear;

Dr Charles Bennington, Chairman of the Human Rights Society, says that the Archbishop is 'perfectly right' and that 'the function of all medical treatment is to restore people to health and if that is not possible it is wrong to continue the treatment'; the British Medical Association says the Archbishop's speech was 'helpful because it emphasized the difficulties'; and Mr Robert Sessions, Secretary of the Voluntary Euthanasia Society declares that 'we would agree but he does not go far enough'.

I myself have asked the ward sister our Archbishop's story exactly, but all she says is he is the Primate of All England. Persistent efforts to conceive of him leave me with an image of this unusual primate humping about on his knuckles in a tall gold hat eating a banana, a picture which surely cannot do him justice. It's typical of my state; the limits and defects of my experience. The more the certainty and calm with which others move about me, the more things seem to gyrate.

I'm getting a false breast.

'IPP!'

A lady with an imposing clipboard appeared.

'May I see your bum, please?!'

Hum? I said, spellbound.

'Your bum. Let me see it.' I lowered and hoisted my pajamas briskly, to which she exclaimed 'Clean as a whistle!' and wrote something down. 'We'll get as much skin off that as we ever need,' she intoned to herself and then declared aloud, 'IPP, International Prosthetics Programme, you are entitled to one artificial breast, how do you want it?'

My gender doesn't bother you? I said cautiously. On discrimination you stand firm.

'You know the law!' she said with withering scorn; 'I don't care if you're a poached haddock, do you want it nylon-filled, oil-filled —'

But why a breast, why not say a leg?

'– Most people want a breast, read the statistics. Oil-filled, fluid-and-air filled — ?'

Will they deduct it from my pension? I said suspiciously.

'It's on the National Health, I have you down, it's the system. Do you want it in nylon, oil, fluid-and-air, or with a very light terylene stuffing?'

43

With a very light terylene stuffing, by God! I said.

Squeeze the most out of the bleeding system, that's what I say. Turn it around. The American way, the great way – got to turn it around!

This afternoon they decided I shouldn't be lonely or sad. 'Now one of the first things is,' they said, 'you mustn't be lonely or sad.' Determined to 'augment the quality of life' for me, gesturing to the Archbishop of Canterbury's suggestion – also in *The Times* – that there is a loneliness about dying these days that is not healthy, they took me and the other two people who'd been declared unmitigably mortal this week and put us into a room in the basement with a seven-piece steel-string and jug band and exposed us to 'simply loads of fun'. It was the full treatment; isn't this loads of fun? I shouted, leaning to the other two – both looking alarmingly warmed-over and inert; each nodded vigorously in turn; in the end I had to confess that it was all the fun I could ever want in my whole life. Then they wheeled us back to our wards.

On the bedstand, poised on the edge:

Greetings from Hinkle.

On torn paper, the same twisted hand.

Why must he remind me? What does he want from me? What's Hinkle to me?

Peculiarly, I find I've been developing what the house doctor calls pica. Unnatural cravings – for chalk, iron, things like that.

I'm convinced that the entire affair is psychological – and that it's a damned shame I didn't point out this likelihood, the obvious really, to Dr Wall. Sooner – before he'd gotten this idea, this fixation about – you know — I'd no doubt be home now – could have saved everybody a lot of trouble.

The house surgeon and his staff file daily past our beds in review, eyes front. Today stopped at my chart. 'Good news!' he bellowed, 'blood pressure's back to normal.' He thumbed my flesh. 'Mmm, halfway from the symphisus pubis to the umbilicus, sister'. And paraded away.

It's then that I experienced the first unpleasant feeling you might have when, passing briefly down a shadowy alley before coming out into the sunlight again, you realized that you were not alone. The slightest shudder, an instant's nervous sinking of the stomach, and then it was over. Only leaving the residual new sensation – of *having someone in here with me*. Company. A 'roommate'; a 'blob'; what *is* it? If I am – if I *were growing* cells, *more living cells*, how could anyone conceive me to be imminently living less? Some sponge, leeched onto me? some multi-eyed fleshy aspect of myself, is it – is that what they want me to think?

Growing? how can they possibly mean? What – if it's there at all – what are its limits, its terms? Does it do as the tissue did – in the Harvard experiment? Like the minute section of liver they took from a hen, that they kept alive for years, nourished just right, warm and moist in a culture, in a growing tank? remember? it was in the news every year or two: TISSUE DOING WELL. Remember what happened...? I do.... Forget it.

I want to run. Say it's not happening – not happening to me. Steady, man!

Shut it out – run and hide —

Where to, home? can you shut it out there? *Use your head.*

Poor chap, mishap, lost the use of his right mind.

It was Captain Blood's performance that saved me. At 8:56, as they were serving the usual hot drink as their parting gesture of the day, Mr Pike burst into the ward waving a sheaf of papers. The House of Lords had just voted Captain Blood twenty points for his whole body – the first time anywhere that any court has authorized a one-hundred percent replacement; the doughty veteran, even allowing for depreciation and after taxes, was to be worth a cool sum in thousands to be spread backwards and forwards over sixty-five years or his life, whichever came first. In a single sweeping gesture Captain Blood flung away his catheter and his ventilator tube and cried, throat-flap coiling and wagging, 'By goom, I've doon em! I've doon em, I've doon em, I've doon em!' Embraces went round, and he lay beaming back and closed his eyes. The house doctor, having come to join in the festivities, cast an eye on the electrocardiograph which was still connected. 'He's spiking', he said in a rush. 'He certainly is,' said a nurse gazing at a point midway down the bed, where the sheet was rising to untold heights; 'why the dirty old —,' said she, 'the sloppy bugger's having a wet dream.' With a soft shuffle of stations, Captain Blood's radio galvanised to the ruffle of drums, and with a mounting swelling throb there came forth the soul-stirring chords of *God Save the Queen*, accompanied by Captain Blood's ardent geyser through the sheet. 'As you were, Sister,' said the doctor, 'stand aside, it's piss, and he's dead.'

Without going into the technical features of the case, Captain Blood was indeed, as it turned out, deceased. That it happened screened from my view and I know of it only secondhand in no way veils from me the triumph that it represents. It's a matter of character. What – hide? *Use your head.* I am going to make a study – *learn* about these physical matters, this complaint they claim I have, the material details. Determine whether what I'm dealing in here is a product or a service. Gather the facts, observe, take a positive line – get a second opinion, *form an opinion – my own.* It's only a trial, this situation, some kind of exercise, I know it. I have asked a senior enrolled nurse to get me every book there is on the subject first thing in the morning.

I was hungrily perusing the best and most up-to-date treatise the patients' lending-library could produce this morning (*But Why Cancer, Sally?* by B. Stoll, 1976) when Treeza came in. The nurse whispered cordially and confidentially, 'Mr Wall is doing just fine!'

'I'm so glad!' said Treeza. 'And my husband?'

That's me dear, I reminded her discreetly. It's a term of endearment, it helps them keep track. What's in a name so long as we have each other?

'Why are you reading *But Why Cancer, Sally?*' she said.

I'm studying, I said.

'Why?' she said.

Dear Treeza, I thought, as she sat opposite me there, small hands clasped neatly in her lap. Look at you now. Not like the old days, are we? It was different then, or so I've been thinking, these years. Then – the old days – she was one of those who felt snug if not secure in proportion to the amount of clothing they'd slipped off, plausible if not convincing in a ratio fixed to the square yardage of her manifest skin. Take the morning we met, that town by the shore. The first day for each of us, there. What a day. Her flashing boobies more or less out on their own and foraging each in its best way (I fell in love); I see you're just unpacking, I said (she fell in love). For three evenings running, she averted her lips from mine; on the fourth I cracked and wept, Must we keep not meeting like this? She lay down, disbanded her straps, set adrift her knees, and produced a form to fill in. Her family sent a fanatical number of ice buckets. Simple as that it was. Or so I seem to require to see it, from here. One thing at least; we've been consistent. In our amorous golden days we gave to each other prickly heat; so do we now of an altered kind, in our more typical moments of brass. With her talcumed secret organs and yellow patent-leather shoes with matching cinch-belt, playing house each hour in more mortal earnest, she performs as though her ceaseless tidy activity makes the world go round. These days it scarcely makes the merry go round. Between noon courses of lettuce sandwiches and bedtime complexion packs (lying face-up covered with sliced cucumbers and mayonnaise), she appears in need of nothing but herself; if all mankind expired on the spot she'd have enough to keep her busy through geologic ages – picking up after us. But this faintly unclubbable devotion to genteel efficiency on the part of my darling is a mechanism of defense, I swear (year in year out, with appropriate secret oaths). Within that mother-of-

47

pearl shell, dainty, fine, translucent, mucid, there is a raw oyster (you thought, perhaps: a pearl?)

And why do I betray her like this? Slicking our lives into shape with masterly thoughts I don't feel? that aren't even like me or the person in childhood I dreamt one day to become. As if I begin to find in the writhing shallows of the facetious the only honest words around. What *has* become of me?

'What are you studying?' she said. 'Why are you studying?'

I want to do the right thing, I said.

She looked down at her hands.

'I got,' she said, 'the gamboge organza for the study curtains.'

That's good, Treeza, I said. That's very good. I know you love the gamboge organza for the curtains.

'But you don't,' she said. 'You hate it.' She began to sniffle.

I don't hate it, Treeza.

'You hate gamboge organza for the study curtains. You said they'd look like great splats of chicken shit on the garden doors.'

But I don't hate them, Treeza.

'How do you know you don't until you've seen them?' She burst into tears.

Treeza don't cry, I said. The people can take back the gamboge organza if you're unsure.

'I have to tell you,' she said, recovering with gratitude and some skill.

Yes?

'I've been having one of my awful headaches over all this.'

Good lord, no, I said.

'What do you mean by that?'

Just – Good lord, no.

'But what does that mean? what do you mean?'

I mean, well, about your headaches, they can be awful.

She thought. Then she went on.

'If you were home – if you were at home instead of here – I couldn't, I wouldn't be able to lift you, or turn you —'

No, I said. That's true. Why? Would you want to lift me and turn me?

'I mean to say, if I had to. If it came to that.'

Ah. If it came to that!

'I wouldn't be able to help you with a – a bedpan, or a – one of those bottles.'

I imagine not, Treeza. I can see that.

'You might need it sometime, a bedpan or a bottle, that's what they say, they all say you might, that a person does.'

I hadn't thought of that, it shows foresight in you to think of that. It's good of you.

'And if you – if you got restless, in the night, after I'd been lifting you all day —'

– and turning me, with the bedpan and all —

'If you took to restlessly wandering confusedly at night – I simply, I simply couldn't cope!'

Dear Treeza, I thought; you and your separate dishes. Fear not.

'And to know that people *know* that your husband —'

Dear —

'I feel like a leper —'

There's not the slightest thing leprous about you darling.

'I feel tainted, eaten, the way people look at me.'

We'll see what ever we can do, Treeza, I said.

What is this draft you felt, Treeza? this chill; could it possibly be Reality?

Don't worry, I said, darling.

'And your brother Lloyd is back from the United Arab Emirates and I haven't got a thing in the house,' she said, bosom heaving.

'How's this for timing, hey?'

It was brother Lloyd doing a panama-and-soft-shoe up the ward floor.

'In an X-hours-in-the-day situation, can't stop. Well, podner!' He rubbed his four-hundred-dollar prescription sunglasses with his shirttail, held them up discontentedly to the light, and put them on to have a squint at me. 'What's all this I hear?'

Couldn't be better, I said, as Treeza, blushing, tiptoed away out the far door.

'All kidding aside,' he said.

He stared at me, did a brief buck-and-wing, and returned to give my left foot one of the most solemnly intimate and tender nudges I'd ever had the pleasure of between us. 'Where does it hurt?'

Where — ?

'Where does it hurt? I mean, you know...why are you here?'

To tell you the truth, Lloyd, nothing hurts.

He stood shaking his head. 'Look at you! Lucky as hell – get to meet it in the flower of your youth, all senses there, in your prime, got your intelligence, got your savings, got your health, what more do you want? Should write a book about it! give you something to pass the time. Think of it – TV rights – millions – you'd clean up!'

Nice, I said.

'Nice? what is this "nice"? it's fabulous! you sound like a goddamn limey stuffed-shirt butler, no wonder you've got troubles, you're going through an identity crisis over here. Come on, look at you – you're beautiful, baby! You'll be out of here in nothing flat – good night's sleep, plenty of fibre and away you go!'

It's easy once you know how, I said.

'Well,' he observed. '...It's probably symbolic. These things are psycho-phenomenological now, you know.'

I'm sure they are, I said, respectfully.

'Existence is dichotomous these days, you realize – I know you've been out of the country quite a while now. Mind-body, black-white, sun-moon, you know, good-evil – and the best of them all, male-female, eh?'

Another nudge to the left foot.

The gist eludes me, Lloyd.

'...Look, you're in real trouble, I want to tell you that, you're not well. Knew it as soon as you left America. Now what you want to do – you want to remember that you're attempting to become an integral part of the whole universe, fulfill your full capacity for humanness, harmony and love.'

I'm easy, I said.

'You've got to let every flake of your deepest being express itself through the spectrum of your whole thing emptied of self and selfness, and filled each moment with all that exists – through the power of *breathing*.'

There's no answer to that, I said.

'Breathe, boy, breathe!'

I took a deep breath.

50

'You look rotten,' he said.

There's no answer to that, I said.

'And it's no wonder, too. Have you got a lawyer? What is this kind of place you're in, a hospital? I mean, what kind of hospital is this, a socialized medicine hospital? Boy, do you need a good lawyer! Now you listen to me. What am I, a cheapo? What do you think I am, some kind of piker?' He cupped his hands to whisper, looking over his shoulder. 'We've got *rubber petrodollars* up the *kazoo* now! And I'm holding, and Treeza's going to be holding, and I want you to be happy – now let me finish – so what I want you to do is get the hell out of this damned National Health place —'

But it's the best hospital in the Northern Hemisphere for what I've got, I said.

'I don't care what you've got – back home, prices what they are, you'd be lighting out for the hills lickety-split let me tell you, you couldn't *afford* to die, let me lay it on you right now. Free doctors, free medicine, all this British bull, no push no incentive, no wonder you're lazy and apathetic! Now I am going to make sure — I want you to do this for *me* — I'm going to make sure you get the best, most expensive private doctor and private medicine and private bed in the whole goddamned whatever it is, and that's no bull, because you are my brother, and if you die then, brother, your ass will be grass around my house, let me tell you!

There's been no time to think. Lloyd presiding – or his lawyers – I've been transported everywhere, seen every 'best damned specialist money can buy', including a Viennese internist advising complete and total bed-rest for thirty years, a Swiss surgeon prescribing tuberculosis, a French professor ordering carrots, a Syrian veterinarian recommending a French professor, four American pathologists urging white sound, and a Turkish savant delicately if obscurely suggesting a horse. And all, when pushed to the limit, ending with the same – at first astonishing, finally noisome – refrain, put most succinctly by the monumental White House neurosurgeon

51

whom they keep attached to a platinum hotline in a concrete silo beneath the mirage-smoking sands of Almagordo, New Mexico when he said over the crackling wireless:

'Have you seen Wall?'

I am Wall, I said, to coin a phrase.

'No no,' he said; '*the* Wall.'

You don't mean, I said Doctor Wall, of London? you're joking!

'Shmegeggy,' he said, 'if all I had for you was a joke would I be talking to you from beneath the mirage-smoking sands of Almagordo, New Mexico?'

'Not to put too fine a point on it,' said his Whitehall liaison and legman Professor Sir Desmond Clerk-Maxwell, 'Wall's your man, and no mistake. Wall is the Supremo.'

And this he was, it seems. So I'm back at St Mary's, in a private room now, in the private custody of Dr Wall's high-voltage, special 'team'.

'Mm-hmm,' said his surgical registrar this morning, 'anh-hanh. Slight weight gain. It's at the umbilicus, now. No signs of pre-eclampsia?'

What?

'Protein in urine?'

I wouldn't know.

'Apprehension?'

Of what?

'Irritability?'

No.

'Noise bother you?'

No, dammit.

'Mm-hmm, anh-hanh – I can offer you some sedation.'

For what? I said.

'Prevents convulsions, fits.'

... I don't want sedation. If I have fits I'll let you know.

'I'll tell Dr Wall!'

Tell him. If there's anything I won't be, it's sedate.

'Just you wait.'

What for?

He left.

At last, in private, I can take up my research.

* * *

Began reading, thinking, eagerly, at sunrise this morning –
only to be sabotaged by the visit of Sister Dingle, the physio-
therapist, with her steam inhalator. 'We're going to teach you,'
she said strapping me into a cough belt, 'how to breathe.' She
turned on the steam.

Impossible to get down to it after the imbecility of that. Sat
giggling in the twilight. Tomorrow must exercise more effort
toward self-control.

'Telly' in one's room; the vicious temptations of private
medicine. Watched it today, hateful thing, until the head-
phones broke down. Didn't want others to hear me watching.
Sat in silence then in the chair by my bed, watching the picture
move, the mouths and things.

Hinkle, the filthy bugger – in this artificial dusk another
'Greetings' has found me here. What does he want from me?
Forget it. I crush the paper and throw it skittering beneath the
bed.

Today, played with myself. Let my right hand never know
what my left is – let my right hand never forget — what ever
was the verse?

The news is that in the matter of mortality and its management, the Pope has declared his accord with the English Primate.

There's some movement afoot.

I've a slight thickening of the gums, with hairline trickles of blood running about them, at the base of the teeth. The house doctor says it's perfectly natural.

Inexplicable cackling, somewhere.

Picked up this private phone of mine and called my wife, seizing the free moment to advise her to ask all our friends to enquire of me through her, instead of harassing the switchboard with their calls. Could hear her staring perplexedly at the earpiece.

Cackling in the halls. One Sleeney, male nurse and self-styled gazette, has consented ambiguously to relate the tale. Mopping in an operating theater, someone on nightshift a while back kicked loose a couple of hoses by accident, and reconnected them wrong. Eight a.m., top of the docket, a fellow was brought into the theater with gallstones. In the middle of things, the operating surgeon ordered oxygen, one hundred percent, and they'd turned the proper switch and administered nitrous oxide instead. One hundred percent laughing gas. It blew, they announced later, the man's mind. Further measures failed to bring him out of his stupor. Then, Tuesday, an attendant wheeling him into an elevator left him for a moment, sitting in his now customarily motionless and speechless way, and forgot. The man sat in his chair in the corner of the lift, going up and down, the door opening and closing and opening – and was he brainless? or was he still giggling inside? – people drifting in and out, appreciatively withholding their stares under the spell of the look he had on him, a certain careless, languidly detached, even stately air of disinterest, until this morning, when eventual subsidence and an uncommonly bumpy halt of the lift laid him definitively askew between the opening and closing doors. The immediate cause being simply dehydration, said the autopsy, a severe case of thirst. Always leave them laughing.

I don't like it. Something in me shrinks — the laughter fades.

* * *

My gums are improving.

I've discovered that everywhere about my body the hair, moles, and freckles have been growing darker.

'Welcome to the Near East.'

Today I've met the much-winked-about legendary Lench. The one no one can look at.

He comes into my room with this cryptic phrase, 'Welcome to the Near East'; I understand he says it all the time, especially first thing in the morning and last thing at night, in this peculiarly amiable yet somehow privately dark way, whether in company or in an apparently empty room.

No doubt he was once, not so long ago, one of those power-pack hucksters, spinners of twisted verbal yarn you spot from far off as you lean at the bar trying to have a quiet drink by yourself. 'Flash', as they say, grinning and calling the barmaid 'luv' and 'darlin' and fondly breezing in and out of the center of things, taut and hirsutely muscular, repeatedly reported sunk in passion in the archipelago of his luvs and darlins, claiming to dream to be the first to cram and recount it all for posterity in Esperanto, Sanskrit or Manx. A secret lapsed schoolteacher from Letchworth Garden City, precociously defrocked, he'd easily abandoned the erstwhile militant-liberal's comforting habit of wornout leather flying-jacket and simulated East End accent in favor of the dazzling drip-dry shirt; 'in business' for himself by twenty-five, hawking used yachts, swamp tracts, scrap jets, whatever he could lay his hands on, whatever he could 'move'.

'I'm getting the word,' he said holding out two fistfuls of privately-ordered books, 'going to gen up!' I could see he was planning an encounter with someone called The Pelican Nietzsche, joined by the You Can Lick Lacan Companion and Do It Yourself Foucault together with a Short Guide to Being and Nothingness, and Fear and Trembling Made Easy.

Great, I said, playing it on the safe side.

In evident stages, they've not only removed his teeth but seen fit to whip off one ear together with modest portions of his lip, cheek, and nose, thus lending him a unique and quite adamant smile. A young man with plenty of vim and vigor, nurse says he'd first had to be straitjacketed when they'd brought him in, and had taken to batting flies – real or imagined – against walls and bedbars with his face. A day-porter's view is that Lench's case is one where, looking at him with unbiased compassion, the best you could wish him would be that an earthquake would pass quickly through and swallow him. And yet you wonder. There's no way he could be kept down; he takes out his energy now in incessant postulation and expostulation, and there's reason to believe it's by this that he's lost what friends he'd ever had, though how exactly I've yet to learn. 'My disease?' he says; 'lingua sempivirens. Symptoms? compulsive speech, obsessively rational.' And it's true – from the minute he comes in you're clinched by the awful charm of his wagging tongue's clickety-clack in the cage of his naked mouth.

'Children, squire?'

None, I said.

'Wife?'

Some.

'Bloody hell!' he said. 'You're right there, mate! She's a red herring, isn't she, the wife?'

I hadn't supposed. Do you think?

'Kids, wives, sod the lot. Red herrings, every one of them, hey?'

I'm prepared to keep an open mind, I said.

'How can blokes moan we've got no purpose? Furthering a species that's got no purpose, *that's* the purpose, hey? cranking out more of the same, that's what's flaming obscene, if anything is, what do you say?'

Doesn't bear thinking about, I said.

'It's not on,' he said, 'it won't wash. It's why I've given up old nooky – sex shackles you to an obscenity, that's why – and do I look a saint, do I?' How he looked at present, humanity told me, was beyond my compass to argue. 'Ha! Abstinence – now abstinence, that's more like it. Abstinence is saying No and Blow you, mate, I'm no slave to the inane.'

I thought he spoke extremely well for what he was, and told him so.

56

'Got an asset, I have,' he said, pleased. 'I come unladen – now there's a word – I come unladen with hopes, see! Makes me a lovely patient. I cannot be disappointed, squire. Makes me a doll to live with, a veritable pussy-cat. There again, though,' he said, tapping his head with a forefinger, 'it's one thing to say "I'm not bothered", and take no notice of dying and all, because life's so sodding unpleasant. But if you've no – no distaste for death, sport, you've got no defenses for life. Which is heavy going, have you thought about that?'

You could get a hernia thinking about it, I said.

'You could do yourself a mischief. Because then what do you refer it all to? life, I mean. Nothing relative, every unpleasantness a horror, got to fight the whole war over at every new buggering ditch, it's an absolute nightmare, you twig? Absolute.'

But you said you've no expectations – you take it easy.

'Ah well,' he said ironically. 'There you have it.'

Have what?

He looked at me appreciatively.

'Right you are, sunshine,' he said. 'I did say that.'

I'm afraid I looked at him rather blankly.

'Of course,' he said, 'the real answer in a depraved-universe-with-a-simulacrum-of-order is to give them back the simulacrum in the eye. Madness with method – it's two fingers up and say fuck-all.'

Addressed to whom?

'You haven't picked up your proper English yet. Saying fuck-all is saying nothing.'

I see.

'Right.'

But you're hardly saying nothing.

He supercharged his inimitable grin.

'Don't you downrate my hard-earned distance from the reeky facts! I'm creating! It's the Arse Moriendi, squire! Death's not just the tail that wags the dog, the ultimate necessity, it's – as you and Darwin perfectly know – the true mother of invention. Only novelty outruns it – here I am, I offer you broad inklings of an art of dying, a dying art – the tilled imagination and a well-manured sense of despair – and all you can say is I should lower my voice.'

57

You believe in despair?

'It's the cardinal sin, do you think?'

I'm very undecided about sin, I said. But I do know that of all the forms of self-indulgence I intend despair to be the very last of my resorts.

'Oh splendid fellow!'

Like fighting-wolves, lions – submission's the last resort.

'Oh noble heart! you've got it back to front! they bare their throats first – *fight* as a last resort.'

Okay so we've both got things to learn.

'And fast.' He grinned. 'So you're one that fancies an order in things? Like – better things, worse things, would you say?'

Only that despair's the least imaginative response to any situation!

'Living's a matter of style, then? You live with more style?'

Imagination's your own recipe, you said.

'Well damn it, man! as a bit of surprise muck to smear on the face of death – it's glitzy slurry at best, it doesn't make bricks, you can't build with it — you can't "improve" life, life's nothing, it's just us, old bean, it's made out of us! It's the bag of tricks, the X we're made of, that makes us behave *as if*. As if we've got more than X or could ever get it. Climb off it – you think too much!'

What else – be a vegetable?! To live is to think – to see yourself, know yourself living!

'Welcome to the Near East,' said Lench, quietly setting aside my rhapsody with breathtaking – and I thought, ill-advised – lack of tact.

Go screw yourself, I said (to my surprise) with that easy malevolence one wastes upon friends.

'What do you think of survival?' he said.

It's here to stay.

'Seriously.'

What's to say about survival? You've got it or you don't.

'But *should* we?'

Apparently unable to supply a ready answer himself, books in hand, he left – me speechless and unsettled.

* * *

I sit here – sitting up, walking about, sitting down, feeling the passage of the damned one-and-a-half tons of blood that *Time Magazine* or somebody says go pouring through the locks and canals of a man's brain every day – shamefully vital and even somewhat stern in my goddamned hospital cell when I could be about in the world — waiting. And what am I, I who sit waiting here like this? Where precisely am I embodied? in the slither and lash of this still ostensibly vorpal tongue in the cage of my head? in the swish of my blood? in my decisions and deeds? What, let the clock decide?! At 30 I had my way, have I lost it at 35?

It's Hinkle. Take Hinkle.

I unscrew and screw up the note from Hinkle I'd thrown away and that's reappeared between my thighs on the chair.

The time, for a start, he was seen pushing the old woman from the plane.

Hinkle. What, in my place, would he do? Once early aspiring, scant of cash and of diminishing expectations; a reject of the gentlemen's clubs of the left, right and center; apprized of certain precarious misconcealments in the high government office of which he was an ill-vetted hireling, he had one Monday morning knocked on his Cabinet chief's mahogany door, uttered a single sweet-honed untouchably many-edged lie, and slipped through the loophole of statutory truth into the vestibules of power. Turned up from under some dank genealogical stone by an ad of Treeza's in her search for Our Roots, Hinkle, appearing one night in my office when all the desks but mine were dark and I'd thought the outer door locked, an unheard-of cousin insufficiently removed. Hinkle, in the fatigue of the hour, numskulledly I'd agreed to traffic his interests with the firm should 'the need arise'; his living unwritten dossier, the fathomless iceberg's unwriteable hulk, becoming mine. What use he saw in the liaison – had even he thought it through at the time? He didn't work like that.

But Hinkle is nothing – he's immaterial to me. Why does he follow me like a shadow?

You don't know?

What do you mean, don't I know?

You don't know yet why he shadows you?

I strew the shreds I've made of the paper into the last scum of gravy on my dish and shut tight my eyes.

Ten days in this room.

Clarity – work for clarity!

If I concentrated on this supposedly growing silent partner in me – made it real, I thought, reduced it to its simple material reality... pullulating polyp, proud flesh, vegetating, dividing and multiplying... to drag the beast from its lair, into the light of day —. Only, when I got around to it, they were bringing me lunch, and I couldn't get the first bit of meat into my mouth. There, with its strains of gristle, rivulets of fat, and pulp, there could be but for the grace of — there but for the grace of —. A lump of my leg, of my gorge, of my ass.

It's this insufferable self-indulgent privacy, it's *this* that'll do me in. Excrescence, increscence, branching, mushrooming. Mad, I've been mad, paying myself such attention – it's unhealthy, abnormal – must bust out of this private house of correction inside me. Get back where I started, back to something innocent, even for a moment — something simple, something pure.

Remember, reach back —

Nothing comes —

She sang me a cradlesong, of an evening. Before she'd go out. The sum of the knowledge I have of my mother firsthand. An evening I feel I recall. A sole conversation I've always believed us to have shared, when I was an infant or possibly shortly after she died. The song's principal part was the rhythmic, persistent empty refrain, 'Lullaby-by — by-by — by-by — by.' Abruptly that night (in one of those word-searching fevers that may take a child's mind) I said to her aloud with a cry, 'But I'm *not going* bye-bye!' And her voice's tender response (quietly penetrating through the portentous element of my verbal misjudgement to the very heart of the matter): 'Yes, darling, you are – to the land of Nod.' And at that instant – I'm sure my memory is right that I was lying in my crib, I can recollect the twisting shadows on the wall – I glimpsed for the first time that there would be states, dark conditions, a whole serried range of them, like that one then of approaching moonless sleep, which one was to enter without hope of redemption by any companionship whatsoever. And such thresholds did in the sequence of ensuing time present themselves, certainly, eclipse upon eclipse – and of course I hardly noticed them, they're scarce worth the thought, as things go. For – as my mother surely cheerily assured me even at the time and as anybody knows – one always simply awakens again come daylight, there's the morning after, and you can always forget the shadows of the night. One always awakes.

One and a half tons of blood, slushing perpetually in restless circles through these shafts and galleries....

You're going merrily along, reading the menu; and suddenly you find that you're on it.

What is the *size*, what *are the dimensions* of what's ahead?

Stop thinking. Start thinking. *Do something*.

Get out of this perverse scummy room!

And they've agreed.

How nicely they accede to my whims.

At last. Ward G again, and my old bed.

'How've you been then, yourself?' Mr Robinson said turning with difficulty around to see me. He's just the same. Well, not exactly. A few new nerves have been affected it seems; it's caused his eyes to go awry, the right one permanently crossing left, the left straying further left, so that over-all he appears continually extra thoughtful, gently pondering something – offscreen so to speak. 'No pain yet,' he said, 'I hope?'

Me?! It's not that kind of thing! A joke my being here, to be honest – false pretences. Still – a person welcomes a short break, chance to examine his life!

'Aye...' he said. 'How's your brother Lloyd, then?'

I laughed. He thinks I'm here, I said, because I'm 'sick' of things outside!

Mr Robinson shook his head slowly. 'I don't know what it is, perhaps it's just what I'm used to, that's all,' he said politely.

What's that?

'Getting on with things. I like it.'

Well so do I, I said.

'Can't keep me from it!' he said with embarrassed pride. 'Doing a bit of gardening. Putting in a good day's work. Collecting the family round a nice roast-joint of a Sunday.'

But in hospitals now half your life – ! I said, and bit my tongue.

'Well, this is it. This is the thing, really, isn't it?' he said.

Yes, I said vaguely.

'These things all come out in the wash, don't they? at the end of the day.'

It's good being back in G, idle chat . . . relax, relax.

'Greetings from Hinkle.' The newly arrived bit of paper with the same mechanical message lies on my pillow. It's not what he wants from me – it's what he *doesn't* want. Somehow that's it. Somehow.

Hinkle – embezzler then, toady, extortionist, liquidator, scam-runner, suborner and ministry nark – *why did he tell me those things?* – so he'd found his métier, then. Am I to blame for all that? Two-faced? he's a hydra. Take the brothel he came to run for a time, his funhouse for embassy queens; Hinkle on show – deanly, seraphic, avuncular, something for everyone – well I pictured Hinkle parading and screaming in earrings and lace, whipping the men into plumed frenzies, three Freemasons and a Swiss attaché beaten senseless by a visiting Canadian Elk – so the bailiffs arrived. Years ago that was, long before he appeared in my office, and the bailiffs now all have government posts. Hinkle, graying, carious, gouty, self-serving, self-observing, a pinwheel of mirrors – why fret over him? Him and his gambits – men's funds he plundered, was it, or their minds? Like the tale he regaled me with of the old woman — You're making this up yourself — I'm not — the old woman he pushed from the hired plane, this was not his grandmother in the least but merely an anonymous someone on the way to the loo, heaved into the jetstream — you're

62

making it up – I'm not, *he* made it up and *he did* it, listen —
the small old woman tossed in the jet-stream as a token in
earnest to a certain business associate effectively soused and
cajoled aboard at the time – a syndicate man and incipient
blackmailer – it was a gesture only, a demonstration, 'a Hinkle
hindered is a Hinkle unleashed'; and as it happened, undis-
cerned by the drunk in the half-dark (though he sobered
remarkably then), she was not actually anyone at all but a mail-
bag, in a woolly coat and tam-o'shanter come conveniently
to hand. Yet – and here's the rub – who'd explain the jest
should 'the need arise'? The people of Milan and surrounding
region, whose post to the Rotterdam Dutch was so strangely
delayed? or the simple country folk who saw this little old
lady land with a puff in a patch of waste ground on the outskirts
of Frankfurt-am-Main? a mailsack still wearing a hat. What
– Hinkle's dupe explain? who (how Hinkle must have grinned
up his sleeve!) was subsequently moved in sterling faith to
commit genuine murder in Hinkle's honour? should *he* be
arrested, weak of wit and small of will – what then? Ah, this
is typical, Hinkle, and the worst yet to come.

If only – minion of reason and bourgeois that I am, beast
of the common herd – I'd have thought the better of him if
only I'd known for sure he was working to some manifest,
palpable scheme.

Why does it have to be me, to live with it all? By sheer and
stupid chance – just one of those unsolicited burdens-of-knowing
one's lumbered with in the hum and drum current of daily
business and blood, each man has his, this is mine – the Hinkle
account. If only, if even at least I could have believed he did
it for the pleasure, the spoils.... And now these new rages of
his, enormity upon enormity. Why lay it on me? He knows,
he knows – the higher he spins, the harder he'll fall – without
some semblance of sense, if it comes to a hearing he'll get life
if not worse – how could I, why should I find him a plea? Will
they let him out again, on the loose out there, on his own
tightwire, his strings of puppets stretching and tangling?
what's he up to? He's nothing, nothing to do with me.

He's less than nothing and you know it. Stories, words – it
doesn't sound right, the whole ring of it phoney – you've
snatched a name you heard and stuck a person to it, snatched

a person and stuck a meaning to it. A horror-comic man.
Listen to the sound of what you're saying —
I don't want to hear.

They've moved a new one into Captain Blood's bed. Some kind of bone disease. One leg huge, heavy and misshapen. Restless. Ten or fifteen times a day he picks up his leg like a club in both hands and lumbers up and down the center aisle as if he's looking for somebody to hit with it; he stares at me like I'm one hell of a Martian, an evident source of irritation to him because I haven't too few or too many parts, because of my obvious comfort. In the far screened-off corner where Mr Austin was, before they took to keeping him in the Special Cases room at the end, there's somebody now who doesn't move very much, lying flat on his back; I've never seen his face, though I've had the pleasure of watching the nurse aspirate his stomach contents often. Is it a young boy? He appears to dread the confinement of the screens they persistently slide round him.

Mr Robinson can't seem to stop thinking about his grandad and the Duke of Wellington. Of the Sundays in his childhood when his father would take him with him on long journeys in search of where grandad had been mislaid; and they would inevitably end by standing, caps clasped in hands, before the tomb of the Duke of Wellington. 'It's not that it were grand,' he says drifting, in surely his father's voice, feeling in memory the peace of that connection which his father felt; 'but that it were there.' Later, through an oversight in his handwritten will and delays in the Christmas mail, they had subsequently burnt and scattered Mr Robinson's father in some unnoted place. 'A stone,' I heard Mr Robinson say. 'Not as I'll know. Just to leave a little sign, that's all. As may last and be true.'

Sure enough, I said.

'Just so anybody as might happen to ask . . . at least they don't need to look any further, they'll know, "This is where Jo Robinson's trail ends down here". They can rest easy and know it's done, this were the last door Jo Robinson went through.'

64

Sure, I said, pretty much at a loss.

Mr Robinson turned his head and looked slantwise at the wall. 'Our Harry,' he said. 'What our young Harry didn't get to know, before he was taken from us – that'd need a book to tell.'

Yes? I said.

'He didn't know if I didn't do certain things I'd had a mind to, it was because I had so much else to manage.'

What was that, then?

'Now don't you start!' said Mr Robinson with half a laugh.

No, not at all!

'Thing is, I forget, now, what else it was; all I recall is what it kept me from doing. But,' he said, 'it's always the way, isn't it?'

I don't know, I said.

Afternoons, he recites to me whole lessons he's tried to learn 'by the post' through the years – how to invest his savings, how to build a model airplane, how to retire gracefully, how to think about Ode on a Grecian Urn and The Rime of the Ancient Mariner – pushing the years by after Harry – and Molly, then – died. It seems much on his mind, inside there, quietly.

'These things can't be helped,' he said. He raised his hand slowly and scratched his head. 'Do you know what I think about, sometimes?'

No, what?

He seemed embarrassed and had trouble putting it. 'Well –' he said, scratching his head again '– did you ever go along a road – did you ever see any road where there wasn't these... along the side of the road, these things that used to be... something else? something run over. Sometimes a rabbit, sometimes a bird? Sometimes something bigger even. A cat, a dog, a sheep? Some wild thing, even, lying there, the further you went... a badger... a fox?'

Yes?

'It's just *there*. Flat, and – empty, like a rag. Not itself. It sometimes makes you think life – is just – what living things have. I don't know. You wouldn't even say it's – "lying" there. Not the way you'd say you or I are lying here – you can't even make out what it is, sometimes....'

65

I suppose, I said uncertainly.

At times I almost wish he'd leave me alone, when he speaks like this, duff old elkhound that he is; and then I feel instantly sorry and confused, and I smile.

Dr Wall flits briskly, vivaciously, lightfootedly by.

There is an increased general crowding throughout the hospital; they tell us it's owing to the holiday climate outside.

The 'boy' lying on his back in 'Mr Austin's bed', and who's afraid of screens, is a girl. A casualty of the overflow, it appears, from the female ward; a woman or a girl. They turn her now, and on my way to the 'loo' I can see her face. It is ageless, very white, and unmoving. I also think it's very beautiful; but no matter how many times I pass the bed in its corner, half behind the partially open screens, I of course always see the face from one angle only; and perhaps I'm prejudiced by its stillness.

'It's never as bad as you think,' said Mr Robinson today.

No? I asked.

'... It's only being in a strange land,' he said, looking over at me thoughtfully, sympathetically, 'that you feel strange, Mr Wall.'

How do you — ?!

'You're in a far off, unexplainable —'

— You see that do you — ?

'You're in England,' he said, nodding.

Oh. Yes, I said. That's true.

'Do you think, Mr Wall,' he said, 'that we might be in an allegory?'

Pardon? I said, startled.

'Do you think that maybe this whole experience that we're having – this dying is an allegory?'

I hadn't thought of that. It gives you pause.

'That – I reckon – do you think we're only dying in a – in a literal sense?'

I'll buy that, Mr Robinson —

'That we're – symbolic, you and me?'

That would be nice, Mr Robinson.... Would that be nice?

'Sort of heroic, really.'

Awfully nice.

'Or is it maybe about *life*, that life is all like this —'

Like which, Mr Robinson, exactly — ?

'And we're – we're Everyman!' He looked at me with a complicated sort of satisfaction on his face.

It's a terrific idea... Mr Robinson.

In a little while, he was chuckling away, sputtering and chortling to himself. 'I was just remembering,' he said, 'when our Harry – the week our Harry was born! That excited, we were! near wet my drawers, I tell you! Well, there we were, and the midwife would come round every day – a rosy lady, that one, all smiling, I'll never forget – and she'd say to our Molly, "Haven't you started yet?!" I can hear her to this day. "*Haven't you started yet?!*" And then our Harry still didn't come, and we had to go into hospital, and the sister would turn up every hour and say to Molly, laughing like, and frowning, "Are you still here?!" Oh, I tell you, that was a time...!'

And then he did come along! I said.

'Sorry?' he said.

He did come along, your Harry.

'Yes. Yes, he did. Did our Harry....' Mr Robinson lapsed into a dream. Soon he was laughing again, laughing out loud. 'And I – I used to read him – I used to read him from *Winnie-the-Pooh*!'

You didn't!

'Yes! Yes, I did – *Winnie-the* — !'

I loved *Winnie-the-Pooh*! I said.

'– About Pooh visiting Rabbit's house, under the ground – and how he sat with Rabbit and ate all Rabbit's honey and ate and ate —'

And ate and ate – I said – remembering and laughing —

'– And when they said goodbye —'

— Pooh got half up the hole, and couldn't get out —

'"Oh help!" said Pooh, "I'd better go back. Oh bother! I shall have to go on — !"'

– "There's only one thing to be done," said Christopher Robin, "we shall have to wait for you to get thin again, a week —"

'"A week!" said Pooh, and a tear rolled down his eye —'

"It all comes," said Pooh crossly, "of not having front doors big enough."

'"It all comes," said Rabbit sternly, "of eating too much".'

– Eating too much, I chimed in —

'– And so for a week at the North End of Pooh Christopher Robin read Pooh a Sustaining Book, such as would help a Wedged Bear in Great Tightness –' Mr Robinson went on, me nodding in beaming unison with him, '– and Rabbit hung his washing on Pooh's legs at the South end —'

– And after a week Christopher Robin said *Now!* and took hold of Pooh's front paws —

'– And Rabbit took hold of Christopher Robin, and all Rabbit's friends and relations took hold of Rabbit, and they all pulled together —'

– And Pooh said Ow! and Oh! and then —

'– And then all of a sudden, he said —'

– *Pop!* just as if a cork were —

'– were coming out of a bottle! And Christopher Robin and Rabbit and —'

– and all Rabbit's friends and relations —

'– went head over heels backwards – and on top of them came Winnie-the-Pooh —'

– Free! —

'– "So," ' said my bedmate, reciting, laughing and with tears in his eyes, ' "with a nod of thanks to his friends, he went on with his walk through the forest, humming proudly to himself, and Christopher Robin looked after him lovingly —" '

– and said to himself —

"Silly –" we said together "– Silly old Bear!"

The two of us sat there shaking and laughing and wiping the tears from our eyes.

The auxiliary who was setting down the afternoon tea coughed gustily up her sleeve and ran away.

'If that is an – an allegory –' said Mr Robinson —

Do you think it is — ?

'If that's an allegory about a – about getting born –' said Mr Robinson, a living tribute to adult education '– then what does eating-too-much mean?!'

Birth, death, heck – I said. Why haven't they given you any tea?

'No no, I shan't, ta very much!' he said, but the spirit of the moment was too precious – I insisted he take some of mine – 'No no, I couldn't' he said, 'I oughtn't –' but I persisted, and finally, with a tender look as if to say he was only taking it so as not to hurt my feelings, and with a glance over his shoulder, he leaned shaking from his bed and took my out-thrust cup and drank the tea down with a quick gulp. 'That was just the job,' he said, 'thanks ever so much indeed,' and I felt ever so close to him; 'feel a better man for that!' he said; 'that went down a treat. That'll just do me! Cheers!'

And he dropped down in a heap on the floor between us.

I perceived immediately and with awful regret that Mr Robinson wasn't meant at the time to have tea, and as I bellowed a nurse came. 'Not at all, take no notice,' he said coming around groggily with the shot she gave him, 'having a bit of a nod, mustn't grumble,' he said as we helped him into his bed; 'as right as rain, bad patch but take the broader view, don't give it another thought, it all comes to the same thing' and he lay back and stared slantwise at the ceiling, breathing heavily, tremulously, the words coming frailly through his lips. 'All comes to the same thing.'

I'm going to leave. Discharge myself first chance in the morning. The whole affair's a farce, I'm here under false pretences, and screwing up other's lives as well – put my foot in it, forever got one foot in it these days – I've got to get away. First thing in the morning.

Dawn. It's arrived: a small ache – between the eyes – and vision's blurred. I've tried already to get going, but can't quite make my way among the strange flashing lights. I'll lie back a while. Mr Robinson is breathing softly in his sleep.

It's stupid, ludicrous. Of course the thing's all in the mind. You feel hurting about the man next to you, you want to run away, and so you get a little headache. It's my own fault, it's psychosomatic. The nurse comes rattling on her round. I'll just keep still. Mustn't squeal at the drop of a hat; keep still.

The imagination will stop raiding the chickens now quick – you've got it outfoxed.

Just lie back.

* * *

There. There now. Evening. That didn't last long at all. Lying back. Looking back.

The only funny thing is – how oddly sluggish the body feels. Ligaments, all over my body, seem slowly to be softening. As though the joints might be subtly coming loose, disarticulating, softly coming apart.

But I was right, no? This frigging head of mine – wasn't I right? It's all in the mind.

So you've all the time in the world – the old psyche's still at work, familiarly clattering and ticking away in there, by turns doltish and canny, business as usual. It's a trial. It's a test run. You don't turn down a challenge. Never. We'll have to stick it out.

Right where we are.

Sister Dingle seems concerned. Twice today she's had me put my head in a steam bag. Or maybe it's just a thing she has. 'Let me see,' she says to herself as she butters her scone at tea, 'I could go and drum up some more phlegm in Ward G. Get Mr Wall's head into a plastic bag, you never know —' Undoubtedly it's a thing she has.

It's from her this afternoon that I learned about Hope Holliday. You probably knew already; I still haven't read all the books. She's upstairs, in a laboratory on the seventh floor, or part of her is. Hope Holliday is a girl that died of a tumor fifteen years ago; I heard where she died but I've forgotten, and it doesn't matter a whole lot. In the cellular sense, they have kept her alive, her cells alive. She's still called by her old name in laboratories all over the world, Hope Holliday; because after all she – this line of cells of hers – still has all the same genetic attributes; except in some places they give her a code name, they call her HoHo for short. She still has the cancer that killed her. Only now there's a little bit of her in New York, a little in Stockholm, a little in Tokyo, a little HoHo there, a little HoHo here – here, upstairs, in close proximity, Hope Holliday in residence in a container of unspecified dimensions somewhere on the seventh floor.

My face is changing. Some kind of pattern, a darker pattern, has begun to spread from the nose over the cheeks and brow. Melanin, they say – unleashed in the system by the cells at work within me. The outline of a butterfly is spreading, imprinting itself in a mask upon my face.

♦

They came in a convoy, a wedged gaggle, like goslings across a bog.

At their head, attired all in pinstripe, came Mr Blyth, fully fitted out with red, bony hands and a habit of standing with these cupped behind the close-knit meeting of his buttocks as though in personal dread of an imminent goose; Mr Blyth, the Registrar-General Himself ('Heavens!' he adds with appropriate pshaws, 'I'm just a general dog's body around here!'). With him, in a handsome cerise tie, shocking-pink shirt and cream jacket, the spit and image of a strawberry shortcake, came one young Mr Lovelock, Secretary of the Complaints Committee and 'the Principal's right hand'. He had long nibbly teeth and – not to be outdone – his own personal habit, which consisted of endorsing each of Mr Blyth's remarks with a quick brainward suck of nasal catarrh and a coy if indecorous furl of the lip accompanied by a low roll of drums from an adjoining room, or so it seemed. Following came Dr Wall, with Sister Dingle and her steam inhalator.

Mr Blyth took up my chart.

'Well!' he said. 'You're just fine today!'

Terrific! I said.

'Relatively speaking,' said Mr Lovelock.

'Been getting plenty of orange juice, have you?' said Mr Blyth.

Oh yes, thank you very much.

'Good good. Well! We've been hoping just to have a quick word!' said Mr Blyth. Mr Lovelock moved smartly to my bedside and gave my internal organs an authoritative grope, with secondary nods of perfunctory agreement directed at Dr Wall.

'Half-way to the xiphisternum,' he said officially over his shoulder to Mr Blyth. 'Weight nominal plus. Oedema steady and rising. Say two hundred days.'

Is that – ahead of me, you think? I said.

'No.'

Would you care to elaborate on that? I said casually.

Mr Lovelock glanced toward Dr Wall. The eminent surgeon stood with a particularly dreary and misshapen look of empathic distress on his face, avoiding my eyes, his hands awkwardly wringing each other.

'Something rather fearfully awkward's come up, Mr Wall, concerning costs and things,' said Mr Blyth with a big smile, looking me level in the eyes, brows well arched above his polygonal silver specs.

Oh yes? I said.

'We're a bit up a gumtree on this one.'

'A spot of bother,' said Mr Lovelock.

'About the style of treatment *in re* this indefinite-duration approach, if you take my meaning.'

'A technical hitch' said Mr Lovelock with a snuffle.

'We're having to take a tuck in our expectations, and we thought we'd just have a word about your death.'

Welcome to the Near East.

Uh – I said, sinking unobtrusively — hope springs eternal — ?

'Well said, Mr Wall, well said!'

Welcome to the Near East. Why did Lench's phrase keep floating to the surface?

'Now then —' said Mr Blyth.

'Now!' said Mr Lovelock enthusiastically.

'Actually, it's about your – about the interim.'

The interim? Ah, I said.

'That's it.'

You can't keep me in the manner to which I'm accustomed, I said, trying under the circumstances to be helpful.

'It's something like that,' said Mr Blyth.

It's something about comfort – you can't keep me in orange juice? I know: you liked me better as a private patient. You want me to pay my way.

72

'I'm afraid it's beyond that, to be quite honest.'

A miracle! I exclaimed. I've got you! you said miracles! It's the old chance-in-a-million shot, isn't it? you've got an operation up your sleeve that'll make us or break us, haven't you? I should've known – I grinned with a giggly wriggle – You tricky buggers – it's the old double-or-nothing, the old stake-it-on-a-throw, the good old go-for-broke, why you've been dying to try it for weeks, I'll bet, heh? How about that! The secret weapon?! Hell! shucks! you listen here – you want to know if I'm willing, you want my permission to take the risk for a complete cure? you want the big go-ahead from me? Well you've got it! Say no more, you've got it, let me tell you right now, you've got it, fire away, you have got it, *shoot the works!*

Mr Blyth shook his head.

When do we start? I said.

'It's later than you think, old fellow. We'd *like* to operate. Don't think we wouldn't like to operate on you. Dr Wall here would like to, Sister Dingle would like to, I myself, speaking personally, I would love to get in there and —'

'We'd *all love* to!' said Mr Lovelock.

'But it's just a lit-tle later ideally than we'd like –' Mr Blyth winked '– a bit far along –' wink wink. 'It'd end up just a downright mess, I'm afraid, all round, Mr Wall. We'd be jailed, you'd be off to the Great Beyond, and it'd play havoc with our records.'

I understand, I said.

'No, our hands are tied,' he said. 'Still!' he said, bucking up, 'can't complain!'

'It all comes to the same thing, really! A question of priorities,' said Mr Lovelock.

Well, I said jovially still, at least there's the scientific interest, in my case!

'Actually,' said Mr Blyth, regretfully, 'it's not all that interesting, your case.'

'Bit of a bore, really,' said Mr Lovelock.

'That is, no two cases are alike, and yours has its idiosyncrasies, its anomalies, there's no doubt about that.'

'Absolutely!'

They both turned pointedly to Dr Wall.

'And there *are* things we'd like to understand better....'
said Mr Blyth.

Dr Wall stood nodding with a vaguely labored, sickly smile.

Meaning, I said with a spark of insight that rather pleased
me, things you'd like to do that the regulations won't let you
do to a live person.

'This is the thing, really, isn't it? That's to say, objective
modern science, you know – correct me if I'm wrong, Clive –'

'I couldn't agree more,' said Mr Lovelock.

'– The truth doesn't *out*, you know, until you can take a
thing – well –'

'Apart.' Mr Lovelock smiled.

Can't I –

'Oh –,' added Mr Blyth with a chuckle, 'some will make
gestures – Let's study the subject's "behaviour", they say, or
his "mental process", and the like –'

'But then there are so many variables!' joined Mr Lovelock.

Don't I –

'It's not worth a heck of a lot.'

'Not worth a cat's willy, really.'

In point of fact, I said, I'd be worth more to you dead than
alive.

'Poppycock,' said Lovelock without conviction.

Admit it, I said, if I weren't keeping you stocked in fresh
parts, I'd be nothing to you, alive.

They gave me a string of blank looks, one by one.

For the future, I said, I *am* darned handy that way, aren't I?
You know – I mean, I've heard – everybody's heard – about
the baboons – ?

'I'll grant you,' said Mr Blyth civilizedly, 'we're having
much better quality hearts in Britain –'

'– Since we've been getting them from still-breathing
donors –'

'But there again –'

'We come by more lungs than we can handle –,' put in Mr
Lovelock. 'We've got more brains than we know what to do
with.'

'And the liver and kidney situation what with the Common
Market –'

'I think we're in for a glut in livers, frankly –'

74

'Not to put an ungrateful face on it,' said Mr Blyth, 'at the end of the day, as a parts-storage facility, we *can* operate a baboon at a lower cost margin.'

'It's a question of priorities,' said Mr Lovelock.

You mean – I said: Who comes first.

'There you are.'

British for the British, is that it? You think I'd do better back home – *America*'s got the answer for me!

Mr Blyth coughed.

'You have *had* the American treatment, Mr Wall.'

I've had the American treatment.

'You have.'

The latest.

'All the latest.'

'Except, of course –' said Mr Lovelock, with a wary glance at Mr Blyth '– the Lever approach.'

The *Lever* approach? I said.

'The Lever approach is a treat,' said Mr Lovelock with an obvious thrill.

It is?

'However,' said Mr Blyth definitively. 'It is not a treatment.'

'Not at all,' said Mr Lovelock. 'It's not a cure. You'll love Dr Lever, Mr Wall.'

I'm sure I will, I said.

'If it comes to that,' said Mr Blyth.

'This is the snag, really...' said Mr Lovelock.

'... Perhaps,' said Mr Blyth with a clarification of the throat, 'perhaps we ought to brief you on the background a bit, the history of the thing, let you have a little look-in — behind the scenes, as it were.'

'Yes! yes!' said Mr Lovelock, clapping his hands.

'Once upon a time,' said Mr Blyth, rising on his toes, closing his eyes and putting together the tips of his fingers before his breast, then settling back with his hands behind him in the accustomed position, 'there was a stage when one didn't think twice, it was perfectly normal, it was standard, in fact it was quite routine to do everything in your power to keep a chap going.'

'It lasted oh a few hundred, a few thousand –

'A few million, really —'

'– yes, years —'

'There came a time, Mr Wall,' said Mr Blyth, 'when we'd *got the technology*. When we could keep a fellow like your good-self ticking over, so to say, forever. And without ever an uneasy moment, without losing a moment's sleep.'

'Butter wouldn't melt in our mouth!'

'A little pump here, a bit of wire there, and a person went on living ad infinitum.'

'Ad nauseam!'

'Grotesque as it may seem, looking back –' Mr Blyth and Mr Lovelock traded a reminiscent smile – 'we'd got obsessed with *feasibility*, would you believe? If we could do it, we did it. We built machines instead of looking the picture square in the eye. Well, I don't have to tell you, Mr Wall.'

'You can guess the rest.'

'Getting down to the nuts and bolts of it —'

'– Not to take you through the swings and roundabouts —'

'It's uphill, but we're pushing back the darkness, Mr Wall. "Living"? What is "normal", what is "health", after all? Hidebound custom? Routine, sloth of mind? take the obvious way, the easy way?'

'We're no reactionary stick-in-the-muds around here, the grass doesn't grow over *our* feet —'

'Vis-à-vis the rational progress of man, we can't afford habit's ruling our objective moral intelligence —'

'Fair's fair!'

'– We can't be caught whipping a dead horse —'

'– Not for one minute — !'

'Things are filling up, if you follow me.'

'Man on earth is a living biomass now second only to the krill, a small shrimp-like creature consumed by whales, seals and penguins.'

'One reaches a point of diminishing returns.'

'A thousand million tons, these krills.'

'Hospitals and the like have been filling up —'

'Certain teething troubles.'

'– With people lying about, well, you can imagine —'

'– Alive and all that.'

'In any best-case projection from the alternative actionable futures, the population-timeframe constraints have escalated

76

us into an infinite-bulge, triple-feedback, dive-dive-dive technology.'

'And that's why there's been a change of thought,' said Mr Lovelock. 'A slight shift in protocol on this mortality-decisions business.'

'From now on we're keeping an open mind. From now on it's honest-to-goodness realism, flexible management,' said Mr Blyth, bringing out his fingers once more to count on them, 'the merit system for all, no lazy taken-for-granteds, no automatic tenure, and – Mr Wall – we must trim our ship.'

You're sure you aren't – you wouldn't be suggesting another hospital? another country maybe?

'To be honest with you as the day is long, Mr Wall, to put my heart on my sleeve, I'm afraid it's not just a matter of local authority. This is an international revolution. We're riding cheek-by-jowl into the rising sun of a better tomorrow with the Yankees, the Germans, the Nipponese – it's mankind – it is mankind against the resources-and-expenditures trade-off.'

I'll admit I gave them a glassy look.

They gave me one back.

So that's it, I said.

Welcome to the Near East.

You're not talking about not being able to keep me comfortable, I said leadenly. You're talking about not keeping me alive.

'Take us as you find us, Mr Wall.'

Easy come easy go, said I.

'Once bitten, twice shy,' said Mr Lovelock cheerily. 'A stitch in time saves nine.'

'The thing is,' said Mr Blyth, 'do you have anything special on?'

I suppose not, I said. You catch me in an off moment.

'Not many of us can say, after all, that there's anything that simply can't be done by someone else.'

You put it with quiet elegance.

'Because with all the good will in the world, old fellow, beyond a certain point —'

'There are people waiting up to two years for goiter and prostate operations,' said Mr Lovelock, 'on account of chaps like you.'

I'm sorry.

'This is the National Health, not National Death!'

'– And besides,' said Mr Blyth, 'it's a pound to a peanut you'll come to seeing it our way! Why one anemic lady from Tooting, we stopped giving her blood —'

'– She said it was spot-on – she was absolutely delighted!'

The mind boggles, I said. And you're sure there's nothing I can offer you before I go? A tongue? a piece of ass?

'Recycling's dubious, frankly, in the case of metastatic invasions –' said Mr Lovelock apologetically —

'We don't want to make too much of a meal of this, do we Clive?' Mr Blyth interrupted.

'– Ugly cells turn up anywhere everywhere —'

'You're not to worry in the slightest, Mr Wall.'

'– Riddling organs and things —'

Dr Wall in his corner gave a heavy start; a person felt somehow that Clive's words struck an intimate chord; the surgeon's pallid hands were no longer wringing each other – one hand had disappeared mysteriously within his clothing. 'You're in the best hands possible,' Mr Blyth continued, 'and your consultant surgeon has been observing aberrant cases for decades —'

'He's El Supremo!' said Clive Lovelock.

Dr Wall's hand was going for his stomach.

'Your case is – I don't want to say ordinary –' said Mr Blyth '– a classic of its kind, shall we say – unconventional generation in a standard host? but you yourself are a sensible man, an honest man, a decent man, a man who by his own lights was never about to set the world on fire, a man when all's said and done who claims no more than his due – common ordinary justice, a decent day in court, no more no less, isn't that right, now? A jolly good fried kipper is a classic, but you just don't go and pay hundreds of pounds for a kipper, with respect. You'll want to keep everything in proportion to the last, I'm sure. And we, on our side, mean to do everything in reason for you!'

Only, I said, my condition may just come to exceed the limits of reason, is that right? I mean wouldn't you say, just for curiosity, tell me – I said in the direction of Dr Wall, whose activities in response to ours now really had my eye – *mightn't* it? My condition may just exceed the limits of reason?

'Not at all!' said Mr Blyth, 'that's not how I'd put it.'

The eminent brain, lung and derma surgeon was leaning thickly against the wall – his expression flushing and dissolving through a rare and awful series of contortions – discreetly gripping his testicles inside his white smock.

Then why, I demanded, is El Supremo gripping his testicles?

Messrs Blyth and Lovelock looked toward the brilliant surgeon and away again with ill-concealed distaste.

'Life's like that, isn't it?' said Mr Lovelock.

'You do grasp,' said Mr Blyth, 'that there's nothing personal in this whatsoever.'

I do, I said.

'Death is something the individual has to achieve for himself.'

Quite, said I.

'Of course you're responsible for yourself, entirely and utterly.'

Oh yes.

'And as long as you are, we're prepared to do our part.'

That's fine.

'Look here, I'm bloody sorry about all this mess,' said Mr Blyth heartily. 'If I were at the stick you'd see some changes around here.'

I see.

'That old coot over there, for example,' he said, waving a hand at Mr Robinson, who was dozing in the next bed, '– he'd go before you any day!'

'Any day of the week!' cried Mr Lovelock in a glowing spirit of fraternity. 'Old, worn out! look at him!' He kicked the legs and feet of Mr Robinson's bed a few times inspiredly. Mr Robinson sat bolt upright, shouted 'What? What? What?' and lay down again.

'You'll soon get the hang of it,' Mr Blyth told me.

Before – I half-muttered, grinning and nodding obsequiously – before it gets the hang of me?

Dr Wall was now sagging over considerably, and he was trying to cover his mouth with his one free hand.

'On balance you'll have to agree,' said Mr Lovelock gaily, 'the glory's not in winning, but in taking part.'

Smashing, said I as they sloped away.

* * *

Welcome to the Near East.

I remember it now. If it's not the version Lench has in mind, it's close enough.

'Carry me,' said the scorpion, 'across the river Jordan' (or was it the Tigris, the Nile?); 'carry me over the river,' said the scorpion, 'on your back.' 'Never in a million years,' said the soft-eyed frog. 'Here! you'll be safe as a bug in a rug,' said the scorpion, 'how could I ever sting you, out there on the water where I'm helpless? it would be the death of me!' So – and you know the tale as well as I, it's in everybody's mind – the two set out over the waves, and halfway across, with all the venom he had in him, to the heart the scorpion struck the frog. In their lash and whip and writhe in the froth of the water as they went down, the dying frog gasped to the drowning scorpion: 'Why – why did you do it – why?!' 'This,' came the bubbling reply, 'is the Near East.'

They found me in the john.

It was hours before they spotted me squatting in a corner there, my fuzzy bathrobe belt providing the lock on the cubicle door.

I had thoughts in there, between those grey walls. Vain thoughts. I thought: *They* got off, my parents, well away to the nether lands, and I didn't mind – I managed. I thought: but this time, *this* person, *me* – this is too close to home. Or too far from it.

It was an idiotic slip, that run of thoughts, and I'm ashamed.

I thought: You on one side in the first tug-of-war, them on the other with rope-knotted fists, they bloody pulled you through the slough, over the line, across the fetid skidding greasepit into life. Now, I thought, they've let you go to the quicksand edge of the sudden second pit, and they'll leave you slipping, sliding there, voices trailing off, if you don't call out.

Hold, hold on! I felt like shouting, All hands round, hold tight! Lock arms, dammit! Lock arms, dammit all to hell!

But the bastards are right, of course. It's yours, all yours, and you've got to face it, the thought is yours, you've got to gulp it down as it comes, straight, neat, no chaser, swallow it to the lees.

I even thought bad things about you. *You*, out there. You ghoul. I thought, you ghoul, eavesdropping, keyholing me, just to sniff what it's like, you carrion-scoff, you sucker-of-neck, you geek, you.

But I blush now to think what I thought then, a simpleton babbling to himself, and I 'came along quietly' with gruff, good-hearted Matron to my bed. I am not a child, and I will not be caught behaving like a child. Have a care! I said, sinking to one knee, and she let go of my ear.

I've borrowed Matron's mirror. It's the mask. The wings of the butterfly mask spreading over my face. Umber about my nostrils, faintly; a growing mummy brown beneath the eyes.

I practice breathing on the mirror, watching my moist spirit alternately haze and go clear.

The street-dressed visitors hustle and drift through. The young man's gone who comes to see the person – woman, girl – in the bed in the far corner. Each time he comes, he stands for the hour looking at her blanched face. I hear stammering, I see his lips moving, I can't make sense of his words, there is something desperate in the motion of his shoulders. He tries to hold her hand; tries to make sense of his holding her hand; stands there; is told to go. I understand that he performs faltering attempts to communicate with a nurse, with a doctor, with an attendant; he waits in the corridors, in the cafeterias, in the lobbies, walking aimlessly, and standing.

From my own wanderings in all the wards on the floor before today I recall now the smiles, the glistening eyes, the little gestures, the empty look, the thin laughter, the sudden glance of bewilderment and shock, the outstretched hands.

So I've no uses in this world, did I tell them? Have I nothing special on, did they say? This Wall, oh physician of mine, keeping me here, me feeling just fine – this vampire Blyth, this Lovelock, this Matron, treating me like loose change, where do they get off – what are they, playing me for a fool? Okay, I say in my heart of hearts – okay damn you. I'll get the bit in my teeth – I'll blow you a bloody raspberry all right – I too, I can snap a garter or two. Just watch!

God it'll make me happy, God I can't wait – to hear them say it, to hear one of them shout it loud and clear: 'Jesus, he really snapped my garter that time!'

Upstairs, Miss Hope Holliday vegetates, floating suspended in her container, cryptic and idle. . . .

81

I can feel it coming, a kind of aura, something's coming on
– just let me catch them once, I'll get them all, I will – I feel
it come on —

Aaaaaaghgh.
It started something like that: Aaaaaaghgh!
It was the evening meal. The tray sat before me. I had already
devoured my boiled-suet pudding lustily, vengefully. I was
working my way through the fish fingers, one by one, doused
in brown-sauce, heading relentlessly toward the rhubarb in
hot custard. There were two fish fingers left when it happened.
A bizarre sensation came into me, entered me with the inexor-
able certainty of a wave of granite, a sensation of nausea, of
mystery, of a whistling song, of horror, and there was no
choice about it, the scream came up out of me, towering
through the ward, Aaaaaaghgh! It's not that I don't like fish
fingers, at all. The scream stopped, leaving an awful hollow
in the space around me. Which I promptly, in the splitting rift
of a second, fell plummeting into. I don't even mind fish
fingers all that much – in fact, I rather like them, especially in
brown-sauce. Someone came, they came, running. My tongue
had fallen back into my throat, my jaw locked up like the
portals of a throne-room. I mean, naturally if you stuffed me
into a trunk brim-jammed with fish fingers I'd be put off my
stride. 'Hold – give him air –' I heard voices say '– jaws – get
Doctor —' On the floor face-up I lay so rigidly arched that I
touched the cold linoleum with only the crown of my head
and my heels, arched up and breathing with a powerful snoring
sound. But things being equal I can give an unqualified yes to
a good fish finger and let that be an end to that. 'All right –
okay –' the anonymous voices said, and soft things were being
thrust beneath me, pillows, God knows what, and pressure
was being applied in front of my ears and my jaws pulled
open, 'he's going clonic – get a thumb in – all right –' my
bulging tongue was grappled out and for another instant I
could breathe, churning foam up now. To hell with the
rhubarb and custard. And the shaking, body-torquing and

twisting part began – 'Don't hold him guide him, he's out, he doesn't know' – the muscles all bundles wrenching, racking against each other – '– guide him, for Christsakes don't let him break his arm, easy, watch the table, steady, watch the bed – okay – all right –' and I lay there, still. 'All right now, stay with him —' I could sense the subsiding, easing breath and soft perspiration of the person exhausted half-lying on me, withdrawing gently, then stopping. '– Oh hell – oh hell, will you look at his lips, his nails – Mr Wall – he's cyanotic – Mr Wall – get some help —' I've no idea who they were calling to. I loved, I wanted to weep for them. Another voice came. 'All right Sister, all right orderly –' '– he's stopped breathing –!' '– all right, move aside a bit – Nurse, quick as you like, my compliments to Dr Jones will he please get us some wheels in here plus Digoxin point 5 mgms to go I V and an Avertin tray if it's not too much thank you –' and this new body was upon me, placing a rapid hand on the top of my head, a hand in my mouth freeing my tongue, fingers tasting faintly of salt and fear, grasping my teeth and chin, lifting, struggling slightly, the cheek against my nostrils, the lips about my lips, the mouth about my mouth, the breath anonymously entering, swelling my lungs, releasing, swelling my lungs, my life, reconfirming my life.

It's then that I came to.

'*Good* morning, Mr Wall!'

I was back in the bed, stinking of chemicals and ignorant how I got there, and it was Mrs Timms from the lending library standing before me with a small bundle of books clutched gaily to her bosom. 'And how are we this week?!' I sluggishly let fall an unexpected term of abuse or two and apologized. 'Had a ropey night, have we?' she said chipperly; 'well, we'll soon put that right – I've some goodies for you!' With twinkling eye she held the books for me to see.

How very nice, I said, reading the titles with more facility as my eyes slowly cleared. *You and Your Feet*; *What to Do When Someone Dies*; and *Treatment of the Stump*! Thank you, Mrs Timms.

'*De nada*, Mr Wall. *Il n'y a pas de quoi!*'

Mrs Timms stood twinkling.

Mrs Timms –, I said hesitantly.

83

'Yes Mr Wall?'

Mrs Timms – I asked with deference – are you comfortable?

'I'm comfortable, Mr Wall. Are you comfortable?'

. . . I was just wondering, I said . . . because I think you're leaning on my crotch.

'I'm not leaning on your crutch, Mr Wall,' said Mrs Timms politely.

On my crotch, Mrs Timms. On my groin, I said. Because it's cutting off the circulation.

'I would never lean on your groin, Mr Wall —'

It's my – it's my external iliac artery or something – it's a pressure point or something —

'I haven't *touched* your pressure point —'

I am not wholly unknowledgeable, I said more crisply, I've read *But Why Cancer, Sally*, and if you want to augment the quality of my life you'll get off my —

'I've got both hands on your bed-crank, Mr Wall — !'

– It might even increase the *quantity* of my life, I added, I can't move my left leg – I can't move either of my legs for that matter —

'You *look* peaceful, lying there. . . .'

You're right. You're goddamned right. My arms aren't moving either.

'. . . It'll pass, Mr Wall,' said Mrs Timms comfortably.

I lay there, the two of us looking at each other, waiting quietly for it to pass. I sent an assortment of familiar impulses out from my brain to various parts of my geography; and increasingly less familiar and more exotic impulses, to darker principalities, chieftainships, outlying settlements. Mrs Timms hummed a little to herself. Silent plains, headlands, gulfs, fields, dry-stone walls, ditches. Mrs Timms stopped humming. I hummed a little, and stopped.

Who do you blame, Mrs Timms? I said then.

'Whom does one blame, Mr Wall?'

Who do you blame, Mrs Timms?

She thought a moment.

'My father, I think, mostly.'

I was able to nod my head.

But she could see that still that was about all, so she went away.

84

In a moment a bevy of attendants came swooping.

For twenty-four hours they wired me for sound, tapped my spine, and had my members levered, swiveled and jacked – me with my books obsessively before me, flicking pages with my chin. It didn't pass. The gauntlet is down. My opponent shows his face. It's the double dare. From the neck southward, the motor nerves are on the blink. The union's on strike. I hear that the autonomic system, whatever that is, still ticks – the skeleton crew's on hand, the guts are for the time-being discharging their duty; with a helpful hoist and a grunt or two and some shrewd alignment of vessels I'm still able to perform simple and not unfamiliar tasks with both bladder and bowel. And that, my friend, is a great deal to go on when at last you've the advantage of seeing your enemy's face. Sickness: he is fat, ignorant, and wears a short skirt. He is the epicene existence I've led up to now, the unshelled slug, my own near-miscarriage, sitting on my chest. Death itself can be scarce more than this, eh? Sloth, death is, if I'm any judge of things; some more exquisite, tropical brand of dullness, stupor, surrender. Temporary motor paralysis? Right hand lost its cunning? It's a fair exchange. My *mind* is coming to life now! No grass grows under *my* feet. No tongue of mine cleaves to *my* mouth. I can beat them yet. The ball is finally, as they say, in my court.

My head I can move around quite a bit. Also, increased stillness makes it possible for me to observe and appreciate many things I'd taken for granted before, some sights, more sounds. The orderlies and nurses rolling things here and there, swishing curtains and screens, carrying bottles and pans, gossiping, giving enemas, serving meals. Sister Dingle has come into her own, she arrives with her steam machine and cough belt – it seems lungs go stagnant, may flood or something when one's like this – she shoves me about and beats my chest, plumping me up like a lumpy, flocculent pillow and I cough for her, all right, and spit; she must chart the volume of my phlegm, and flatters me gruffly on my breathing style; her place in history is assured.

85

A small lectern rigged on my tray, I've already finished the first of my new library of books and have made scrupulous mental notes, turning pages with my nose. When Treeza arrived I was limply propped and pleasantly dribbling, in the middle of *Care of the Stump.*

'Darling darling,' she said.

Darling, I said.

She kissed me and wiped her chin discreetly.

I've so much to say! I said.

'Me too!' she said. 'Darling, I've been looking and looking for some of the trunks and boxes we sailed here with. Where are they?'

In the loft, probably, Sweet, by the window. Planning a trip? I said, laughing.

'Dear, really!' she said. 'Just straightening up, a little Spring cleaning!'

Is it Spring?

'You know me, Dear!'

Darling —

'Darling, do you recall where you left the savings books?'

I think they're in the rolltop, bottom left, I said. Listen, Darling, I've had a silly fit of some sort, and I can't seem to move anything from the chin down —

'I *thought* you had a nasty loose cough!' she said.

Yes, I'm sorry, I said.

'I didn't know whether to pamper you or if you were just after attention!'

Now Darling, the last thing I want is pampering, and that's what I have to talk to you about.

'How about the tax papers?' she said.

What Darling?

'Our tax papers, where are they?'

U K or U S?

'Both.'

In the top study closet shelf, I think, Dear.

'Oh good!' She sat down with satisfaction and folded her hands, unfolding them to brush down the hem of her skirt, and smiled at me, folding her hands again.

I love you, I said.

'I know,' she said.

Treeza, I said tenderly but firmly, unless we're strong, there can be difficult times ahead, and I want you to know that – however lazy and unassertive I may have been in the past – I'm going to make it up to you now. I'm taking on my responsibilities, at last, as a husband, and as a man. I want you to know how *good* I feel about it, no matter what kind of – kind of strain I may be under, I feel just plain, well – *good* about it, because I'm, by God, Treeza, I'm *taking over the controls*!

'I got a rubber plant,' said Treeza.

Treeza?

'For the master bedroom,' she said rather archly I thought, 'I've got a beautiful rubber plant growing in there.'

Good, I said.

'What is wrong with a rubber plant?' she said. 'What have you got against a rubber plant?'

Nothing, I said. Nothing. Many people find happiness with a rubber plant.

'I've got one in the bedroom,' she said.

Treeza, I said, I want you to be strong, and to be realistic with me —

'I'm being strong and realistic,' she said.

Now, Treeza, I said, there are certain things that I've been studying, finding out about, planning against the worst – against *every* eventuality, Treeza, and I'd like to share some of my thoughts with you on this subject.

'You're not going to do anything silly, are you?!' she said suddenly.

Like what?! I said, startled.

She looked at me soulfully, or so I imagined.

Do you mean – ? I said. You mean – to myself?!

She didn't say anything.

I shook my head from side to side. I actually rolled my head from side to side, savagely, to show how forcefully I felt in this matter. To myself, would I do anything? I said. Do violence to myself? I said. Treeza, here I'm – here I am lying here, Treeza, and I'm thinking, why would I ever do violence to myself? As a matter of fact, I'm lying here and I'm thinking, *how* would I do violence to myself?

'I just thought....' she said.

You poor darling, I said. Now I want you to wipe such ugly awful and sad, dreadful thoughts from your poor head, Treeza, you promise? I'm going to beat this! I'm going to win do you understand? Win! Or I'll know the reason why! Now how about that? Is that better? Do you feel better now?

'Yes.'

A lot better?!

'Yes!'

Good! Now —

'But if you die?' she said.

Treeza!

'Or shrink?'

Shrink, dear?

'Oh I don't know.'

. . . Treeza?

Her tone was different.

Treeza, look at me.

She looked at me.

She was struggling with something.

'Nights . . .' she said. 'You don't remember.'

I do.

'We used to lie . . . like . . .'

I remember.

'You don't.'

I do, I said. 'Like spoons.'

Her pupils seemed to dilate. That bright-oiled efficiency, I thought, all those years . . . I grew warm to the thought . . . all her sleek erection of decorous parasols, screens. . . . I looked at her. It had been her cover against the deepening rain, the gradual loss of us.

Treeza . . . .

'But that was long ago.'

I withdrew.

The Stone Age, I said.

'The age of flowers.'

I know – flowers and candy.

'I don't mean that,' she said. 'I mean flowers.'

I gazed at her again.

She was really – was she truly revealing herself? could we be bare – we could be naked again together — ?

88

She looked away.

Treeza, can I bare myself to you?

Her eyes flicked to me and away again, darkening further —

'What if I need – want – flowers a little longer?'

Yes Treeza!

She stood up.

'I don't know.'

Treeza, there are things we could say – I don't know the words – things we could try —

'Yes,' she said, 'I'm trying!' And she turned and fled from the ward.

Her feelings – her running, full of life, of passion – real *wanting*'s there – have we honestly a *chance*, now? To talk, to see – next time she comes – to turn over a new leaf!

What does she mean, 'shrink'?

So much to talk of, to tell her, to say.

Once we simply understand – it all changes!

Before my eyes, an empty envelope, the 'greeting' this time on the inside of the flap, jagged and sprawling. And suddenly I understand about him.

Him and his ideas. What an idea, that Hinkle's vein-blotched impostures are nothing – some kind of gift to humankind. That we like it. That we've all got our warts and veils, all dream ourselves in some fable, all live our secret agendas, that the whole thing's a costume carnival, an immorality play – that we're all impressionists, impersonating persons, that everybody's somebody's fiction, that our trouble's all of our own making, with him there but to play his part and collect his dues. Yes, I'd tell him (and it was early days then), like these invented tenants, burning your own buildings, bogus deaths – what kind of insurance, what indemnity is this? That was his ace – victims with more to lose by their truths than he thought he could ever lose by his lies – his foothold, and how long could it last — ?

Listen to yourself. Phoney, it's phoney. Queen among ministers, incinerator of tenants? he's a banal wretch, failed shopkeeper, petty crank —

He's pathological, a mythomane!

You, besotted with your image of prudence (or was it the funk?), asking no one – where have you ever had any of it but from him? what makes you think his lies aren't for *you*? You the chief receiver, the defrauded one.

It's happened, all of it.

You make even his avowals of lies sound like lies.

He's a wrinkle, a twisted fold in my reality, my comprehension of how things work, what's true and what's false —

It's what you make him – you take an insignificant tipster, devourer of court circulars and tabloid tattle, bootlicking frequenter of police stations, seamy exhibitionist, dirty old man – and you make him some monster demon. The footprint in the sand, an arrow in the sky. A Figure, an Idea, a Symbolic thing —

They're just lying in wait for you, I told him, natural enemies by the hundreds. 'Waiting for what?' he'd snort with scorn, 'for nothing.' *Just one stone on the track – you'll go off the rails*, I'd tell him; what sort of rebuttal is this to the human condition, to say 'Try and catch me, I don't exist'! it's nobody's answer – it's a sickdream. 'Mine?' he said 'or yours?'

He's got you stitched up in his talltale and you can't for the life of you see the seams.

I accept – he's the person about whom everything I say is a falsehood and has to be —

There – generalities – you see — !

– nothing I say about him can be true, everything he stands for is that no one can describe him —

– you surround him with epic, tragic phrases –

– no one can say anything about him but Hinkle himself.

– you make his world an amphitheatre when it's a toilet.

He's the man with no existence but his own.

– Abstract! Synthetic! *Lifeless*! A fairytale, a melogothic Theory – a mental contraption, a distant chattering, a stab in the dark – nothing to do with what's happening here, now — you complicate everything. Simplify!

I've no time to think simply! Be realistic! I'd tell him. 'Realistic! my danger's in *your* script, not mine,' he'd say, glugging down his coffee. 'I don't need you,' he'd say picking up his battered gold-headed walking stick, snaffled out of hock for the tenth time. 'It'll all be better in the next chapter and no fear, it'll all work out in the next scene.' There ought to be a law, I said. 'There isn't,' he said with a mordant wink; 'it doesn't apply.' But the truth! what are you doing? what are we doing? 'The truth is no answer to the questions that you ask.' His sudden look was almost austere, tormented. But what kind of living is this? I said as he went out the door. 'The truth is not an answer.'

Testify for him? Attest to what?

That's right – what's the difference?

Forget him.

That's right – he's a myth! where is the man? the face, the flesh and bones – what have you done with the body?

But his messages are real —

How would you know?

I know. Today I know. The unvarying message, finding me wherever, designed to keep me taut – his fail-safe switch, him like a locomotive plummeting on. Handling me like some private object, his deadman's switch, some springloaded brake in the same fist as his throttle – once faint or weaken, once lose his grip and the lever flies – I retrieve him. His messages say Hang on and keep away, my grasp's tight, I'm in my element, stand back!

So you say.

So I leave him to it then. Forget him.

Then why these mind-convulsions? these eruptions into opera?

Forget him.

You can't. And you *don't know why*.

Not true!

This *peril* he's in. *Is* it the *law*? *are you sure*?

The sisters and the cleaning women were bustling and drifting, making beds, dressing incisions, arranging flowers, cursing, mopping, changing infusion bottles, cleaning lockers, rattling about, always looking at their watches. The ward fell into a hush.

91

Everybody knows the rumor. Mr Austin's been going berserk.

A health officer had come to say they were bringing him through on his way to another operation. I don't buy her theory about his behavior, her 'explanation' that down the road he's traveling there must always be some inner – some 'clean out' – some fundamental, 'primeval process'. I don't accept that when people – in their sheer good will – reminded Mr Austin of things such as love and beauty they were only setting explosive mines in some otherwise distant tranquil landscape of his own. Silence has nothing to do with 'finding some kind of peace', 'making peace' with yourself; he was always the odd one out; defective, dissolute, an ill-mannered, scurrilous surrender it was, a debasement of the man; you don't give up the ship. And now this new thing. For days, he's still as a lamb. Until they prepare to stretch his life a little, with another operation. And then Mr Austin is transformed. He goes psychotic, he becomes a wild beast – he has demolished two operating theaters – silently bellowing, flailing his arms noiselessly, shrieking without a sound, however that may be, he shatters and crushes everything in sight. He has graduated, if you believe what they say, from a condition of remote quiet, to a state of estranged abomination.

The report, as of this week, was that – his skin in several places having revealed itself to be of 'poor quality' – they are initiating a round of grafts. Rumor has it that 'poor quality' means in fact that he has begun to shed, slough, or generally 'jump out' of his integument much in the manner of a gekko or newt. (The unfortunate image is not mine but that attested by his perhaps overly enthusiastic consultant psychiatrist.) If everything they'd so far collected and organized inside him wasn't to fall out and go thoroughly to waste, something had to be done. Following the techniques of Dr Felix Nagel of Pforzheim, West Germany, who has grown the first living ear on the back of a rabbit using his wife's ear as a model, they tried to work up some suitable patchwork for Mr Austin out of the epidermis of various local hares, stoats, gerbils, and finally a wallaby or wild imported yak, but in each case – owing, they claim, to an allergic response – Mr Austin jumped out of his new skin. Now, understandably, they have decided

92

to use Mr Austin's own hide wherever possible – so that, should a better ear be needed, for example, they will simply embed a dental-plastic mold of one of Dr Nagel's wife's ears into a flap of the still tolerably good skin on the inside of Mr Austin's arm, they will then stitch the inside of Mr Austin's ear-bearing arm to the side of his head, and when this has properly grown into place, the arm will simply be severed – that's to say, the part that's become an ear – and left attached to the head; the only real difficulty being that of centering the patient's new arm-ear precisely around his old earhole or he risks ending up looking just as attractive as he could hope, but either partially or totally deaf, depending on whether this has been done with the same degree of success to both sides of his head. The growing-process requires, of course, that the raised arm be strapped for stability to the side of the head, or the thigh be belted to the shoulder, et cetera, according to need, but is said to take no longer than six months and ought hardly leave time, they declare, for the provocation of unnecessary comment ('he doesn't know his ass from his elbow', etc.).

The other explanation given, however, for the awkward position in which Mr Austin carried himself when he finally appeared this morning, was that they had set to work on his brain.

This is as open to conjecture as the suggestion that his present behavior stems from his putative acquisition of a monkey heart.

Nothing is known for sure.

When Mr Austin emerged through the archway and came down the center aisle of the ward, he was standing, or doing something like standing, upright. He was raised some distance above the floor in a wheeled apparatus consisting of bars, springs, safety nets, and motorized sprockets, himself so arranged within, somewhat like a spider – bound in self-protective restraints, his hands and feet taped securely into twelve-ounce maroon boxing gloves – that he might be maintained in a state of continual exercise as they rolled him along. Flocked hopping and skimming around him on tiptoe, the specialists harkened wide-eyed through earphones and wires plugged into his various organs as they went. Spread-eagled, silent, his mouth gaping and closing and gaping, Mr Austin went whistling past, his wheels squealing discreetly into the distance.

Night. On the small table by this bed, and always glowing like an eye, a mouth, the large red button hungry for some convulsive's panicked thumb.

But there are always compensations, aren't there? I've discovered something else. Amidst the fairly endless sounds of my fellow patients' coughing in the dark, conducting their low solo conversations, muttering disconsolately, moaning, and generally carrying on, I have feelings in the now immobilized regions of my body; but far-off, and changed, or changing, in quality. Not feelings in the normal sense, it's true – to feel a leg in the way that one feels one's leg, the leg feeling the sheet on the bed, its own weight on the sheet on the bed. But there *is* feeling here, somewhere. This 'where?' of course, causes trouble. Having no motion, from 'place' to 'place', *'place'* makes progressively less sense. Yet – this now subliminal spread of sensations seems definitely at times to be referring to *something* somewhere, something *else*. To itself, almost. And at moments, to my mind (in its occasional turmoil, such as you might expect) trying with revulsion even not to feel it. The way, after an accident, after an orgasm, a part of one may echo the event, saying senselessly over and over, 'hit! hit! hit!' or 'here... here!' or 'this, this, yes,' or 'love, oh, love!' or, confronted with the instrument again in motion by which the part had been struck here before, saying in a throb of anticipation, 'not here! not that! not here!' A feeling in me longing to stretch beyond itself – as if in a yearning toward the previous, *last*, obliterated feeling, and toward the *next* feeling as yet unfelt. Almost as though referring to the past and even to a future it cannot know and that may never be. Phantom sensations – something my body has on its mind – is actually doing – in its affrays with the new colonies advancing within it, intruders rowing in their swift outriggers up the rivers toward the vibrant darkening heart of this luminous and radiant continent, dare I say? Intensely alive, I can sense its striving beat, in rhythms of a closing and yawning sort, a narrowing and distending, a kind of clenching, clenching and reaching.

Listen! I said to the night nurse as she was going off in the morning, I've got feelings! She backed away. Come here! I cried, I've oodles of feelings! I clamored on, lying there. It caused a stir, you may be sure; I don't know exactly which of the details I revealed sent her running for help, but I do recall that by the time I got around to 'hit me, hit me!' and 'phantom kisses' she was gone.

In a matter of instants, a new star whisked brusquely into my medical firmament. Outside of my now restricted range of sight, he emerged thumping rather unforeseeably from what I'd always have sworn was a closet, accompanied by a titter and a scamper of feet. He came gliding up, smoothing his hair, a pencil at a precipitous tilt behind one ear, and between his teeth, a rose. He began instantly to write on my chart with this, and stopped to glare at it piquedly. 'Damned pencils!' he growled, and absently offered me the rose. Thanks – I declined. He found the pencil in his ear, replaced it with the rose ('Bloody secretaries!'), and jotted a few evidently creative remarks on the chart.

'So,' he said, sizing me up, 'you're looking a bit off color still – feeling a little dicky, are we?'

Depends on your point of view, I said. I *have* been feeling things —

'Yes well that's why I'm here, we'll get to that. And otherwise?'

What else is there otherwise? I asked. What's happened to me?

'You mean?'

Before. What happened?

'You had a touch of eclampsia – a kind of seizure. Not to worry.'

I want to thank the genius that saved my life, I said.

'No genius about it, I'm sure, and no one wants thanking. All in a day's work.'

All night, more like, I said. Honestly, who was it who — ?

'— The resuscitation, you mean?'

The mouth-to-mouth.

'He wouldn't fancy your bringing it up, I'll wager.'

It *was* Dr Wall?

'I think he would say he happened to be there, yes. But it was hardly the work you'd put a "genius" to!' he said. 'Just happens the others weren't really fit for it, by the time it came to that, pretty much of a mess, so everybody chipped in. Now the thing is —'

What mess? I said. Who?

It took me four tries to worm out the truth about that night: that of the ones who'd reached me first – a student nurse and an orderly ('all right, all right, steady – !') – he'd sustained shattered teeth, a split cheek and a concussion and she (withdrawing gently, 'oh hell, oh hell, Mr Wall, get some help', soft breath and perspiration) had got three broken ribs and her pelvis cracked. 'It was done, that's all,' he said, 'outside the norm, a bit extreme but not really your fault. And they were glad to help.'

You were there too, weren't you? Admit it. What did you have to do?

'Nothing at all, I administered your Bromethol. It's a rectal infusion. It's nothing at all. Now —'

Except to say you now know me as few do.

'It comes of arriving at the tail end, so to say. Now about these "feelings" you've been having. We must just keep our nerve.'

You keep yours, I'll keep mine.

'It is indispensable for your well-being that you come to see that everything's going right according to plan.'

But whose?

'What I mean to say is, all is on schedule, we are on terms with your neoplasm, things are absolutely in order, our predictions have been immaculate, everything is foreseen.'

You're not just a pretty face.

'You must see the beauty of it. Nature. Like the movement of a fine clock.'

All right so I play your silly game. When did it happen, then? What did I do wrong? How did I slip up, for argument's sake? Where does the slip happen, between being a living person and being —

'A dying one?'

It's your idea, not mine.

'Nothing happened,' he said. 'There is no slip. No change. Once you've got the condition, everything is on course.'

But where did I get the condition, just supposing? What kind of contagion are we talking about?

'It's an auto-aggressive disorder.'

I've only myself to blame.

'I didn't say that.'

Then how did I catch it? Why?

He looked at me, or at the edge of me, where the bed and I were lying together. It was a question he clearly did not understand. As though its structure was somehow logically unintelligible, grammatically incomplete, non-functional, and strangely, weirdly so. As though *everyone* knew, as one knew one's own face or hands, that dying was an inclination or aptitude of the order of bodily excretion – a sometimes but not always unpleasant yet necessary side-effect of being alive. This, then, was the 'condition' I had, and that was that.

'I've the awful feeling,' he said, 'that we are diddling with each others' most cherished definitions.'

My definition of "doctor", I said, and your definition of "life".

'That's it.'

I know – doctors 'face facts', I said. *I* am interested in their implications!

He busily pawed about himself in search of a pocket for his pencil.

Like what about these phantom sensations, I said doggedly.

'It's all in the mind.'

But —

'Legs, arms, eyes, hearing, tongue – in the womb you start building up a big picture of yourself, you see, it's like a jigsaw, from all the little bits you're learning to feel. Experiments have been remarkably successful on this subject.'

I can scarce contain my pleasure.

'Now that one's grown – take away some of the little bits —'

I'm not losing my bits.

'– Cut off a man's leg and he feels the leg still – the big picture stays perversely whole in the brain. It's called being a person.'

Listen, I'm no amputee.

'This big picture will give you trouble from time to time, it's to be expected – it's part of the "puzzle", if you'll pardon the pun.'

I want my bits back.

You *are wicked*!

I'll get them back!

'In essence, I couldn't agree more. I won't say I'm not damned sorry, in a sense. Dreadful, really.'

Unspeakable, I said.

'Hard lines,' he said.

A losing wicket.

He looked at me uncomfortably, calling a halt. Then he came out with it.

'I mean to start you on something. A little "cocktail".'

Ah! I said. A tranquilizer —

'A lytic cocktail.'

– You're Dr Lever. And this is the Lever approach.

'You guessed it.'

I don't want to be tranquil. What are you all so afraid of? I mean to get better. How can humanity expect to improve its situation tranquilized?

'It calms psychotic activity without undue depression.'

What psychotic activity?

'You don't know what pain is.'

I do. It's you. Hence the saying, leave me alone.

'In an advanced country like Japan, Germany, America, they'd have you —'

I thought *here* was the advanced place.

'Where you come from they'd already have you in a state where you wouldn't notice a thing from here on in.'

I *want* to notice!

'Look here —'

I won't be drugged!

'Steady on, old chap.'

I'm trying to get hold of this thing, and you're trying to screw around —

'Now don't get shirty.'

Why do you think I keep asking questions, stupid questions – I am just trying to get hold of the reality of my – my own – condition! Damn!

'No need to mince words —'

Hell!

'No need to tiptoe.'

Fuck!

'I'm sure we all have our views on this.'

It's *my reality*.

'*Cobblers*.'

What?

'You people confuse yourself and your reality with a silly, simple-minded, somatic concept of your identity.'

Look who's talking. Are you saying now that what happens to my body doesn't matter?

'Well, the whole thing *is* a bit of a curate's egg, isn't it?' said Dr Lever. 'Crikey, I mean – what is it? A bag of bones and a hank of hair, to quote the poet? It's disposable, it's expendable, isn't it? Look at the bother it gives you – why cling to it? Good riddance to bad rubbish, eh? Heh?!'

All right: What *does* matter, then?

'Ah well, for that we must turn to our odd – our old friend the preacher, wot? The parson. The chaplain. The right reverend doctors of the church, mm? Not our line of country, really. Not my cup of cha. Not my pigeon! Ha! —'

Quite, I said.

'Now listen here,' said Dr Lever. 'I don't like your having to pack it in any more than you do —'

But you'd defend to the death my right to do it, you self-righteous sonovabitch.

'... There is *no need* to lose tone.'

Okay, I said. I got carried away.

'... I find that most people die with astonishing style.'

Don't rush me!

'Of course not. It's *your* death.'

You bet your ass it is!

'But you're not to expect too much. I mean really, you tourists! expecting all mod cons, *tout confort*, sending back perfectly good food, banging the porter's bell at all hours, making an ungodly row about nothing at all!'

You know, I said, you've got what I would call an extravagantly prurient taste for the up-and-up.

'We make do, in our own little way.'

But at what a price! I tell you I would like – I hope I learn in time – to be able to say 'It's-nothing-just-a-scratch-I-set-the-bone-myself' like you all – but how for Christsakes do you make it out that any – any ostentatious manifestation of pleasure, of displeasure, of success, failure, taste, distaste, in fact any incontinent damned display of *life* is some kind of – of felonious assault on the human spirit?!

'That was marvelous.'

Thank you.

'Really super.'

You could see he was decidedly working to keep a grip on himself.

'Have you got a better idea?' he said.

I'm thinking! I said. I'll let you know, believe me. What do you think I'm *trying* for?

He shrugged.

I mean – how do I know this devil-may-care anti-heroics brand of heroism of yours has a payoff? that it's not a put-on? turn the other cheek! Murder! Listen *Doctor*, what if one day I was to look into your *eye* once instead of away, when one of you's putting your needle into me —

'Here now —'

– What if one of us did that, when you were feeling up his leg to saw it off, what if he looked into your eyes instead of away, just once? What would it be? Obscene, would it? bedlam?

'If I were you I shouldn't —'

– Would it make a shambles of everything? Or would *you* manage to look away then, just in time, to save the scene from utter chaos?

'Mr Wall —'

Why is it like that?

'*Mister* Wall—' He was reaching toward the table near me.

– Do you know why? I said. I think it's because you – you haven't sufficiently examined your own attitude toward malignancy and death, what do you think of that? Hunh? Ha!

'Do you know, I don't much appreciate your brand of sarcasm.'

Sarcasm! I said. He was unpocketing a large tongue depressor.

'If you think we're involved in some sort of jiggery-pokery here –' he was coming at me with his spatula '– there's something I feel I ought to make –' he had hold of my mandible 'perfectly clear —'

Ahhh, I said without conviction.

'Cheers!' With a clever thrust of his stick he had me pinned by the tongue. 'Now I think I can say without fear of contradiction,' Dr Lever said, peering down my larynx, 'that one understands completely how the instinct of those of your race – essentially proud monoglots in a universe that's rarely better than a Babel at its best – is to lift up your voice on high in well-worn curses, Mr Wall, and pound the countertop for service; I am personally happy that you're habitually hog-fat with wealth and health and I sympathize wholeheartedly when these assets fail you and you go shopping and haggling through this straitened and stony realm for the best deal in salvation as you would for a genu-ine handmade Morocco-leather necktie.' He smiled blandly as my gullet went dry. 'But if anything we've said or done has led you to think for one moment that all we have to do is give you touches of first aid from time to time and you'll live forever, with all due respect, why you're in for it, Mr Wall. It's my job, it's our job together, to accomplish nothing and to hope for nothing but to get you used to this idea.'

You mean *dead* to it! I said, yanking loose from his stick. And – ahh! He shoved in the stick.

'And as to your suspecting us of silence, dear chap – of indifference – ? you're thoroughly right – it's quite genuine indifference, and floundering perhaps but indispensable and profound.'

You – ahh.

'– Understanding and indifference are the first two fingers of our hands here, Mr Wall, the very finger and thumb. The rules of the game, the law of the land. You'd best post a watch, or you'll run aground on this one.'

Ahh.

'Oh sickness is one thing, we're marvelously vocal on that, but —'

Ahhh!

'There is simply nothing to be said as to your death.'

Dr Lever paused, deliberately withdrawing his stick.

'You — !

'– You must somehow start,' he said, 'to manage to separate any grievances, any doubts you may have about your treatment,

Mr Wall, from your irritations about dying.'

And why? for what?!

'You must sort things out.'

Why?! What does this mean, sort things out? It all comes to a *head* now, to a *point*, doesn't it? Where's the time, now, for one thing now and another later? It all comes to the boil at once, doesn't it, this time! I'm not obliged to sort anything any more, and you can't make me!

'Well – if you're going to take that line. Throw away reason. It was our last game-plan, all we can offer – but go on —'

– I don't know, I said.

'Opt out, write-off our help, decamp if you like —'

I don't know, I said.

He seemed satisfied. He looked at his watch.

'Time for our elevenses, time for you to have a nice hot cuppa, Mr Wall,' he said. 'If you took the medicine now, it'd be a lot easier on all of us. Think on that, while you have your tea.'

Oh you think I'm not thinking enough, do you? I said. I'm flat on my ass and you come in here all hale and rutting with a rose between your teeth and ask me to 'think on' your damned convenience and your cup of tea, but you don't want me to think on the – on the one-and-a-half tons of blood or polluted effluent or whatever it is babbling like a happy brook between my ears without a particle of any clear and fathomable use ahead —

He stared at his watch.

... I'm sorry, I said ....

I was fumbling the thought.

... I'm sorry .... It begins to look serious, you see? I said. So I take it out on you.

'Not at all ....'

... I'm sorry.

'So you won't have my little cocktail just now, then?'

No.

'Right. Just so you know the position. I can't have responsibility for the little itches and scratches of fallen angels in my ward.'

No fallen angels, I said.

'One's aware what "to doctor" means in some countries; but we can't just airbrush the nasty bits away.'

No airbrushes.

'A nod's as good as a wink, then.'

You've a phrase for everything.

'That's it. And everything in its phrase.'

There's something you never admit, all of you, I said, in all your phrases — are you scared of it or what?

'I know what you're going to say.'

You know there are cases of another kind. Every human, every child knows. A brand of remission.

'Name it if you must.'

The patient who comes through – because he wills himself to.

'The power of positive thinking. You had to think of that one, didn't you?'

And why don't you? I said.

'It's not in our line. You'll see we don't go in much for the afterlife —'

You know what I'm saying – I'm saying *in* life, dammit. In *life*.

'A "miraculous comeback," I know – and as I say there's not much room for resurrections in the professions —'

It's a whole shipload of doctorates gone to waste when it happens isn't it?

'I do think it's a pity you've got us mixed in with your problems still.' He made an ostentatious display of having run out of time. 'You really oughtn't to let yourself be fussed with our little blindspots and caprices – we have our wee crazes, our improvisations and redecorations, this policy and that, we trim and tack – it keeps our hand in.' He made ready to go. 'It's a kinky business, mortality, as you'll come to see. But you must get on with it, don't bother with us. Get on with it, in your own way!'

And if I decided I wasn't interested in dying —

'Have you?'

– If I decide interrogating this thing's my one chance in life —

'Whatever it is, you must get on with it, old boy.'

– that it's all an exercise?! For the future of my life — ?

'You'll know in future, won't you?'

You mean 'on the day'! You're not talking about what I'm talking about, damn you!

'Oh! These things tend to even out, on the day. You may

take a rather dim view of things, on the day. Of course, if
you could adopt a constructive outlook, on the day, it'd be a
help – but not essential. Heavens no! It's the in-between I fret
about – you could be making it easy on yourself. Otherwise,
you see – it's a cracking pace for a gelding.'

Cheeky swine, I said.

He gave me a slow look of chilling gloom. 'Extreme measures can be dreadful.'

What, for preserving life?!

'– You don't know about the Nightingale cure.'

I'll take it.

'Oh, it's not for you. It's for the doctors.'

For the doctors!

'And the others,' he said, 'all the others.'

You've lost me.

With a shrug he brushed away both my curiosity and whatever 'dreadful' wind had just blown through his mind. 'It's
one thing you'll never have to worry about.'

That's nice, I said. It makes a start.

'I'm glad you think so.'

Take your rose when you go.

◆

I lead a charmed life, I said.

I've these sores growing, on my back, over my hip bones and heels. 'Don't worry, it's normal, bedsores,' says the lass they've sent, rubbing my buttocks and heels with alcohol, 'it doesn't hurt? Aren't you the lucky one!' And never a truer word; what is this obsession of theirs with pain, whatever have they in mind? One headache, have I had? it's nothing. An occasional tic, a tickle I would have stilled with a scratch but can't just now – a twitch for a moment, two moments, an hour or two, whatever takes your fancy, it just continues; then it stops. A charmed life.

What if it came on like that, death? with a little click, a tiny tic that one simply couldn't settle with a scratch, with the proper fingertip at the proper time? And out you went? What if life, one's life itself, had come *on* like that, as well? Damn fool silly question! A distant recurrent cramping and releasing – it's nothing at all. A thickening and thinning of sensation itself, rippling in me, through the hours of the days? Birth, death; tick, tock; it's nothing.

Dear Treeza, what a chance we have here! Come soon – at last we can speak. Who you are, the roles we played, who I really am or could be. Me, I can stop pretending I don't bend and don't need you, and you, will you tell me what you hope too?

The Blob and I, a fine-feathered pair. Sneaking silent non-committal crud, inching, deploying, deepening, reproducing, consuming, twisting and turning indifferent thing. Brought

105

it on myself, of course, that's it; healthful antidote it is, really – to this baffling new mania of mine for some absolute resolution of matters, of issues. Is there something in the principle of life itself – ? some potency at its very center that wants to feed on, eat up, engulf the plenum of this jammed mental space of ours? Some puffing, winding, streaming plethora of potentialities – fomented to devour and dissolve by its radiant boundless procreative force the margins of all fixed resolutions, all straitened reason, all mere reality?

Shrink? what does she mean 'shrink'? Wait now: bare my weakness, my need – will she take me wrong? her soulmate reduced by circumstance and battening on her pity? I'll show her! I shrink from nothing! I'm not a tracksuit, Treeza – rest assured I'm a man.

'You sent for me?'

It was the Reverend Eustace Griffin rushing in – flourishing a newspaper, tripping the light fantastic amongst his flopping soccerboot laces, one undone, the other neatly tied but broken and trailing its perfect bow along the floor.

MR WALL COMFORTABLE
said the newspaper.

> Informed sources today disclosed that Mr Wall was resting comfortably following police reports that his mother had crushed his skull with a Hepplewhite chairleg in the Brompton Road this a.m.

It isn't me, I indicated.

'Thank God!' cried Reverend Eustace. 'I thought, "This on top of everything, the poor soul!" And then I heard you needed me, so here I am!'

I want to thank you, anyway, for keeping me abreast, I said, of world affairs.

'His name –' he said, taking back the newspaper rather bashfully, gesturing to the headline, '– his name *is* "Mr Wall" —'

Undoubtedly there is something in it – I said – but it's not me. It *is puzzling*, I added sympathetically.

'It does after all –' he said '– in threes – come – often – what with this and that – if not always – and then –' he said in a lowered voice '– there *is* your *wife*!'

I'm not sure I follow you there, Eustace, with respect.

'It's this grief thing,' he said confidentially with the utmost tact. 'When you're – when you're – when it's over – she's *bound* to be upset. Pretending "nothing's changed" is a charade, you know this yourself —'

So you've told me.

'Yes yes. Modern times, we must wipe out this awful *stigma* that we attach to – well, I don't have to tell *you*. Hell's bells.'

Speaking of which, I said —

'Our Primate himself, you've heard what he said —'

– Yes, *about* Our Primate —

'– We must clear the air of this general embarrassment — the way that, um, you-know-what, has, so to speak, in effect, replaced –' he whispered behind the back of his hand 'has replaced – well, *sex* – as the great, the Great Unmentionable —!'

– About the Archbishop of Canterbury, Eustace —

'So we've got to, we'll simply have to remember when the time comes that a woman's grief is perfectly – the *perfectly natural* thing – and I want you to feel that I'm with you on this, I'm right behind you and you must give me a ring, give me a tinkle any time, any time at all, when the time comes, between nine and five, before nine, after five, after six —'

I won't be in, myself, I said, 'when the time comes', come to that.

He looked at me disconcertedly, and started to wobble at the knees.

Will you be in? I said. Because I won't be in.

He bent over and began tying his broken lace.

I'm sorry if I've upset you, Eustace. I mean this is it, isn't it? I won't be around, as you say, 'when the time comes'. . . ?

He sat down heavily, flushed and deeply baffled.

'I don't know what's wrong with me,' he said.

It's a kind of a problem in logistics, isn't it? I said.

He was shaking his head. 'The traffic getting here, and everything. . . I must really be addled.'

It's a poser, I said gently.

'*Of course* if you've – if you're – then you won't be —'

It's tricky, Eustace, the whole situation.

'No no – ! give me a wedding, a christening, I'm fine, just fine – but I never seem to be able to – to – to – I'm really put out with myself.'

107

It *is* a real doozer, though, Eustace. It's a tough nut to crack.

'Oh don't tell me a lot of bally twaddle. The Lord knows when I've been a right nit.'

He sat still quite a while, trying to get hold of himself. Pulling a hand out of a pocket he produced a little book, awkwardly, and looked at it.

'Can I interest you,' he said hopefully, 'in a copy of the *Book of Common Prayer*?'

Thank you, Eustace, but I'm in the middle of *You and Your Feet* at the moment.

He shoved it back into his pocket.

'Well!' he said conversationally, in a spirit of comradery, to uplift my morale. 'So!' he added on an affable note, casually clapping his hands about his knee, foot up, squash sock slipping, revealing a lengthy expanse of idle white leg, 'it'll soon be time for you to pay the debt of nature!'

Why, I said, exhibiting alarm, am I leaking?

'Haw haw! A jest!' he said, 'Good show!' He tugged up his sock with some concentration. 'Actually what I mean to say, it'll soon be time to take one's true place in the great cycle of life!'

It's not just a big yo-yo, I said, you don't think.

'Goodness me,' he said, throwing up his hands and slapping them on his lap. This seemed to make him feel more content, and he sat leaning forward, alert, palms on thighs, elbows out. 'I say, you don't mind my – that's to say, I don't know what your religion is, but it doesn't matter, now does it? It all comes to the same thing, wot? Tell me if I'm too ecumenical, not enough ecumenical, or just right.'

To tell the truth, I did want to ask you, I said. What about this Archbishop of Canterbury business?

'You read that one, closely, did you?'

I did notice, I said, he doesn't seem too perturbed about folks dying.

'You do see, don't you, that most of our chaps are dead keen on getting all you other chaps into the Next Place.'

On getting us 'into'? I said. You mean 'moving in'? or 'believing in'?

'Well, even to have an interest these days, under these circumstances, it does take some of the pressure off, do you see. You do find that yourself, don't you?'

When in doubt, punt, you mean, I said. "Anyone for a hereafter?!"

'Haw haw!'

So who's pushing the herebefore, these days? Who's in the *life* line, anybody we know?

'You don't want to go putting all your eggs in one basket though, do you?'

That's catchy, I said, Eustace.

'However we may fail with these bodily eyes to see the meaning, Mr Wall,' he said mysteriously, proudly, 'we must live like those singers, you know.'

Which singers?

'The captives, you see – by the river of Babylon — ? "How shall we sing the Lord's song in a strange land?"'

Some dim recollection slipped in at the windows of my mind – fierce men with harps, flinging them away, harps hanging silent on trees – and vanished.

'Let my right hand forget her cunning,' I said inadvertently.

'That's it,' he said, 'that's it. You know, Mr Wall – however far we may stray – we must fix our sight on what's precious behind it all!"

Which is?

'Sorry?'

What's precious behind it all. What's that?

'It remains to be seen,' he said.

There's no two ways about that.

'Yes.'

Meantime, I said, what is death, Eustace.

'Ah!' he said readily and with confidence. 'It's when the soul has departed.'

The soul's departure – is that the cause of death?

'– The cause? I don't think one would claim —'

It leaves life behind when it goes, the soul.

'Exactly.'

What sort of life will I leave behind, do you think?' I said.

'Could you rephrase that?'

Certainly. What sort of creature's left when I go?

'I'm not sure I —'

– Like Hope Holliday upstairs, say?

'I don't believe I'd – care to speak at any great length about Hope Holliday,' said Eustace, looking a bit wan.

I mean – I said – if my soul's departure doesn't kill me, what — ?

'Oh no, you're *quite dead* then – at that time —'

But what makes me dead, then? How will you tell, to look at me?

'Well gosh,' said Eustace with an uncomfortable squirm. 'As the Fathers say – Canterbury, Rome – it's not within our competence to decide that.'

Whose competence is it within, then?

'Ha! we'll have to leave that to the lawyers to fight out amongst themselves, shan't we?!'

What about the doctors?

'Oh – the doctors, without a doubt!'

Without a doubt what? I said.

'But then,' he said with a homey wink, 'it all comes to the same thing, really, doesn't it?'

I shouldn't have thought so, Eustace, I said.

It was at this point that nameless parts of me ceased in effect to hold to the regularity the staff and cleaners of St Mary's had come to count on.

But soft! I said, detecting the first vile odors as they issued from regions of myself beyond my control. I am at this very moment paying the debt of nature!

I don't know why at all, but tears began to come splashing down the sides of my horizontal face. Sisters appeared, and as they tended to me, Reverend Eustace Griffin stood stout-heartedly by and dabbed surreptitiously at my cheeks with a free edge of my pillowcase.

'Thus we see,' he said, when they'd gone and he dauntlessly remained to console me, 'that it will very soon be time to Return.'

In the Great Cycle, I said.

'The Great Cycle of Creation.'

Always went for that one, I did – I said —

I was glad they'd left me propped up, with some dignity. – But what if now I said to you, No? What if I said No to the goddamned Time-to-return and the goddamned Cycle?

Reverend Eustace was looking apprehensive.

What if I said to you, Eustace. Look at me! what if I said,

Soon enough, at some hour very soon, while you're walking up and down this ward with your finger up your *Book of Common Prayer*, I will be changed – unrecognizable, smelted down, altered *beyond recognition*. Do you get the picture? What if I said I do *not*, in fact, as it transpires, I do not *need* to be melted down – just for some toothsome notion of continuity? that I do not owe myself any added fillip of suffering any whiff of effacement and annihilation for the sake of what turns out, and let's be honest, to be an only mildly relevant, only very moderately interesting *fantasia about things being connected*? I mean, what would you say?

Eustace looked distressed to the point of dismay.

I don't know – I said – I mean, I'm only asking.... I'd be nuts, probably, wouldn't I? running wild, a frigging coward, yes, and no style, to boot.... Forget it.

Reverend Eustace Griffin wasn't about to forget. He stood picking at his cuticles and finally said shyly:

'May I ask you.... that comment... about your being – melted down – and the like? Smelted, melted down. What... what gives you the strength... the inner strength... to make a comment about your own future... like that? I mean, that's a very remarkable figure of speech, I find it, personally, strong, a remarkably strong figure of speech, myself, I mean, one pictures heaps of rubble, and bones and flesh, and rubble, and heaven knows what else –. That is to say, what gave you the inner... power, and... glory... to say a thing like that?'

The sweet was too much; with renegade whimsy, before I could stop myself, I said:

I've seen God.

'You're joking,' he said.

And he blenched.

This morning, I said, before my phlegm exercise.

'You're having me on!' he said, turning sheer greenish white.

'How can I know what you're believing, inside?' he said.

'But then I know,' he went on, reasoning with himself hastily, '*I know* that *you* must be serious, because you're – in that condition, you're – *in that way* —. You must be —'

And I am. I am deadly serious, Eustace, I said.

I suddenly saw – as the conviction washed over his face –

111

that now he would not come visiting me again. The excitement was too much, the burden – I'd seen the last of him – nature's played a cruel joke on him, I thought, and all the worse mine – have you noticed the eyes? a cruel trick of faith: one resurrection was enough. I tried quickly to smile —

'Oh I see,' he said, 'I'm onto you – you're actually joking you're pulling my — haw haw!'

Hee hee, I said.

'Blasphemy,' he said. 'Haw haw.'

Hee hee, I said. Excommunicate me.

'Wot? Oh yes! Haw haw haw! Ripping!'

I had run out of hee haws.

So had he.

There was nothing for it, as he would have said. We'd salvaged face. But we'd irretrievably lost touch, if we'd ever had it. (Or did he see that I would *save myself*? – another doctorate going to rust?) He had to leave.

'I'm awfully sorry, old knee,' he said valiantly, not looking. 'It does seem you've got yourself into a dreadful jam, as to values, and things. Hogtied, as it were, twixt the devil and the deep blue sea.'

How's that?

'Wanting to live, I mean, and wanting to die.'

That's crazy.

'Anyway . . . try to remember what's precious behind it all!'

Who do you blame? I said.

'My mum. My mum,' he said.

I'm sorry, I said.

'These things happen,' he said. 'Well —' he collected his prayer book and his newspaper. Halfway down the aisle, he turned and lifted his thumb. 'Keep your pecker up!' he said.

Will that help? I said.

They've started plugging things into me – a few minor tubes and the like, just to tap off the overflow, they say, the nasties, the dross. Books heaped about me, my studies go apace.

* * *

'Sweetheart,' I heard, and Treeza had arrived.

I'm here sweetheart, I said, craning to see her.

'About the curtains, I want to tell you –' she said '– it doesn't matter.'

I know, darling – I feel that way too — !

'It was silly our fighting over that,' she said.

I feel exactly the same!

'I was protecting myself.'

I know.

'From worrying, and all that.'

When we understand the reasons, I said warmly, it makes all the difference doesn't it?

'You've changed. You're different.'

I *am*.

'Very different.'

I'm getting stronger by the minute.

'Are you?'

Definitely.

'You don't think you'll die, then?'

We all have to die, dear – that's what I wanted to talk to you about. We're going to have our whole lives together, when this is straightened out. But I want you to know you come first in my thoughts —

'I'm too young.'

What dear?

'... I want to dream a little longer.'

Of course dear. And that's why I want to show you I've thought everything through and there's nothing we can't handle. I want to show you that *I'm* all right, *I* can take the worst thoughts and get on.

'Do you think — ?'

There are certain things you should know, unpleasant things but —

'You wouldn't happen to remember where the insurance papers are, Darling, would you?' said Treeza.

Which insurance papers?

'You know. Fire, accident, life, things like that?'

I think they're probably in the office, Darling, I said somewhat impatiently. With my stamp collection.

'Oh good,' she said.

113

Now, I said, one of the first things is – I hate mentioning any of this, but there you are – I'm afraid there are certain things you might have to be bothered with if I – well – it's part of an exercise, you see.

'Let me just ask you, Darling, one other thing – before I forget – where are the conveyances?'

The — ?

'The deeds. You know, for the house, and things?'

Look, if you don't mind, Darling – I'm trying to get down to something important, here, down to the hard, practical nitty gritty, the facts of life, however stressful it may be for us both —

'Of course,' she said, sitting back, 'Dear.'

They're in the larder, I said. In the Jollyfine Biscuit tin, in the larder. It protects them from fire, and damp.

'Thank you, Dear. I'm sorry to have interrupted.'

It's all right, I said. As I was saying, then. If it ever were to – happen —

'Don't speak of it, Darling.'

You'd need to bring a suitcase to the hospital. To pick up my things.

'What few, simple things you may have here,' she said.

Yes.

'Your toothbrush, and your slippers.'

Yes, now —

'Your Lulu-doll.'

My — ?

'Have you told them about your Lulu-doll?'

I wouldn't make a scene about my Lulu-doll.

'It's all right, I know you're —'

I thought we had an agreement about the Lulu-doll.

This brought a smile to one of her lips.

Now I want you to remember, I said unfazed, to look through all the pockets of my clothes before you do anything with them. There might be anything, laundry stubs —

'Don't talk about it.'

I've got nothing to hide, I've got no secret life. You'll have to turn in my passport. They'll give it back after they've cancelled it.

'No.'

– Then there is my season ticket to the underground – you'll get a refund for this backdated to – to – you know, when it happened. And my library cards and library books – you'll have to return these immediately or you'll get an endless series of reminders and possibly a fine.

'Don't you worry at all, Darling, I've already taken them back.'

The books?

'And the cards.'

Oh. Good for you! Okay. All right, now Darling, there is a death grant.

'Don't tell me, I don't want to hear.'

It isn't much, but –

'A lump sum? or spread out.'

It's a lump sum. But it seems it's only thirty pounds altogether.

'I don't want to hear!'

Well, Dear, we have to face these things.

She tidied her skirt.

Now, there'd be some nasty paperwork....

'Yes?'

Darling, you'll need a Disposal Certificate. You must have one, or you'll be stuck with it.

'It?'

The – body, Dear.

'Oh, I see.'

Of course, after fourteen days, the local Environmental Health Officer will want to remove it, he'll want to get rid of it for sanitary reasons, but I'm sure you wouldn't wish to wait that long. Not with Rover the Third, and the cats, and everything. Darling, could you push me over a little? my left leg seems to be falling off the bed. Thank you, Dear. Now the next thing is, what to do with it?

'Don't you worry about that,' sitting back in her chair again.

Dear, I want you to be strong. And I want you to know I'm always right behind you! that's why we've got to be frank, last but not least, about the undertaker.

'Do we?'

Absolutely. Now, he'll use terms with you, dear, such as "preservative" or "hygienic treatment". This does men "em-

115

balming" – involving, you know, replacing the blood with something called "formalin", and so on – but you mustn't get overconfident or expect too much, here. In this country they don't use cosmetics, they don't try for a lifelike appearance, so don't be upset if you don't get one.

'I understand.'

Yes; on the other hand they're very efficient in their own way, it seems; he'll embalm anything that doesn't move, so don't wear your fur wrap, and leave the alligator shoes at home. Ha! Ha! It's always good to find the amusing side, Treeza – that's one message I want to be sure to leave you with.

'You're testing me,' she said.

I'm not.

'You're testing me.'

I'm not.

'You're trying to get my attention – you *said* you're not dying – you think I haven't given you enough – you're challenging me!'

Treeza, I think *I* haven't given *you* enough.

Silent. She didn't respond....

It's just a kind of – drill. Like basic training, I said. Builds new muscles, toughens the nerve. A sort of – ordeal by fire!

She dabbed her eye with a hanky, and smiled.

Yes, well, I said. Now about the actual – the actual disposal. First things first. If you erect a monument, dear, just remember that this does not confer exclusive use of the grave.

'A monument?'

Well, you know – I just thought – anyway, if there's a stone or anything, that says, Sacred to the Memory of Me on it, or anything, there's no law – it doesn't mean they can't also stick Fred Binson down in there too, along with me.

'Who is Fred Binson?'

It's just a name, Dear, it's nobody, I want you to erase Fred Binson from your mind. Okay? Completely. Now. Next, there will be digging charges. These can be higher if an organ is used.

'An organ is used?'

An *organ*. You know, tiddlypum toot-toot, an organ. But you mustn't worry about the gravedigger. If the parish doesn't have a gravedigger —'

116

'– The undertaker is obliged to find one.'
– Yes. How did...?
'Is that all, Darling?'
There is one other thing, dear. It embarrasses me to mention it. I don't know why it sticks in my mind so.... But – if the undertaker, when the undertaker asks you if you want to "pay your last respects" – that means he's going to close the lid. Do you get my meaning? *He's going to close the lid.*
'Yes.'
So you'll want to be sure. I can't emphasize this too strongly, it means a lot to me – you'll want to be sure, before you let them close the lid.
'What about –' said Treeza '– cremation?'
.... Yes, I'm glad you brought that up, Treeza. I want you to feel free about that. I don't mind. If you find it more convenient or in any way desirable to have it burnt.'
'It's cheaper.'
There you are, you see, there's a perfect example of how it might be more desirable—. Right. You're so *brave*, Treeza!
'I'm not.'
Yes you are, I can't get over how brave you are!
She shook her head.
So —. About getting the ashes after —
'They'll post them.'
Hm?
'They mail the ashes.'
Oh – that's good....
'...Anything else, Dear?'
Well...., I said, I guess not.... Did you know about – about the Value Added Tax situation — ?
'What about it, Dear?'
Well one of the *benefits* is, the coffin, the burial or cremation fee and the shroud are exempt from V.A.T.
'It's a put-on,' said Treeza.
What?
'It's a con – you can get a shroud on the National Health for free.'
Oh. That's great.
'Still, it's good to know. I didn't know that.'
You didn't know what?

117

'About the V.A.T. exemption on shrouds.'

It was just like Treeza, decent down to the points of her nails, to insist on my having the last word before putting me away.

There now! That exercise didn't hurt did it?

She was still.

Now we can get on with *living*, can't we?! Unless – is there anything on *your* mind, dearest? I said. That we can take care of right here and now?

'Only that –', she began, and she was dabbing her eyes again, '– only —'

Yes, yes? I said tenderly, encouraging her.

'– You won't — ?'

Do anything silly?

'– You won't – I keep having these nightmares –' she said.

'Yes — ?'

'– Of turning over and seeing you lying there all – all – *dead* and everything —'

My poor Treeza – ! I cried.

'– you won't – I mean some people ask to – you won't suddenly decide to –' she said, and a ghastly shudder passed visibly through her whole frame, 'to – to *die at home*, will you?!'

... Go and mind the rubber plant, Lucille, I said.

'I'm not Lucille, I'm Teresa!' she said, blubbering. 'Who's Lucille?!'

Nobody, I said.

Who is Fred Binson after all, I thought as she went down the aisle. And who is Mr Wall?

Oh Treeza it's hard. Turn a new leaf? I can't even talk with you – buried in banality, passive, impassive these how many years, what – yes – craving attention? Speak with you? never even learned the words yet, not yet. But we can! if at first you don't succeed —. We *can*.

'Greetings from Hinkle'.

The brain's lurch. The back of a cigarette packet's foil liner, the letters spilling and blurred. Him and his loco-motives, let Poole handle him and be damned.

It was a year ago, after all.

Still, why didn't I speak out then?

He'd got himself invited, it seemed, of all places, to the prospective PM's country seat. Why didn't I see?

Do you see even now?

What should I think – what's there to see? It's simple —

Over sun-up gammon, dinner duck, and midnight brandy and cigars, he had sustained the ever-leaking dam of his obsessive social and politic falsehoods with streams of lies on subjects stretching from fortunes-found-and-lost-in-juvenile-journeys-to-Mukden-and-Samarkand, to sleekishly vaunted forthcoming billion-pound tidewater barter; from whispers of still-negotiable nuclear missions to Johannesburg and Tehran, to memorable disclosures on the ingredients of his hostess's rival's cuisine – each extraordinary floated deceit more glitteringly, hushedly received than the last.

So you believe all this then.

It was on the climactic Sunday night that he was discovered cryptically foaming at the mouth on his way down the long carpet to his room. At an undersecretary's bewildered and hasty expense Hinkle had to be taken by padded van across moonlit country to a well-known private rest home or madhouse, where I found him in what they called a state of nervous collapse. 'I'm splendid!' cousin Hinkle breathed to me, winking jitterily, sedation wearing off. 'They loved me!' he said, tugging shut the collar of his borrowed gown over his frayed undershirt's grease-dark neck. But this – I said – look at you —. 'A ploy!' he said, 'just a shift to play for time – an entr'acte, don't you know?' Patently he couldn't see his own distracted and harried face, *didn't know* he was lying. You've got to stop this, I said, you've got to break this chain. Before it's too late. 'Too late? for what?' There's a way out, I should have said: *give them what they want.* But I didn't. The moment was perfect; the press had just received new technical guidance on the benefits of silence, the judiciary was taking instructions, there was a spirit of discretion in the air; let me file a deposition now, I could have demanded, entreated. For as much as I knew – for all *he* knew – his intentions might have been honorable all along; I could have entered an affidavit forestalling the lot, putting his side – his delinquencies, his dreams, whatever they

119

were – the court's mercy, his ghosts laid in time. And I shut my mouth instead. I somehow believed him, that's it. 'You, you can't tolerate contradictions,' he'd say; 'but I am *an amphibian*. I'd suffocate, drown, in your either/or world.' I couldn't help buying, and he couldn't help selling. 'Don't worry,' he said; 'I know you, Cousin, you can't stomach me, and everyone knows it; you're my salvation. If anything ever happened, you'd come off your deathbed to save me, and they'd fall for it, every one. You'll be my bloody *keeper, won't you!*' he hissed. I didn't argue. Wildernesses, enigmas were never my strong suit. We understood this much – in his web I'd be worthless to us both. In the hired room in that asylum he straightened restlessly out of his vexed slouch, turned his back, and gathered his street clothes, his china-silk tie. 'One day,' he said, 'you'll *live* for lies.' Someone else came, and swept him away in a limousine.

You like this story.

Carry on then, Hinkle. Leave you alone? Leave *me* alone, and to hell and be damned.

You love this story. Have you finished — ?

I hate it.

– Houseguest – brandy and duck weekend? Maybe he'd clambered over the orchard wall, furthest from the gates —

No —

– an hour before you arrived. 'Regaled them with tales,' had he — ?

Leave me alone —

– yes, tales for the security guards – of petrol, a breakdown, missed his way – lost in the garden maze —

He's a lunatic —

You're attracted to him.

I'm not!

Drawn to him – he has you hypnotized.

It's not true.

Make up your mind – you're building him into the past —

No he's —

– out of terrors of the present —

I'm not!

All right then – *how long have you been carrying him around inside you? What unspeakable insensate desire is this?*

* * *

This morning, here, there, impossible to say where: a kind of dim, dull supplementary disturbance, a sort of eddying of fluids – nothing that bears mentioning – it came in a pulse, hung over me like a dirty sky, and cleared.

TISSUE DOING WELL. I remember, all right – the Harvard tissue test. The tiny slip of tissue from the liver of the hen. What they didn't tell, in the early days of the experiment, a small matter: the test tank was only so big, and naturally, the living tissue grew, every cell times itself in minutes – they'd had to keep surgically sectioning it, throwing half of it away. The experiment continued with spectacular and then mechanical success; two years, they'd hoped, and when that had been achieved, another two years they planned, and so it went. And finally, ten years past, most of the people had gone on to other projects, and whoever was left in charge – as had been agreed – terminated the test. And one of the details of the final write-up was: that the mass of living meat they'd thrown away, destroyed in sum over the years, was equal to twice the volume of the city it was grown in – buildings, parks, people, and all.

What's growing in me – does it die? a kamikaze roommate, a superabundance of life, suicidal, having done away with its host? Or is it like the great Harvard liver, will it simply outgrow me? and will it stop there, my roommate, taking all the room, the space? – there *must* be *limits*, surely – will it outgrow us all? the egg and I – becoming me, till I am myself a blob? an egg? is that it? is that to be me? a great single cell compounded of all cells, the egg of all existence, a vast fluid edgeless glutinous spreading mass—? Must ask someone, be sure to inquire.

'Look, you want to do me a favor?' said my brother Lloyd, just back from Oslo and Aberdeen where he's been looking into the possibilities of blowing up the North Sea oil-fields, returned to find me in my unusual new state. 'Don't bother me,' he said, 'with the chicken liver story.' Always attentive, Lloyd's brought me crossword puzzles, coloring books, a large assortment of simple building games, and a lawyer. 'Go easy on the chicken liver, hold the chopped liver, will you?'

121

What's the lawyer for? I said.

'Don't you think you're making a meal out of this dying bit?' he said. He was patently uncomfortable. 'I mean, look – you've got to admit, deep down inside, you're a sensitive person. We've all known that ever since I took your little red car.'

So why a lawyer?

'I mean, for the sake of your nerves and my nerves, let's not overplay it. I mean *temperamentally*, let's face it, you're an irritable guy, now aren't you? A supersensitive guy, you always were. An *irritable personality*.'

And for this you bring me a lawyer?

Standing respectfully out of the way behind my brother Lloyd, Jim Fitz was fiddling with the locks on his attaché case.

'If you talked to Teresa, boy, like I've talked to Teresa, you'd know you've got big problems – and Jim Fitz isn't just a lawyer, he's the best damned lawyer in the business. What do you think, I'd bring you a cabbage?'

So what?

'What do you mean, so what? Listen, what've we got here, a breakdown in personal communications between us? Rates, insurance, joint properties, inheritance taxes, death duties – your life is a mess! And Jim here is going to help you get out of it. This is what relationships are for, man!'

And what is he supposed to do, brother, act your part?

'What are you saying to me, here? what are you saying?

You're not coming back.

'What do you mean? What do you mean what do you mean?'

You took one look at me in this condition, and you've had it. You're not coming back.

'What do you want me to do, do you think I don't care? You want to talk to me about your condition? go ahead, talk, let's talk. Where does it hurt? Tell me, I'll listen.'

Where does it hurt, I said. It doesn't hurt. It doesn't hurt anywhere, look at me, am I feeling any pain? Who's complaining? I don't feel any pain, I can't feel a thing.

Lloyd looked at my limp body under the covers with nausea.

'This is doing things to my image, you know,' he said. 'You know, my image of you? and I don't like it, so stop doing it.'

I'm sorry.

'Look let's face it,' he said, 'the last person a person wants to spend a whole lot of time talking about these things with is a person who's – who's —'

A person who's doing these things, I said supportively.

'It's sort of demoralizing, the sight of it puts a person off his – off his concentration. Look, I'm an active guy – I like to get into action, I'm a go-getter – I do my best, and I'm not one of your intellectuals, I'm not a good conversationalist.'

So you're not coming back till I've finished talking.

'Look, you think this is easy for me? This is not easy for me. You – you're in your element, dying, what do you mean? You were always bored, looking for something to happen —'

I snorted.

'You've got it made,' he said. 'Now *me*, me I —'

You feel you're just not up to it.

'It's just not my style, you know? Too confining, too limiting. I like –' he looked expansively around the room, around the world with his keen and clear eye '– I like variety, I like looking forward, a little something here, a little something there – every day in every way I'm getting reborn, *reborn* – can I help it? I'm American, and proud *of* it.'

So you're not coming back till it's done.

'You've got to – we've all got to *feel* it, in here,' he said, thumping his chest, 'we've each got to become intuitively conscious of our cosmic destiny, which transmits its energies from very high levels into the pulsating center, like one big universal pipeline, and if you don't feel it in here (thump thump) there's no use forcing yourself, you shouldn't force it.'

Okay, I said. I want to talk to my lawyer now.

'Don't think we're not together, you and I, we're all pulling for you, we're behind you one hundred and fifty percent – give it all you've got, baby – you've only got one life.'

An untimely stupor was slipping unexpectedly over me.

'– But like you say, just in case we both get tied up in our various things – I'm not worried, it doesn't put *me* down, don't think we're not together you and me, it's not merely the outer vehicle that counts, we'll recognize each other in some other planetary round – I'm already starting to recognize you, believe it or not, I can see you in some other plane, smiling away like you always did, you old Cheshire cat you!'

123

Who do you blame? I said.

'Both of them,' he said. 'I blame the both of them.'

I lost the trail of my brother's floating face.

'Excuse me, Mr Wall...' I heard a voice say. I snapped to.

Thanks, Lloyd, anyway, I said, for the jigsaw puzzles, the coloring books, and the assortment of simple building games.

'Excuse me, Mr Wall,' the voice said again as the vista cleared. It was Jim Fitz. There was a small-eyed prospective sparkle behind his shiny hornrims.

Hello, Happy Jim Fitz, I said.

Hello Mr Wall!

Thanks for standing in for my brother, Happy Jim, I said.

'It's a pleasure, Mr Wall. Now I've got some of your documents here —'

What are you, Jim? Are you one of us or one of them? Amurrican or what?

'I'm like you, sir.'

A man for all nations, I said.

'Right!'

No more race, color, creed. The new generation.

'I have high hopes.'

Well here's looking at you, Jim.

'Thanks, Mr Wall. Now about these other things, Mr Wall—'

Jim, I tell you, I said. I don't want to know about joint property the inheritance tax the death duties. I want to know about death. Now what can you tell me about death?

'I'm afraid I'm basically a torts man, Mr Wall,' said Happy Jim regretfully.

Don't be sorry, Jim. Only I really would like to know about death, and you come highly recommended. Now what do you say you tell me what that is, will you?

'Legally speaking?'

In your own words, Jim, I said. Legally speaking, failing that.

'Well strictly off the record, Mr Wall, I'd suggest that you have a word with your doctor. The doctors'll tell you whether you're dead or not, and all.'

You can certainly turn a phrase, Happy Jim.

'Well no kidding, Mr Wall, what can I tell you? These doctors are pretty great these days, pretty terrific.'

This is speaking off the record, now, or on?

'Off and on, Mr Wall. What can I say? We had a man die once, in a liability case. It was awful.'

You didn't know he was liable to die.

'Exactly!'

Well that was interesting, Jim. So what else can you tell me about death?

'. . . About donating your organs, maybe.'

Now this is something close to my heart, Jim. Tell me about that.

'Insurance-wise, it's second class.'

Beg your pardon, Jim?

'I say, if you've given away any organs they won't accept you as a first-class life.'

Fancy, I said; you'd think the owner'd have a view as to that.

'Actually, I think legally,' said Jim, 'it belongs to the coroner. Or – no, that's if it dies of unnatural causes – are your causes natural or unnatural Mr Wall — ?'

Organs, bodies – Jim, do I hear a murky preoccupation here with maggoty matters post mortem? after the fact, shall we say?

'You want to know about – *before death*?'

I want to know about before me, before you, beyond us all – the law – the chart and charter of humanity's faith in what's right, noble and good. What does the law say about dying? Spare me the maggots, Happy Jim.

'Well, I can tell you that without your permission or your wife Helen's —'

Teresa's.

'– Without Helen's consent —'

Lucille's.

'– Without Teresa's consent, if they remove anything before your demise they're open to action for trespass. You can have them up for assault.'

A reassurance few durst refuse. Look at Marie Antoinette, 1793.

'It's the Human Tissues Act, I think, 1961. Except of course —'

But what's my 'demise' — ?

'– there *is* the problem. What if a patient's unfit to decide — ?'

125

What is my dem —, I said, screeching then to a halt — what do you mean, unfit? Unfit to decide what?

'Whether to live or die.'

What are you saying, 'Unfit to decide'?

'Well the problem seems to be, if I remember right, that it's an unfair burden to place on relatives, and if the person can't decide for himself or speak for himself – then the idea is it should go into committee.'

Whose idea? what committee?

'An elected committee —'

What, of citizens, say? Ah democracy!

'Or a judge,' he said. 'The judge decides.'

Jim, I said when the hair-raising roar of voices in my ears began to subside, do you think, I said, as I tend to think... that it's a good idea to work out *one's own* fate?... and to do this with a good solid background of up-to-date information behind one?

'I think it's a fabulous idea, Mr Wall.' He'd started pacing the floor in large tours around my bed.

Then Jim, would you get off your ass in the interest of justice and don't come back here unless you can tell me?

'Tell you what, Mr Wall?' He was pacing and scratching his shoulder blades, the right then the left.

What's it say, the law? What is it to die? Tell me that, if you would.

'Crazy, Mr Wall,' said Happy Jim. He paced, pulled at his cheeks and forelock. 'It's a fantastic project.' He muttered to himself, catchphrases about Happen to me – always knew – happen to me. 'Really fab,' he said. 'Something every profes-sional ought to have at his elbow.'

Do a search, Jim. Work up an abstract, or whatever it is you do.

'Truly marvy,' he said.

As my brother would have you do it. Remember our Lloyd.

'Right!' he said. He tore small tufts of hair from his scalp. 'Fabulous, marvy. Okay. Don't budge.'

I won't lift a finger.

My head falling to one side, gazing on Mr Robinson, whose lids seemed to be opening slightly at last, I began to drift.

'Wakey wakey!'

126

It was a nurse, one of the many. I had meandered way down stream.

'Wakey wakey!' she was saying, her face coming to me through the bubbles, the voice cheery, the eyes firm and cold and averted, the hands taking me and turning me as they do to keep me from going stagnant – 'Time for our roly woly!'

'Well now here we are!' It was Jim Fitz, already, smiling just beyond the departing nurse's shoulder. 'Believe it or not, Mr Wall, I've got everything you want!' He held up his famous attaché case and flipped it open, papers flopping over the bed. 'London, Geneva, Iowa State – the most up-to-date data you could ever want!'

The legal position, I said.

'Right! I'm going to read you the legal position.'

Give me the Word.

'I'm going to give you a blow-by-blow breakdown of the whole darn thing. I'm going to read you your rights.'

Take it from the top, Big Jim.

'Atta boy! Now the first thing is, in the eyes of the law —'

What's dead.

'Right! Well here it is. Item one. Charnley vs Higgs. It seems that as a matter of fact, there are three kinds of things we've got to consider.'

And those are?

'And those are: Live bodies —'

Yes?

'– and mere bodies —'

Swell.

'And corpses. Now a *live* body is easy – a live body is a body that's got sensations.'

Yes?

'Where the sensations have got a body.'

Oh.

'Yes. Presumably this proviso is to cover against crank claims in the name of ghosts, souls, and things like that. A technicality, Mr Wall, you know the kind!' Jim Fitz chuckled.

Of course. I chuckled.

'A corpse, on the other hand, is "a body which is not a person", got it? It is – let's see – yes, here – "dead in that a person no longer lives in it".'

Well that makes sense.

'And then, third, a *mere* body is a body that has no life in it.'

I see?

'Yes, because you see, a *corpse* still has some life in it, are you with me?'

It has —

'It has cells, tissues and things like that, which are still alive.'

Hope Holliday.

'How's that?'

Chicken livers, Hope Holliday, things like that.

'Certainly.'

Well?

'Well that's it, Mr Wall.'

It is?

In the bed next to mine, Mr Robinson, a silent witness to these discussions, seemed to be stirring.

Hello Mr Robinson, I said.

'From there on your rights are plain as day,' said Jim Fitz.

My rights, I said. Yes, my rights — ?

'I want you to know – and I've looked scrupulously into this, I've spent all morning at it – I want you to know that you've got nothing whatever to worry about.'

I'm really glad about that.

'It's here in black and white, Shank vs Brown – the universal principle – the question of death is for the law the question of the death of the individual, of a person before the law.'

It sounds good.

'Here it says, for example' – ruffle of papers – ' "a person is construed as a bearer of rights and duties".'

Grand.

'Now "death occurs", he read on, ' "when a bearer of rights and duties is no longer present".'

– Okay.

' "One then says, for example, 'the patient as person is dead' ".'

But Jim —

' "The person is 'no longer alive in the sense of being the embodiment of a person'. You say, for example —" '

Jim –, I said.

'– " 'Here there is no longer any personal life' ".'

But *those rights and duties*, I said, they make me a person, but what *are* they?

'They're perfectly clear, Mr Wall —'

It was at this point that Mr Robinson began slowly to sit up.

'– listen – here –' said Jim '– Stenton and the Crown – US vs Fleishman – "If no person is present, no harm can be inflicted upon the patient as person."'

Mr Robinson, though I recall it now only with hindsight, was leaning forward.

'You see!' said Jim, 'a person is somebody with the right not to be harmed!'

Or with the duty not to harm any person's rights, I said.

'Right!' said Jim. 'Fooey.'

How's that?

'Feh. Fooey.'

With specious abandonment, Mr Robinson had seen fit in a gush to deposit a volley of vomit at the feet of our Jim Fitz. Amidst the aged patient's tonelessly burbled and wandering apologies, profuse but unfathomable, and the flurry of staff activities on all sides, Jim Fitz maintained an Olympian calm. Sturdy little heart visibly beating beneath his tie, but otherwise unbowed, while Mr Robinson lay back, Happy Jim, almost as though inspired, took up his thread. 'Now let me put your mind at rest this minute, right away,' he said.

If you can see your way clear, I said.

'As far as I can see here – so long as you are a person, the necessary conditions of personhood aside, you haven't a *thing* to worry about.'

Who was worrying?

'That's the stuff!'

And my doctor?

'He'll take care of himself.'

I meant to say —

'Listen. I have here a bunch of papers' – he flourished papers – 'by judges and lawyers in every walk of life – government, industry, religion, health – look here, look here – where every blessed one of them is agreeing that this is an area of such importance that there is just no room for disagreement. We simply can not afford to disagree, and everybody agrees on that.'

It's just that you can't decide.

'What?'

You don't disagree, you just can't *decide*.

'I'm not sure I grasp that,' said Jim.

I'm not sure I do either, I said.

'It's *you* that decides, Mr Wall. You're the initiating party, you're the party of the first part.'

Initiating what, though?

'In the eyes of the great court in the sky, Mr Wall, ignorance is —'

I know, nine-tenths of the law.

'It *is not!*'

That's what you're saying, isn't it? it's that or it's bliss.

'Look, you don't seem to appreciate the quality of *thinking* that's going on around you, for people in your situation.'

I'm sorry – I really apologize. I'm not complaining, mind – it's just that as a layman, a novice in these matters. . . . I'm really sorry —

'All right,' said Jim, 'all right. You want to know? I've been holding out on you' – he dragged a final volume from his attaché case – 'the best part, I've been saving it for dessert, it'll make everything better.'

Goody goody, said I.

'Just listen – these professors know – you listen to this. "There is an important element of epistemic inaccessibility that is characteristic of death." Do you know what that means?!'

Can't say as I do.

'I'll read you some more. "Death," the man says – and he knows, believe you me, Berlin, New York, Rotterdam – "death is something about which I have no direct personal knowledge." Isn't that gorgeous?'

I'm happy for him, I said.

'Listen, you're not listening. This being true, he says, "the actual person never actually reaches death – death, the limit, is unattainable.' Now how about that? Do you see? It's beautiful! "It is merely a *possible* person who is dead," he says. It's the clincher, listen, listen – "Thus," he says, "thus it seems to follow that actual persons" – get this! – "thus it seems that *actual persons – never die*"! Now how do you like that?!'

I love it, I said.

'The very – the very *logic* of it!'

I love the logic of it, I said.

'You don't,' he said. 'You're pulling my leg.'

I'm not, I said.

'Mr Wall,' he said, 'you want to ask me about insurance, or rates, or something like that? Because I'll help you with that. I can help you with that, even though it's not my line.'

I know.

'Mr Wall, I'm basically a —'

You're a torts man.

'That's right.'

Swiftly, rhythmically, and with extraordinary vigor and trajectory, Mr Robinson was disgorging prodigious volumes of puke upon the body and face of Happy Jim.

Who do you blame? I said.

'Ours – theirs – not to reason why,' said Jim, standing rigid.

What would you think then professionally, I said, if I decided to beat this rap?'

'Listen,' he said, flinching as Mr Robinson lay wheezily back at last. 'I can't concentrate with all this going on.'

These are inferior working conditions, I said, and you quit.

I had a dream. A silly dream of Treeza. A message from her was lying neatly in my hands, a telegram of sorts.

> It's the mole. Stop. Fault of the mole. Stop. Are you a man or a mole. Stop. Where has my little mole gone. Stop. Treeza.

Silly wench, I thought. And wondered. And woke up.

It was long ago, I thought. Years back, it was. Where the husbands and the wives sat on the lady's floor and the lady beat the tom-tom. How far back, really, can you put the years – a year like that? When the lady thumped the drum and taught us how to pant and pant and pant and Blow and now Bear down – hold on, hold on – now Breathe, and one and two and three and finally – we never got to say the one and two and three....

Treeza we can change things still! Come! Come and see!

* * *

'Heigh-ho and you're caught at last!'

Careening-about down the ward in an invalid chair, grinning face gnawed and worm-eaten like an old familiar hat, it was my man Lench come visiting from some distant wing.

'I'll give you what-for!' he said, shaking Mr Robinson's hand with an earnest almost courtly deference I didn't grasp as he passed him. 'I've got the thing for what ails us!'

We're in business then, I said.

With a deliberate lordly show, he was pitching the armload of books he'd brought into the waste-bin by my bed. 'Foils! ringers!' he said as they thundered in one by one, 'stalking-horses! poor fools, stooges of the State!'

You find them wanting, correct me if I'm wrong.

'In a manner of speaking,' he said.

I laughed for him.

Lench. They'd removed another detail or two from the fellow; which, exactly, was unclear, but he was distinctly tilting in this new chair of his, favoring one side a cut above the other.

'You think I'm mad,' he said gaily.

That is the word I was searching for.

'But it's not me you're rankling at.'

Who says I'm rankling?

'Your face is creased. It's your wife?'

No, I said. No.

'It's the others?'

Who knows?

'What do you want from them?'

What could I want?

'You tell me.'

What should I expect?

'You tell me.'

Why should I expect anything? I said. Here I lie, I see a mob coming at me with their texts in their hands – doctors, lawyers, priests, inspector generals, Christ knows who all, with their hymnals, manuals and protocols —

'– And you?'

– standing orders and prescriptions – briefs – screeds —

'What about you?'

– everybody with his damned bedside stories, fables, platitudes, rites and bromides —

'And you and I don't — ?'
– and nobody's got an answer he can call his own.
'What can you say? it's homo saps coping with their condition, lovie.'
But not with mine.
'They can't cope with yours.'
Trivia, my condition! Am I hungry? am I dizzy? is my pulse steady, is it racing? — It's not what's important, it can't be what matters, it's all trivia, trivia.
'There you have it.'
What do I have?
'The clue, swansdown. What keeps you going.'
Up yours.
'You can't relax, can you? What's all this gravity? Such introspection – what's your mind, some celestial body? Cutting loose from terra firma? It's a bootstraps game – you'll never do it!'
How do you come furnished with nonstop opinions, right or wrong, and me so unable to arrive at any? How lame-brained, how fatuous am I?
'Rubbish, can't you see? you're sure-fire smarter than me put together. I'm saying nothing – it's a game.'
It's not.
'You won't believe me, will you? you won't believe anybody. Here we are, you and me, flower – like it, despise it – spun out of our sensibilities and nothing more —'
It's about facts, hard facts —
'– You're a – listen to me – you're a life-support system for a portable array of nerve-endings and that's all – a perpetual-emotion machine and built to propagate more of the same! what do you expect? We're decoy and bait to keep you in a state of caring, all of us – each others' red herrings, you, me and all! Your *mind is* the facts, Pandora!'
Okay I'm here to feel – let me feel my life and I'll take what comes!
'Then what's your trouble?!'
We die! I said. This thing may get out of hand. It could be over before you know what hit you.
'You're dying to believe it makes a difference.'
I don't play word-games with strange men.

133

'Like hell,' Lench said. 'That's all we've got – you love it.'
I belched.

'I feel bad that you feel so bad,' he said. 'You couldn't be consoled, I suppose, with general assurances that we're all bound to sustain the same losses and the same bewilderment?'

Is a consolation prize a consolation? I said; I want to win. It's got to come from outside —

'Now who's playing with words?'

– outside the roundabouts of what I happen to think!

'Oh do us a favor – ! he said, bunging both hands over his ragged earholes with incredulous impatience.

– Can you imagine a victory that includes bewilderment?

'You fancy some kind of crisis, hey wot?'

I just want to understand things.

Lench stared heavily down the ward and spoke almost inaudibly.

'When you understand everything. Will it help?'

What?

Will it help?!

Stuff you.

He looked at me with a glint in his still intact eyes that was either savagery or pain, I couldn't tell which.

'You've got the gall to think you can have some shining trial-by-fire —'

And you pretend you've flushed your illusions and stopped hoping for an order in things – you take nips on the side.

'And you still haven't noticed that you're missing something?'

You can just thank your lucky penny, baby, I've a sense of irony.

Lench was poised in his wheelchair with an enigmatic list to the left.

I laughed.

Then he laughed.

We laughed together.

'Well,' he said. 'What have you decided, about survival?'

Was that the assignment?

'Personal survival – are you pro-creation?'

You're all trick questions.

'Trust me!' he said. 'Would I sell you a bill of goods? Like that trash?' He waved to his books in the waste bin.

134

Tell you about the modern predicament, did they?

'They *are* the modern predicament, damn it.'

What – absurdists, relativists are they – 'indeterminists'? I'd think they'd be just to your liking, those.

'Isms! What've you been doing, pansy, you've been skiving, haven't you? larking about, mind on all the wrong things, haven't found out yet, have you?'

Could you repeat the question?

'It's a question of fashion, flower. It was a fad, being born!'

Ah here we come, I said.

'Look, look around you – look at history!'

If I must.

'It was safety in numbers – *safety in numbers* was the thing, the en-tire flaming thing.' Lench was keeling perilously left-ward. 'Christ, they even made suicide a crime. What've we ever done, us humans, I ask you, but hype up some blinding new posture to cover our shortfalls?'

Thus and so — ?

'Thus and so what about suicide now – you follow?' He was righting and bracing himself in his seat with unmistakable difficulty – something of him, I could see now, being decidedly not what it ought in the way of supportive equipment, gim-bals, landing gear. 'You can get how-to books on it, suicide – they're handing out d.i.y. aids!'

Always a bad sign, I said keeping graciously mum about his increasing teeter and roll.

'And gay rights? and the pill – ?' He was wobbling terrifically, as if, below my shortened sightlines as I lay there, he'd lost the foot or two by which one normally kept oneself canti-levered upright in your ordinary chair. '– And abortion? sterili-zation? euthanasia? – all the mod-cons?' With an excited slow-motion glissade he was perceptible slipping, sinking out of his chair. 'Shite, squire! Made a new world, have we – ?' he said, slitherily receding '– too many mouths to feed now? Give over!' Lench disappeared under the bed.

Your arguments have a thick consistency, I said anxiously filling time as he scrambled above the horizon again.

'Life?!' he shouted, clambering onto my bed. 'We've had a falling-out with safety-in-numbers,' he said, arranging him-self. 'The population's exploded out of the cave!' he said, now

135

cleverly disposed on the bed, inescapably but unfussily disclosing the absence of one-and-a-half of his feet, the leg-ends in plastic bags. 'Things change — !'

Are you trying to tell me, I said containing my shock, are you telling me my death now and your death —

'An enactment of the communal will.'

– Somebody's idea of —

'A medium of cultural expression.' His sitting between and occasionally on my legs imparted an undeniably piquant note of fellowship to our conversation.

A master plan, I said wrily – and the master mind?

'Mind? what mind, idiot?' He had a hand in his bathrobe pocket. 'Society has no mind. It's got reflexes, spasms, effusions. Pluralism, indeterminism, "aporia" – freedom to be unborn, liberty to die – it's the new convulsive musk, to mask the eternal aroma of rot.'

So what are you – whose side are you on — ?

'Would you prefer I said it was a joke? Look —' He rummaged in his pocket.

You're what, an anarchist then?

'"Anarchist"! I swear you're more anglo than me! Another sucker for the irrelevant.'

Don't smother me with complements.

'Sod it, blossom, you run like the rest to hide in that holy of holies – "rumblings of revolt? he must be political"! Don't you see? it's a fantasy about *action*. "Anarchist", "liberal", "fascist" – nobody's truly bothered what sort.'

Except the oppressed and oppressors, I hear —

'Dunce! They all back the same myth, the same horse, down to their last penny: *human power*, *action*, is all – anything else is just somebody's pink spiders. What leaves people incredulous and sneering with the speechless horrors is the stark raving reality of somebody of the other kind.'

What kind is that?

'You'll see, I'll have my day.'

Yes Hinkle.

'What?'

Sure, Hinkle.

'It's me – Lench – I'm your friend. I want you to see this —'

What are you selling me?

'Have you seen my memento mori?'

I'm not your mark, you know. You can't score off me.

'I'm not! I'm not,' he said, 'don't go off at half-cock. Look!' He'd dug something out of his pocket and was holding it up. 'It's my memento mori.'

It was gristled and pearly.

What is it?

'It's a memento mori, I tell you – like in ancient times – a man'd carry one around, keep it before him —'

I know what's a memento mori —

'– you'd keep it on your bench or pulpit, under your pillow, plant it amongst your baubles and billy-do's – it's to remind you —'

I know what a memento mori is, I'm not a complete fart – what is *that*, in your hand?

'They got it off me just now, just a while ago, off my foot, they let me have it —'

What is it?

'Bones!' he said. 'What are you, blind? It's my toe. It's my big toe.'

I stared.

'They got more off,' he said, 'but I reckoned this'd do me fine. You don't want to be piggish.'

We stared at it together, for a long time.

What do you figure...I said...a memento mori...what do you figure it was to remind you of?

'That you have to die,' he said. 'That's what it means. "Remember you must die".'

Yes, but – I said – why?

'You plunk a mangy skull or an old dried foot down amidst the crackers and cheese,' he said, 'and you're an odds-on favorite to shake your neighbors out of their "platitudes", as you put it.'

But a man put it at his own table, not his neighbor's. Why?

'It made him think.'

But what? A memento of his own death! – hell, his *death* must have meant something, then. But *what*?!

We looked at his toe-bone and at each other and at his toe-bone. Marbly and directionless, lying in his hand.

'It's not my style of question,' he said.

Why do *you* keep one, then? I said.

He put the thing away.

Are you ignoring me now, or what?

'You're going to do your nut,' he said. 'At this rate you'll entirely do your nut, you'll go round the twist. You still don't see what I'm on about, do you?'

What are you on about?

'Bloody hell, mate! You still haven't once – not even once – noticed people rushing you now?'

I went cold.

He was nodding, his enviable motive power taking him precariously near the edge of the bed.

'You've got it. Comes a time – there comes a time,' he said, 'where one of us has to look at the whole thing. *The whole thing*, do you see what I mean?'

I'm listening.

'And what happens? Maybe it's envy, maybe the funk? we get the wind up? Anyway, the rumor gets out. It's like bees, like ants – like lemmings. One of us, one of our own kind is in sight of *the zone* – he's about to glimpse the whole thing, to *look down in*. And what happens? We can't stop – we have to *push* him, *shove* him. To the edge – over the edge. We have to throw him in with it. We drive the stake through his heart.'

Buried at the crossroads, eh? I said.

'You've found the clue, old tit! It's *trivia* – just like you said – the Latin for "crossroads". At the crossroads – thére's absolutely nothing there. What looked – crucial – is nothing.'

Enough! If I'm there, why can't I *see* that I'm there?

'Getting out of your depth, aren't you – ?' he said.

Why can't I *feel* my death?

'– Sure you're up to it?'

It's *my* damned death, I *must* be up to it, I said.

Something seemed to have stung him. After a second, he sounded almost angry.

'Now's your chance,' he said.

I know it.

'What've you got to say for yourself, then?' He seemed bitten somewhere deep. 'Speak now, sunshine, or forever hold your peace.'

I'll speak, all right. I *must* be up to it.

'I must go pee,' he said, starting up suddenly.

It makes sense, I said.

With a deft maneuver he fell into his wheelchair on the first try.

Right, I said.

In the thin split of a second he was gone, rushing off remarkably in the manner of Dr Wall.

And then he was coming back. Wheeling slowly.

Have we met? I said.

He was glaring at me, in a way that had things like resentment and anguish jumbled in it.

He was not Hinkle. For all that I'd thought it, perhaps even wanted it – was it some nostalgia for unity, was it a case of softening brain? – a single look at him at that moment would have told: Lench was nothing like Hinkle. He was a curse unto himself.

'I've a confession to make, luv,' he said.

Should I cover my eyes? I said.

'You couldn't if you wanted to,' he said. He was having trouble keeping upright.

Well?

'You're so immaculate,' he said slowly. 'Not a scratch on you, ever. And never will be. You won't even have time.'

Oh, I said.

'That's not the confession,' he said.

Get to it, I said with some asperity.

'I let-on I was going to die,' he said.

Yes.

'I'm not.'

A swift welling of different feelings overtook me.

'I'm merely a necrotic. I've known all along. It's a matter of little holding-actions with me, a bit of pruning from time to time, around the edges, see? I'm worth decades like this, another generation or two.'

I'm sorry to hear that, I said.

'It's just one of those things,' he said. 'Luck of the draw.'

I'm really sorry.

'You're not just saying that?'

No.

'Not being just trendy — ?'

Unh-uh, I said.

'Say...?' he said then.

Hey?

'I had a way through, you know, for a while? I was a hustler. Would you believe me?'

I believe you.

His visible tongue clattered – his eyes arrogant, as if barricaded, in a deadlock.

'Do you find me a pariah...?'

It's part of your charm.

'Look you,' he said, 'one thing.'

I'm looking.

'Don't you pity me, and I won't pity you. Don't misread me. I'm an enthusiast. Believing's nothing to do with it. One of the world's great, few remaining, true enthusiasts. Much greater than you. You'll see.'

Still, later, him gone, I have this rather poetic vision of us: enjoying together this mutual shame – scratch partners – one having to die, one having to live. What a choice. But that's crap, sentimental; Lench would shoot it down in a wink. Sure, him and his 'brilliant confession' —

No listen, says my maudlin voice —

– Lench wriggling off the hook —

He's clapped in irons, you fool —

– Slipping the collar with a word —

He can't bear his glitter any longer on his own.

Ridiculous. Hell. Why didn't I confess that I, too, am thinking of not dying?

Somewhere within me now – thirty days, they say, since they laid me out numbly here – a small sound has begun to make itself present. Phlegm in the tubes, perhaps. A little sound, a sort of chirping. Or is it just behind my brow, above my eyes?

Funny about Treeza. Treeza not coming around.

Rhythmic, the chirping, a whistling and sniffing, animal panting – peculiar the thoughts that come into your mind – a one, and two, and three... and pant and pant and pant... and Teresa and I, in some place, in some town, years back now, years back, where the husbands and wives sat on the lady's floor, and pant and pant and pant and... this is too much... this rodent-snuffling behind my eyes —

140

Is it time to play my ace?

Suddenly, compulsively, I stopped the ward nurse.

Who's been delivering me these messages, I said.

'What messages would those be, Mr Wall?'

You know, the messages. From a man called Hinkle.

'You've had no messages that I know of, my duck.'

I've had messages! Regularly! Three, four messages in a row.

'. . . I'll make inquiries, Mr Wall,' she said.

Do, I said.

'I'll ask around.'

Do.

What do they mean, no messages? And there was another, too, now that I think, the card the man Poole brought, the Get-Well from the office – Poole – the one who knows Hinkle — what happened to that card? They gave me a drug, and made me wait, and Poole was there and handed me the card as we talked – and then – I was wheeled away – and where is the card — ? What are they doing to me?

It's time to play my ace.

A new matron's on the ward; I'd found the perfect break. I didn't waste a moment.

I feel I must tell you, I said.

'Yes, Mr Wall?' she said, absorbing my chart.

It's all a mistake, I said. It's not me they're after.

'Oh?' she said.

I'm not Mr Wall, I said.

'Nonsense,' she said.

It's true, I said. It's not me they want. I'm here under false pretences. They've got their records wrong. Everything, from start to finish. It's not me. It's the doctor that's Wall.

'So you're just visiting,' she said.

I just dropped in to collect a prescription, I explained. You know, for my wife —

'You don't like your name,' she said.

That's it, I said. It's as simple as that. I took the name by mistake and the goo hit the fan. I'm afraid I've caused everyone an awful lot of trouble —

'Not at all,' she said, 'what'll it be, then —'

If you'd just get me my clothes, I said, I've an appointment—

'"Mr Fish"?' she said. 'How about "Mr Fish"?'

– I'll be on my way, I said energetically, turning my complete head unswervingly to the left, quick as a steel trap.

'Mr Pratt" is nice,' she said, 'we had a nice "Mr Pratt"—'

Super, I said, deciding on an all-out show of force, call me Mr Pratt, I said, turning my head back to the right, with indomitable snap. Just get me out —

'May I say you're a live wire, Mr Wall —'

– Just give me a shot, a shot of something, vitamin C, I'll be fine as soon as I hit the street —

'Now Mr Wall, what would you do in the street — ?'

Mowgli, call me Mowgli, I said – a breath of fresh air and I'll be —

'We'll call you "Mowgli" if you like, Mr Wall, what does it matter' – the new matron burst into song – 'as long as we-e-e have you-ou-ou!'

Joke if you will, I said, but has it occurred to you you could be laboring under a semantic delusion? what do you think this means, 'have me'?

She gave me a chiding smile out of the corner of a motherly eye as if I should have known better.

Just who do you think I am?! I insisted.

'*This*,' she said, and began kindheartedly, indulgently to pat the middle of the bed, 'this is you, Mr Wall.'

By a series of swift calculations it came upon me that it was not the bed she was patting. It was the body.

Everything for a second went white. 'We habeas the corpus, Mowgli,' said her voice in my head; but when the colors came back there was nobody there and I was emitting oaths like 'You nasty slattern, I'll get you!' somewhat fecklessly to the air.

The bowl of ice that matron had brought for Mr Robinson to suck – in place of the food he was no longer permitted to eat – went clattering just about now to the floor beneath my bed, and Mr Robinson sat up with a lurch. The retch that followed this time, with extraordinary sounds and flying dark watery matter, included great gouts of dayglo-red blood, luminous and astonishing. Mr Robinson sank back.

I lay angrily listening.

'It's all through the cardia, if you ask me,' one was saying in a hushed voice. They were standing close by my bed outside the curtains they'd drawn around Mr Robinson's.

'I'm afraid so, he's got lesions, vessel ruptures right up the esophagus along with everything else,' said another.

'Comes the autopsy, I'm putting my money on lacerations right through the muscularis,' said the first. 'I say promethazine, twenty milligrams every eight hours.'

'You can't keep that up!' whispered the other. 'Can't we try meclazine, twenty-five to fifty, once a day?'

'What have you got in mind in the way of days?' said the first.

'It's safer, meclazine, for longer.'

'Longer than what?' said the first.

'I know,' said the other.

They went away, and the nurses left Mr Robinson's curtains open once more.

Hollow-eyed, Mr Robinson said,

'What did they say?'

Lying there, he said, 'Am I going to die now?'

Well...I said...they're not sure.

'Feeling poorly,' he said in a frail tone. 'Still, can't be helped. Don't want to make a nuisance.'

No, I said.

'Do you know?' he said, wandering. '...My Molly's last one was stillborn, you know —'

No, I didn't know.

'– and do you know, if it's born and if they can't decide if it was born alive or born dead, it has to be reported to the coroner. Did you know?'

No, I said, I didn't.

'Had to go along to the coroner, us did.'

I'm sorry, I said.

'Breasts filled right up, Molly's, with milk. Her breasts filled right up with milk. Didn't know what to do, we didn't.'

I can imagine, I said stupidly, wanting hard, for some reason, not to let his words go unanswered.

'...Shan't see it through,' he said.

Don't be silly, I said.

'Well, dying's dying,' he said. 'Still, takes the stuffing out of you.'

I'm sure, I said.

'Be well clear of this place, though,' he said. 'Well shut of it. Eh?'

Sure, I said.

'Thing is,' he said, 'I've et too much.'

Don't be silly, I said; you've had nothing in days.

He was shaking his head.

'I et too much.'

What? I said, perplexed.

'Always have. Liked to do. That's what's wrong.'

No, I said.

'. . . I'll be going on, said Pooh' – Mr Robinson recited – 'Well goodbye, said Rabbit, if you're sure you won't have any more.'

Is there any more? asked Pooh quickly – I said.

Mr Robinson sort of laughed, and began to cough.

His cough subsided.

Who, I said compulsively and couldn't stop myself, who do you blame?

'. . . A person hates to say,' he said. 'About *them*, after all. . . . Well,' he said, 'it all comes to the same thing, really.'

I don't know if it does, I said.

But Mr Robinson had fallen away into a kind of trance.

What can you do when you've very little working but a face?

Oh where, oh where has my little wife gone, oh where oh where can she be, my wife is my shepherd, I shall not want —

What can you do to disclose how genuinely nettled, rankled you feel by the developing course, the general run of events? How do you put them all, at least, in their place? *What do you do* —

Visiting time at the inn. And everything's chatter and buzz. Aunts and close-lipped uncles and gabbling mothers-in-law, and gazing children in tow.

And at the foot of my bed a stray was standing, a small red-headed boy with a gaping silent look – and a terrible rolling lump betwixt his molars that instantly caught my eye.

We stared at one another.

144

'What's that?' I finally said.

He drew haltingly near, the great lump clattering in his mouth.

Whatcha got there, son? I said.

'. . . Oy weetie,' he said at last, staring suspiciously.

How's that? I said with undiminished terror.

We stared suspiciously at each other. He shifted the lump with a visibly moist tongue.

'. . . Oil fweetie,' he said.

Come again? I said insistently.

He put his hand to his mouth, took it away, and held it up, revealing something huge, green and purple and shining in his palm.

'A boiled sweetie,' he said rapidly, and popped the giant jawbreaker back in without delay.

It inflated his entire physiognomy to a degree.

Who do you blame? I said impulsively.

'How should I know?' he said, taking out his sweetie again.

Good point, I said.

'Mum says *him*,' the boy said, to my surprise, 'he says *her*, 'n' Auntie Ellen says the both of them.' He stuffed his mouth again, his face expanding on the relevant side until the nostril vanished and the lips took on the livid indecent hue of spoiled ham, not a pretty sight and he was scarcely six.

You want to watch that, I said, your mum'll do herself a mischief when she sees that.

He stared. And the lightbulb switched on in my head.

Say, I said. I don't suppose there's another where that came from?

His eyes widened in clear, even proud if wary acknowledgement.

Lend me one? I said.

'Owanee-endoowan?' he said skeptically.

I drew a blank. He extracted the monstrous thing once more with all his fingers. 'How can I lend you a boiled sweetie?' he said with greater clarity and some wonder.

Give me one then? I said timidly. I'm a sick old man.

Slowly, he took out of his coat pocket a large paper sack, and from this withdrew a mammoth red boiled sweetie and held it up.

One more favor? I said. Put it in my mouth?

'In yer gob?' he said.

In me whole gob, Lad, I said. And thank you with all my heart.

When the new matron came passing by at the end of the visiting hour, in a moment of glory I shall recall to the end of my days, I gave her a full frontal of myself that produced a tribute worthy of the princely boy's openfisted bounty.

'Good Lord,' she said, and staggered. When she'd uncovered her eyes, I'd fleetly rolled the sweetie in my mouth from under the lip to a prominent position before one ear. Off she went in a wake of fizz. I heard voices. Wall's registrar appeared; the sight brought color to his cheeks. 'Christ', he said, 'Craddock!' he cried, 'Craddock!' and Craddock came running, Mr Robinson's promethazine doctor in fact, 'would you have a look at this swelling,' he said. I shunted it to a conceivably horrible site up under one eye. 'The devil!' he said, 'it's moving!'

'What is he? is he croaking?' shouted Craddock, going away again and coming back.

'He's not croaking but he's something,' shouted the registrar.

'Like what?' shouted Craddock, going away and coming back again.

'Something peculiar, prop him up, he's gone funny,' shouted the registrar.

'What's funny, funny what?' shouted Craddock, peering down.

'He's gone all funny in the face.'

'Croaked, you mean?'

'I don't know what you call it – what do you call that?'

'I don't know – what do you call that, George? Where's George?'

'Jesus Christ!' cried the registrar as I expelled it airborne with all my might, 'look out! it's a boiled sweetie!'

Shit, I said while they backed away. Shit, shit, shit.

It was my last authenticated word on the subject.

◆

Quietly gathered about my still slightly propped form with its now deferentially bowed head, they took occasion to remark upon the flow of saliva that was running down to my waist. And to comment that the language I spoke was no longer intelligible to them. Indeed, even to me it was a disconcertingly meaningless medley of sounds, leaving something to be desired. The paresis, as they're pleased to call it, had crept up my throat and into the muscles of my face; I seem, simply enough, to be no longer adept at swallowing on my own, and to have lost my voice. The 'power of speech', if you've a taste for abstractions.

The first few minutes were rather fun, really. For all misadventures there must surely be compensations. The staff, for example, gave me every encouragement on this occasion and a general feeling of conviviality went round as I tried to speak. The writhing efforts of my mouth to open itself and pronounce 'I' they welcomed with such phrases as 'Great!' 'Extraordinary!' 'Electrifying!' 'A real eye-opener!' and 'Wow!'

In this position, I'l freely admit, it is more difficult to take the bull by the horns. To make up one's mind, adopt a stand, not to mention cut the crap – it is touch and go, I'll freely confess. But wit must prevail in a just cause; for a time, a new manner of speaking was at hand. I could blink. It should work, after all, computers thrive on it: on/off, true/false, yes/no: you can imagine as the staff and I explored the universe of subtle possibilities: good/bad, in/out, black/white, alive/ —

It wasn't, to tell the truth, all that interesting a proposition.

147

Apart from my quite evidently resembling a long night on a railway siding, blinking right and left, it was bound to prove awkward saying 'It is there' in a series of on/offs, not to speak of 'You're lovely today', 'I prefer classical music', or even the old standby, 'Help'. It's plainly a question of getting the categories right; of people entering into the spirit; of definitely needing to start too far back.

'Note the skewed eye movements,' said Wall's registrar.

'Nystagmus,' said Dr Wall.

'Sir, he's getting wiggly eyes.'

'What I said,' said Dr Wall fatalistically.

By evening of this first day by the new revised standard reckoning, while the eyeballs continued to whirl, my lids ceased blinking. And people went away to think.

I lay in silence to sense the increasing chirp within me, growing in speed to a burble, like the rising boil of the little ball in my brother's whistle. Initially the trouble – painless as always – was nothing. It was merely as if my heart and lungs were squeezed into a decreasing space, my ribs spread up and outward – it was a trifle to begin with; what nettled me was the enchaining of this with a startling loss of air. A small matter of threads forming. A bubbling wheeze of filaments penetrating through and coiling about the lungs, evolving a web of breathlessness, airlessness. A nest. A bird caught and striving in the toils – let it go. No. I was the nest *and* the bird. An intricate, sweetly interlacing network of unfurling fluids, shooting off sparks, struggling, firing, coiling, a cascading and upwelling liquid shower of lights incandescently foaming, filling me, gasping away the air – myself flooding myself – passages engulfed with coagulant mucous mysteries which my body squeamishly displayed a convincing and decisive indisposition to attend to or further discuss. Casually supine in this disastrous flooded state, I heard someone saying 'He's tachypneic, and that's not all'; and they were holding me downside up and hurriedly dumping me out like storm troops doing a quick frisk of a suspect pair of slacks, a hell of a way to clear one's throat.

So you thought, didn't you, that you were safe this time. A handful of jokes, a few laughs – you thought you had it made?

148

Air regained, I lay drifting in oblivion. Wafting, floating. It was gorgeous. A prism, I mused, rainbow colors revolving, a crystal letting windows onto distant shining vistas. And swiftly, interminably, one of its faces comes turning: a blinding mirror. Its gaze like the people's, averted, its light bent away, a mirror without a face.

Dulcet, luscious, euphorial, this blank oblivion. To die, what will it be? like this? A voyage to the bosom of....?

'His poor pulse is bounding,' said one of the staff.

...A bosom of mangoid globes, eyeless, viewless papaya breasts, splayed and blind to the world...?

'The primary's reached the xiphisternum,' a doctor said, 'he'd be in costal margin pain.'

...I lay fondly mouthing the blind nodding staring breasts of my imagination in luxurious rapture....

'He'll be in awful pain now,' said a doctor, 'we can start giving him something now. Bring the tray.'

Pain? I mused, bemused, floating raptly. What, which, whose? The tray? what is it? who needs it? oh do as you like....

'I've seen pain,' someone was saying interestedly as the rattling tray approached, 'where you'd, you know, put your hand in, pull on the hollow viscera or stretch the deep structures such as the heart, you know, or tug at some vessel or other at the base of the brain, and the patient's pain would go quite unrecognized as such —'

'Ah well – !' said another, inserting the needle of drug into an arm of mine '– but you take the *ultimate* pain, now. *Thalamic* pain. Hmm? There is a really *interesting* phenomenon. You take a man with *thalamic* pain – you give him your little tap on the knee, say, hmm? And suddenly he has a feeling – a simply exquisite, apparently indescribable feeling of –' he said as the plunger went slowly in '– pain – pain accompanied by – an astonishing expression on his face of – fear and dismay –' he said, the squish of the plunger sinking '– because he cannot tell in any way whatsoever *where* –' he said, the syringe going empty '– or *why* – or *how* – he's having this – pain – it is simply everywhere, everything – total – unspeakable – pain. There, that'll fix him,' he said, the needle withdrawing. 'But is he – is this one getting –' someone whispered '– thalamic pain?' 'Oh hardly! 'Not that.' 'Not yet, anyway.' 'Not that.' Among

149

them I could view Dr Wall speechless standing there, his right hand complexly, quixotically, inscrutably installed in his left trousers pocket. 'Close patient's eyes for him, would you nurse? They'll get deucedly dry staring gormlessly about that way' – a shadow came up – 'and if he's getting any glim through them at all' – the scene went dark – 'he can't be enjoying it much, there's a good girl.'

An instant later things went light again, my eyes having apparently reopened, and I saw their backs retreating down the aisle, murmuring amongst themselves. 'Let's keep a watch on BP, pulse, the rest,' 'Don't let respiration go below eight a minute,' 'Apneic pauses – under no circumstances longer than forty-five seconds,' 'We'll see if he's still got a sleep-wake cycle....' 'Thalamic pain? Not yet anyway....'

Their lavishly-meted analgesic began its work. From the stasis of peaceful oblivion I passed on into a realm of planetary perturbations, large and small. The side-rails they'd put on my bed, though I could hardly see them, chilled me with intimations of a casket. Treeza? Treeza? The notion that my eyes might close once more and never reopen came upon me – like the conception of entering a darkened hall and seeing the light fall upon a figure just before you, the back of a head, and the head begins to turn, and the dread comes over you as the face veers toward you, the dread of the sight of the face, the deformity of the face, the blank absence of a face. Down the ward, nurses sat at the little table, playing at noughts and crosses, tic tac toe. What have you to say for yourself? someone said. A surgeon drew near me where I lay on the table, scalpel in rubbery hand, lips in a cupid smile, starch-white breathing mask securely trussed across his eyes. Thalamic pain? Not yet. 'It's a dance we do –' Dr Lever was saying '– us lords of the bloody earth –' as the new hulking invincible dinosaurs came lumbering past, herds reeling, jostling a quadrille and a do–si–do, skirting the crevasse, heads armored aloft in the murk. Dr Wall standing there among the blank-made beds, his right hand tortuously, incoherently, unhingedly disposed in his left trousers pocket. What've you to say? It was a snow avalanche – the man was tucked into himself on the table and rolling interminably like a ball – an utter snow range coming down in a rush, rising softly over him as a tidal wave.

'Really hard luck, bad effect,' I heard someone say. 'He's allergic to morphine.'

In the freezing mud, the prisoners stood, pulling their cuffs down over their hands, first this cuff, then that, then this, then that. They stood there in the cold, pulling their cuffs down over their hands.

'Try him now,' somebody said.

The worst was passing, for now. I beheld Treeza dressed as the fabled wife on the desert strand, the giant whooping stork carrying her hooting husband skyward in its atrocious talons with mounting awesome flapping wings, she crying up through mad-cupped hands, 'Throw down the keys!'

Someone was knocking on my skull. 'We've got grimacing, doctor!'

'Ah, there you are!' said Dr Lever turning and approaching me with smiles of relief, 'afraid we'd got out of touch, we were!' He looked down at me. 'Now don't you fret about the allergy, we've got bags of other tricks to try, can you hear me?' He was implanting another needle in my arm, looking at me scoldingly. 'I told you, didn't I? Didn't I tell you? Why ever did you cling so to suffering? Hmmm? Manly, is it? Hmmm? Confused your suffering, didn't you, with your *psychological reaction* to suffering! Now isn't that right? When *will* you sort things out?'

Deeply I reflected, as I lay draining like a cool stream out of the caverns of hallucination into the light of day once more. Yes, there was no way I could convince myself he was wrong, he had to be right, I was guilty of what he said, whatever it meant.

'You're imagining things,' he said, 'All kinds of things.'

You're damn straight I am, I thought.

'You *don't* want to suffer, now *do* you?'

Suffer? suffer what?

There was no doubt about it, suffering and a psychological reaction to suffering were not extraordinarily well discerned from one another in my mind, to be fair – what suffering was

151

that? Not yet. Where was the suffering, exactly, did they think? Clearly they knew – they'd *been around*; surely when they declared me in need of their instant painslayer, theirs was the majority view; the consensus and hence the objective perspective had to be, must be right. But then who – was it my companion that suffered, within me? my shadow, my usher? And how would I know if it did, besides? Thalamic pain? *Not yet.* Not yet. Who, then, was suffering? The others, outside me? The patients – the doctors? those whose community contained *me*, for whom I was the insufferable blob?

What of the pain – of the pain of others – of Lench, of Austin – of Treeza? – of Hinkle? – and what kind of pain was this, the impalpable pain of the others?

A surprise factor reared its head, then; the pain of the others. It's all a game, says Lench; Lench laughs at himself. The gameness of things is a function of the otherness of things; Lench's laughter is a factor of the otherness of Lench to himself. Was I, then, in some unknowable way, an other? perhaps I was, in truth, somehow wonderfully *only* an other? It was all – that was it – it was all – a case of subject versus object. Wall's registrar was frightfully right; one must *learn to distinguish*. I distinguish, therefore I am. The better part of valor is distinction. *I must distinguish myself.* Subject versus object – and which was I — ?

'Haven't you noticed –' Lench had said '– you're missing something?' What – what's that? is it something I miss? something I'm missing? or something that's missing in me? That's what it's all about, I thought with hurried elation. I foresaw fanning out ahead like an open hand of cards, a bouquet of infinite gambits, a galactic universe built of notions that had looming within them – as it had lurked within *me* all the while – this equivocality, these warps of meaning, these mutations and transpositions, this incessant slippage of things into one another's places. (Who am I? what have I to say for myself?) In haste, a whole cosmos of möbius strips and streamers unfolded and coiled up before me, my very own endlessly private syntax, the anamorphic world of the ubiquitous subexistent Mr Wall. That was it. They flushed narcosis into the arm of a contented man – and who was he, to carp? I mean – really; their guess was as good as his. I'd been imagining things.

Death itself was no problem. Even this was no doubt subjective; Jim Fitz had it right; death didn't arise; real death didn't even occur. What actually mattered was so momentous – and so becomingly, perfectly human – that it was beyond, it transcended the concept of fatality itself. The whole thing was simply, I deduced, the exercise by which one dealt – whatever the way, by refinement of optic resolution, sleight of hand, dint of wit – with the intriguing, harmless shapeshifting harlequinade of subjective and objective truth.

What am I complaining about? *I'm probably happy.*

They had put me on my left side, so that my eyes were facing Mr Robinson.

He didn't vomit a bit, this evening.

He was completely tidy, and in fact he didn't even move a lot. He just lay there shouting – with them gathering quickly around him – shouting 'O Jesus! somebody help me!' They drew the curtains, figures passing in and out, one of them fumbling and unable to find his way out through the curtains and cursing and throwing them apart with a screech. Mr Robinson, now quite visible, lay there shouting 'Somebody help me!' and I kept wondering, What can he be thinking, with all these people around him, helping him? I was impatient, even, with him. What can he possibly mean? Then he was quieter, I could hear him breathing peacefully, and they left him with relief, one by one.

Then, in the night, with a single sweep, he threw off his bedding.

I could hear his voice, though I couldn't make him out, part of my sheet happening to cover one of my eyes and the halflight of the ward being dim here. On his bedside-stand I heard the clink and overturning of the glass that contained his set of false teeth. I could hear him speaking, not shouting but speaking in a trembling voice, almost as though afraid of punishment for being heard. It was surprising to me somehow, his voice coming with the sound that it carried with it, out of what had seemed to be a presently peaceful body. He was saying, 'I don't

153

want to'; I can hear it even now, in the stillness of my head; he was saying 'But I don't want to go there'. It was so familiar, somehow, the child's voice. The child being sent on by himself, upstairs, into the dark, alone. The hand I had the impulse to stretch out to him lay languidly somewhere about me, impassive, inert, growing cold. 'I don't want to go there alone,' said the voice of Mr Robinson, trailing off. And he did the thing. In a series of gasps, squirts, shudders, dribbles, oozes, as the dawn came up. By the time the light filled the windows I could see his face, and how the regions of the skin had begun to drain and discolor, the influence of gravity freely leaching the blood into stagnant pools within the limp pajama'd frame. Flustered, the night nurse, evidently discomposed by her own slackness and surprise, bustled on her own about the bed, leaving the curtains open and me lying on my side motionlessly there with immobile eyes, watching still. The bedclothes she tossed into her wheeled hamper, and for a moment the speechless corpse lay opposite me, nude, embryonic and claylike. They sometimes ask, Can a man look forever on the sun? She fingered out the tongue from the back of the throat, and wiped at the corpse's ooze-soiled parts. How long, and to what end, may a man be made to look upon the face of the sun? With small square compresses dipped in a basin and wrapped around a tongue blade she swabbed out the flaccid mouth. She replaced the fallen false teeth in the mouth and, holding the jaw closed with one hand, found a long muslin bandage in her tray, passed this around beneath the chin and over the top of the head, and tied the face's mouth closed in this way with a knot behind the ears. Under her fingertips she closed the eyelids and held them like this for a moment, and withdrew her hand. Again he looked 'peaceful' this way, as he had with only a brief surprising interruption, before. She crossed the hands on the shrunken belly and tied them there with a muslin band at the wrists, and went to the foot of the bed, drew the legs down straight together, and tied these in the same way, at the ankles. Thursday a.m., peacefully, in his sleep, to eternal rest, send wreaths only. With an adroit though cumbersome maneuver she rolled the cadaver into a curled side-lying position like my own, its back to me, cracked a wood tongue-blade lengthwise in half, wrapped it in cotton

154

padding, and thrust it hard and permanently into the rectum. Send no surprises. She nudged the carcass so that it flopped onto its back, found the wizened penis and, with a strip of bandage tied it off. Gone but not forgotten. She quickly jotted things on tags with a ballpoint pen, leaning at the bedstand, and went around attaching these tags to the tied wrists and ankles, then unfolded something that emerged into a hooded paper shroud, pulled this over and down the lumpy shape and tied it neatly at the bottom as a porter came up with a long trolley, slid the closed package with the porter's assistance into the trough within the trolley, drew a sheet smooth and flat over the trolley, and with the porter went wheeling this empty cot down the aisle, out of the ward, as the morning lights were being turned on. Robinson, Mr. Devoted husband, father, son, silly old bear. Sadly missed. Went alone. Services a.m. No surprises, please.

Objective, subjective.
As long as you've got your health.
Object, subject. The crumbling morning remains. I can distinguish, all right. I *know* who it was, dying, Oh God! and it wasn't me.
Speak now, or —

Hinkle? Is that you calling?

I could supply them with no grimaces this morning, when they knocked. And my eyes, from what they say, are now centrally fixed and unalteringly dilated. For exploratory purposes, they've taken to standing about my bed holding up printed signs. 'Close Both Your Eyes' says one of these; 'Close

155

an Eye of Your Choice' reads a second; a favorite seems to be 'Put Out Your Tongue'; some wag insists on waving 'Smile' and another has suggested 'Say Cheese'. They put me a range of questions next. 'Do you know where you are?' they asked, 'what day it is? What month? What year?' 'Who are you?' proved an especially popular one. They rounded off the morning's exercise with the celebrated 'blink-reflex test', performed by means of a sportingly quick jab of the reflex hammer toward the root of my nose; I left them dazzled by the cool of my steady stare, and they're sending for reinforcements.

Is it like someone pushing the door?
And is it opening, or what?
And which would you prefer?
'Midbrain displacement,' said the first, peering at me. 'A space-occupying growth of as-yet unspecified nature, midbrain.'
A new lodger, thought I, midbrain. The germ, perhaps the seed of a new idea.
'Resection, would you say? Open up, reduce the pressure?'
'Have a heart for the patient, man,' said the first. *What* idea *was* it, then, though? 'Where would you start – belly – brain – chest?' A new conception? of what? Like a singer – forgotten the song. 'This isn't 1960 or the Middle Ages or something.' Seem to have the chords – only lost the melody. 'Our job's to keep chaps alive, not muck about white-mousing them on the off chance.' Have chords, will travel.
Or was there ever – was there ever a song at all?
'And his mental condition?'
The way they bob and weave about, you'd think I was blind.
'Akinetic mutism, I'd call it.'
Just less in control of what I see, that's all.
'It won't hurt?'
Lids unclosing over fixed eyes, the muscles probably atrophying, the irises losing their spring; a little less able to focus each hour, or take shelter from the shower of light.
'Mightn't he start feeling kayak-angst?'

156

Things a little more – how shall I say? – wild? and woolly?
Figures blurring, light searing, a little; never mind.
'Kayak-angst? Better that than thalamic pain.'
I won't talk. If there's a need – why should there be a need?
– I'll squeeze your hand. Remember.
'He *does* seem to show some appreciation of his environment —'
'Oh he appreciates it *just fine*.'
A vision came....
'He's got sleep-wake cycle, pulse steady, all sorts of things!'
A cobbled square, a clattering of stones.
'In fact, *I* think he's probably bright and chipper inside there!'
People were pelting and hammering someone faceless with
stones.
'That's right. He's just hiding in there.'
'Who's –' said the first, poking toward me with a noodly
finger '– who's being a naughty boy, then?'

Hinkle? is that you? I don't – I can't hear you.

Mysteriously, Lench has been observed prowling in the
vicinity of the kitchens, with a large paper bag.

Treeza. Teresa. I could swear she was here.
Came in, took a look at me, and – letting out a sound, a
solitary howl – went away.
But no. That's not like her.
But yes – what *is* she like?
Oh give us a chance!

* * *

Ward G is behind me. Moved upstairs – to a long glass-wrapped room where technicians in white stare with devotion at the ticking equipment, the expressionless faces of the patients in the backwater like a scattering of islands, burnt-out volcanic rims and atolls filling gently with shining sea – I'm only visiting, a convalescent weekend, body-building and getting a change of scene. My tiresomely hand-washed-and-dried-and-powdered penis's old rubber draining cap removed for good, they've taken a firm step forward and driven a sturdy indwelling catheter hose straight up into my bladder. They study my stools and irrigate my rectum with gay abandon. A hole's been cut through my windpipe and a cuffed vent flanged into place with a little cloth collar to soak up the stray juices, so I can swallow my tongue or do anything else I like with it and still breathe. I lie in wait for the pert blond sister who sucks out my lungs and stomach with her Hoover attachment and brings me what she fondly calls my 'num-num'. At the bedside she takes hold of my Levin tube where it runs down into the stomach through my nostril, sticks its other end into a bowl she holds, and slushes me a long, a wholesome dose of the gray runny gruel through the tube, until she's satisfied. I don't wish to overplay the bond between us – her somewhat monotonous diurnal refrain of 'Here comes our big num-num', followed by complete silence save for the chance reciprocal gurgle of her tubes and mine, isn't much; but as has been said of the relations betwixt men and women and can't be said too often at a certain point in life, the quickest way to a man's heart is through his Levin tube, and you can't go far wrong with three square num-nums a day.

I'm on a winning streak – living nearer the bone at last, starting from scratch, the spirit's up and willing, and what have I to lose?

Not like the man in the wheelchair, in the lift, going up and down.

Or is it all lies?

But harmless lies?

Is it possible – Hinkle meant no harm: because what harm could be done? If it's all of it lies, what does it matter – if even 'harm' itself is a veer of our imagining?

Hinkle. For all his faults. The only real artist I have ever known. Old Master, macher, fabricator of living facts – if Hinkle was right – then things are what you dream them to be; there's nothing to fear. If you want something done right – you know what Hinkle says – you've got to do it yourself.

You've only to dream your way out.

You old dog, Hinkle – I owe you. You always knew something the others could never grasp. Hinkle, oddly silent these days, I never gave you your due.

Why can't I move?

Want something done right? Do it yourself.

The sisters come and turn me, and leave me, and come and turn me – my sight pinned upon a crack in the wall for a sum of hours – on a fly, on the occasional interloping face or two – outlines growing haloes, glowing and guttering and swelling brighter, retinas decaying in the constant light; next the sudden whirligig again of sheets and pillows as they roll me, and of *them, their eyes*; then the carousel spinning to its halt, my horizon now some other fading seam or stain in a different place, on the spread of wall on the other side, for another string of hours.

Cousin Hinkle calls for your help.

'He's tachypneic.'

'And hypoventilating.'

'Fleshy fingertips? any sign of clubbed or fleshy fingertips?'

'No.'

'Response to prick and tickle?'

'Reaction in one or two muscle groups.'

'That's promising; good.'

'But forehead-wrinkling has ceased.'

'Still, there's a vague waking-reaction, hard to describe. I'd say there is a facial expression of vigilance, there's just no evidence of – his responses just aren't appropriate.'

'You've palpated his skull.'

'Yes.'

'It's important to inspect the skull meticulously – you've percussed it?'

'Yes.'

'And checked his pH.'

'Yes.'

'Stand by the bed and make a loud noise.'

159

A tall doctor stood beside me and shouted loudly.
'*Mr Wall!*'
What can you say?
'Raccoon eyes,' said one of them, 'do you see something like raccoon eyes?'
'Not really.'
'Let's set up for an EEG, chaps.'
'You think there's positive structural disturbance of the cortical neurones now.'
'He'll be raising some awkward waves.'

Treeza?
Have you been raising any? A few waves of your own?
I know you – silly me – you're just home, waving your hair.
Wave to Treeza, boy. Go on, *wave*.

It happened fairly smoothly, then. When this girl was turning me. As she did, I couldn't help but see, or imagined I saw, the little ticking of the silvery watch she had pinned to her fresh white laundered collar a few inches from my eyes, with just above it, the soft pulsing almost lustrous waxen texture of the skin of her throat, the silken down, the slight moisture of – she was so – I could simply have – if I could have – she was drawing away – and – she was fading... fading.... down along my wall I could flaringly discern all the mannikins moving in their wax-museum medical disguise.... And with that, like so many softening and fusing candles wavering and guttering and flowing about their business, in gradually molten pools of white and marbling white and bronze... the scorching sight of the world in my eyes blazed and shimmered and burned itself out.
I am paralysed, and speechless. And also I am blind.
Speak!
About what, about death?

It's not about death.

Whatever comes up, however I think of it, no matter the resolutions I take or what conclusions I draw near to – it never belongs – it never manages to belong properly to the *subject of death*. 'I am blind,' 'I am dumb,' 'I am helpless' – I try everything, and it keeps on being about life. About what makes life life, better or worse life, more or less life, never about what makes death... whatever it is. I refuse, I refuse it. You'll know what you're doing, or there'll be hell to pay. The whole catastrophe, a gaping inanity, you'll have blown it. Nowhere, stuck and floating, a wind in space. A whole half of my human reality, of truth, is a blur, a blank. *I won't have it.* I would rather die than not know what death is – you see? *I am committed.* It keeps coming up Here's bloody life, and more of the same. But what kind of death is that – you die for a point, or *never say die! Where is the way to beat this?*

I've et too much, said Mr Robinson. Always have. That's what's wrong, he said. Why did he say that?

Why should it ring out now?

◆

My hearing, and the phantom sensations inside me, if that's what they are, are now massive and acute, like the hands of a paraplegic I once briefly knew – giant, powerful senses, seizing and holding. Near me, a monitor ticks, the suction machines throatily hum, and I believe I detect the circulating air of the room breathing among the cables and bottles hanging on poles.

'You look a sight.'

It was the voice of Lench.

'Been overdoing it, have you?'

Lench! I thought. Let me tell you! Listen! I've got to tell you! It's never about death!

'Terrific time finding you,' he said. 'What're you playing at, skiving about in your knickers, you don't look half dead, mate, all silent and bleary and all. What is this, the Intensive Oblivion unit? I don't know this part of the Near East.'

I heard the faint squeaking of my bed.

'Budge up, flower, make room for Enkidu.'

Lench listen – I'm trying everything and nothing works, do you hear? It's just never about death, why can't you hear me?

The squeaking went on, and settled.

'They say you've got brain insult, or some such nonsense, say you need talking-to or you'll go wandering off forever. I'm your man, hey? Supply you with buzz till the cows come home. Growl. Great Chain of Being, Chain of Chatter, it's all the same to us, what, babble?' I could hear him scratching. 'Blot the godawful noise of the void, can we hey?'

162

Lench, poor Lench, he wasn't listening; if I'd filled a stadium
with my voice, would he have heard?

'Well!' he said. 'Let me tell you, have I had an operation to
top them all! Resounding success. New, super-radical surgery
they call it, prophylactic or something. They've would-you-
believe cut off the bottom half. Preventive medicine. The
bottom half, maybe two-thirds of yours truly, feet, knees,
ballocks, right up to my appendix scar straight away in one
go – I told them Sure! I am a right clever Dick, and no danger!
I said Don't be daft, take the whole thing! Anything for a bit
of attention. What do you think? Hey? I tell you, it's terrific,
this super-radical stuff. Has disadvantages of a cosmetic
nature, I know – you'll think they're wearing me down,
whittling away at my self-confidence, but that's not it at all!
It's my doubts they're removing! Here I am, further abridged,
condensed, getting to the nub – just like you – I'm a precipitate,
I'm getting down to the Ultimate Me, here, look you.'

There was little doubt about it. The minimized bleat of my
bedsprings suggested him to be a lighter person altogether, a
summary, compact, more quintessential model of a human
being; query not, if they'd cut off the lower half of his body
in truth, or if he was just standing on a chair (a poignant ruse
for a soul in search of something to talk about), I was prepared
to believe him in the name of all we'd been through, and that
was that.

'So you think you've still got a march on me, eh squire?
being all sealed up and marked for mailing?'

He got no ready answer, understandably.

'Well let me say this, into your good ear if you've got one:
Your getting bunged up like that means nothing, mate. It's a
sad story, but *no* stories mean *anything* general – you can say
Piss-off to your theory of just deserts.'

Large quantity of silence.

'This is *your* way out, mine's some other,' he said. 'You're
struck dumb, I'm short on length; I'm long on time, you're
not. Nothing, Daphne, is symbolic.'

What was this nervous yearning in his voice that I heard?

'Mother Nature says "I pass".'

Silence.

'Me not dying?' he said, 'did I say that? What's to do about

163

alligator bite – first, avoid your alligator?' Silence. 'Neither one of us is going to do anything both of us didn't know about all along.' Spasms of words and of silence.

'No comment?'

What did he expect of me? What had he come for, then?

'Hey wot? Takes a lot of stomach, that thought, no?'

Flaked was he? speeding? Lench, what are you looking for?'

'That's life, isn't it? A strong stomach. The essential. Life objective: to develop a strong stomach. Before they remove it. Hey?'

For a single instant I felt as though – as he halted – he was looking deep at me. As if he were looking at me with something I would have to call...compassion?

'A strong stomach,' he said. 'Somebody like Jo Robinson,' he said. 'Here when Austin came, here when I came, here when you came, still. The best-made for life, was our Jo – the best that life had in store for itself. A man with not much, you may say – but he was a man who had a stomach for it, he was. Who could take more of the same.'

And what about me, then – was that why he'd come? As mobs flocked to touch saints, claw clothes from matinée idols, hug champions, brides, fresh-pregnant mothers – praying to tap into their connection with the energy mains, was that it?

'You didn't know we used to talk, did you, Jo and me? Answers, did he have? Or questions, even? He was the best fit for living, and that tells you just about all there is to know about questions and answers and about life.' I could hear Lench shifting on my bed. 'Yeah, we used to talk. Till I couldn't live with his fear anymore and hated myself,' he said. 'Healthy fear he had – not like us. And the gift: he was no stickler for detail. Took it on faith, not like us. You and your wretched Distinguo and your ergo sum – it was plain all along. Born to dissect, you and me, nicety upon nicety, wriggle and lash – and *I'm* a freer man than you, Gungadin, I'm here to tell you – did you know that? I keep mine down to two things, my distinctions – did you know?'

More shuntering about on my bed. Or was I wrong? Had he come to sponge off my 'death'? To taste *that* – soak it up – real or pretend – was *I* his memento mori?

'Jesus you're responsive,' he said. 'Ever thought of donating yourself to geological science as a stone?' What was he after? 'I've heard of the prisoner going quietly, but you are evolution's answer to The Mouth. Do you want to hear my distinctions or not? shall I let you in on the sweet and sour options?'

What do you want from me, man?

'They're What's funny, and What's not. That's what my two things are. 'Ey? What's funny, my lovely, is that it all comes to the same thing —'

No – not so — !

'And what's-not is that there's a delay – a diabolical delay you see — ?'

– no! why had he got to say it —

'– the stay, the stretch, the lag you call Life.'

– so glib Lench, so easy saying that —

'Want to know how it works?'

– him too and his speaking sickness — ?

'If the answer is no, say No, and if yes, stay just as you are —'

– like every other bleak scurrying soul?

'Ah,' he said. 'The correct answer was Yes, and you got it in one, congratulations, I am obliged to tell all. My dear bon ami, death is the Funny Subject.'

Was that why he'd come — ?

'There you are. The all-purpose watertight heavy-duty punchline – makes an instant thigh-slapper of every story ever told – wait, says the funnyman, this'll killya. The original infectious joke, affects the muscles – once you've caught it you can never keep a straight face again, you see? Every time I think of death I have to laugh. Hey?'

Was that what he'd — ?

'It's the gilded frame around the picture. There's only this snag —'

He'd come to laugh, to laugh at me —

'– It's – we fox ourselves. Take *you* —'

Come like the others, have you? to push me – over the edge, redhanded – to push me down in? what are you doing?

'– you bungle – you let things slip from the frame. Whatever for – delusion, bloodymindedness, incompetence, hope — and it all wallows down again into the slough of meaning, meanings, meaningfulness – the ultimate gaffe, the screamer, and there it is, sunbeam. Why keep a skull around the house? I'll

165

tell you, that's why – to keep us grinning, keep us honest. That's the game – getting back to death and laughter. To draw up your chair, inch up on your extinction – if it's not getting funnier, you're out.'

The bed squeaked.

'And what do you say to that, then? You, daisy, I mean you – what do you say? You don't feel the challenge? You don't give a damn?'

I give a damn, you bastard. What are you trying to prove?

'You don't give a damn. You lie there all solemn like. Making a meal of this thing, you know that, don't you? You ought to see your face. Mountain of a molehill. What ever were you looking for, "wisdom" or something? *Another diversion!* It's diabolical, you see?!'

Lench, by the sound, was squirming at my side.

'Come on, speak to me old son! Got to thin down yet, get trim, damn your eyes – look at *me*! Laugh it up, lad, what do you say?'

Say what? *What do you want from me?*

'You know what the trouble with you is?'

The elaborate creak and rattle of springs.

'Still stuck on life, you are, still stuck. So full of yourself – you've been a dilettante right from the off and everybody knows it – you're an overworked idea – like everyone else, cooking up heroisms one after another, squatting sweating on a lump of coal, dreaming to hatch a diamond – how long do you think you can go on?'

Lench climbing about above me.

'. . . You're not making a man – you're making a spectacle of yourself, look at you, whipping a dead horse – "exile" from some other place that doesn't exist – never existed. . . . Dear heart, *this is it* – here and now. *The whole thing.* You! I wouldn't be caught dead looking like you – what're you hanging around for? Hey? *Hey?!*'

If I could see – what will you have me see?!

Something shook. Continuously. He was *laughing*, wasn't he? The swindler, it was a con. Hawker, shark, gone ravening now, his larder bare – me surrounded by sharks? Or was the hungering my own?

'Why should I go on talking to your puling damn body lying there?'

166

Laugh then! Whatever comes, *it's not my fault*, go ahead, laugh!

'Don't feel bad,' he was saying, and shaking, 'don't feel bad, it's a natural mistake.... Everybody's a failure, you know, you must know. Everybody....'

What made the bed quake, it was laughter, wasn't it?

'You think I'm mad? you think I'm scared? you think I care?'

Was it laughter, was it sobs, that roiled the whole bed in convulsions?

I listened for another sound from him. Another word. But nothing.

Performing – flagrantly committing his act of mirth.

They took a long time coming.

Did he laugh, or did he weep?

'What is it?' I heard one say.

'It's that man Lench.'

'What?'

'He's slit his bleeding throat all over the clean bleeding sheets.'

I thought: It's so like him.

I thought: Wouldn't you know it?

I thought: *His* truth, not mine.

In their broken shoes in the freezing mud they stand, the prisoners, pulling at their cuffs, this cuff, then the other cuff—

Don't think about it — !

Knuckles white, standing there, trying with frozen hands to pull the sleeves down over their hands.

Don't think about him – it – blot it, beat it away — !

My skin – my fingers – what is it?!

I can feel my skin – *crawling* – the wrinkles in my sheets, my skin, my brain – I can *feel*! It's *me* – I'm coming back! Somebody – *turn around – look at me* — !

At me — !

Gone.

The feeling of me in the world...

...come...

...and gone again.

'It's not Mr Lench it's a —'

I hear, but can't keep track.

'It's a chicken —'

167

I breathe in. And the cage of my ribs – grotesque – won't expand. From all sides, the cage closes in. Motionless, I count now each single shallow whistling breath.

It's not real, it's not happening to me.

I believe I hear the man's body being carried away laughing, crying, laughing.

I seize a trace of air, and lose it. Somewhere about my person the air is misplaced, dispelled, spent.

It's an illusion, got to be – it's only a dream.

Air all blown out. It's a game.

The wind in the reeds.

Lench's dream. My dream.

My hiccuping brain, sputtering in wheezing heaves —

I can dream my way out, surely I can – dream a different dream. Join acquaintances, poised elbow-to-elbow amid music and crinkling smiles, sipping sweet from an ice-clinking glass —

Through the hollow heaving spaces of inert time, my brain awaits a breath and observes: Myself: body bilging, ballooning: it doesn't perform —

Through an atmosphere of silken scarves, I seek air – scarf upon scarf —

This can't be! my body, forgetting? Can it be I must *think* to inhale? *Breathe in! – breathe out – breathe in* — ! Laboring – in layering leaves of scarves weighing, a mattress of scarves bearing me down — where is the nature in me that knows – to breathe? Deflating, seeking, gasping for the living air somewhere within the massing of leaves, earth, stone – stone growing about me, clinging to the substance of the stone —

What *is* promised, then? what can ever be assumed? Swamping in my own chokedamp – it's some blind pantomime, someone's wild speculation, another penny-dreadful dumbshow – who's on the curtains, the lights, in the pit, who's in the house, who's pulling the strings, who's that – Lench? – who's there? Lench is a chicken? an egg? another caper is it, another dodge – another boiled sweetie – another fandango to placate the – hoodwink the — deepmouthed tunnel roaring — enough of this – what else do you have? sepulchral roaring – can you do Tea for Two –? I'm sick of this one – Melancholy Baby?

168

It's not true.

I'm in here alone.

Miles from the cliff-face, whishing down, sinking, quick-sand of stone up to nostril-sills, I'm a stranger here myself, gulping, gaping in the morass, venting, blowing, it's a bitch – it's a – son-of-a-bitch – am I – let me out – there's – how much is left? is it leaving? all caught in the downflow, rushing away in the outflow of —

'Breathe! Breathe!' the female voice says, 'take a deep breath! dammit, he's deaf along with everything else.'

'Right that's it, plug him into the wall,' says a man's voice.

'Wall hell,' says another, 'city mains is not enough, this man's decompensating, he's at no more than a resting tidal volume, I want that trach hooked to a dependable, heavy-action, volume-controlled pressure respirator for full-time ventilation at twenty-eight percent with postural drainage and the rest. Get him on an Abercromby or I quit.'

I can hear the footsteps, the snapping, screwing and ham-mering very near of metal and plastic, the muted sound of wind through polyvinyl accordion pumps and tubes of pink or white or blue or beige or some elegant and tasteful combi-nation of these erected in an invisible maze about me...and gulps of clean, filling, sterile air swish into me to the distinctive electronic rhythm of a minuet not unlike the one my lungs swayed-to on their own only minutes ago.

'And let's get that EKG going,' someone adds. The minuet slides into a waltz with a pinging bleep.

'Got to hand it to him,' someone says. 'Keeps hanging around.'

'I'm shaving his head for a regular EEG,' says another.

'Pulse very thready, sir.'

'Ye-e-es,' says one ruminatively. 'He's not really got a nice heart picture, either, if I do say so, definitely arrhythmic, I don't like his pattern.'

'Keeps hanging round, I'll give him that.'

'He's not really doing enough on his own, this one, or he's got a kinky notion of what's enough.'

'What would you, put him on a pacemaker?'

'Mmm. Let's see if we can't fix him up with something.'

'Right, sir.'

169

'Oh and by the bye, that Levin tube just isn't staying down, look you. Seems to curl up in the back of the throat somewhere, awful nuisance. I'd go straight into the stomach, if I were you.'

'Gastrotomy, sir?'

'Tha-a-at's right.'

There is a soft mumbling.

'You know what he's doing, don't you?'

A second series of soft mumblings; and I recognize it to be coming from my very own Supremo, Dr Wall.

'No facial mimic,' says someone as the electric shaver buzzes about my ears, 'no more muscle tone, swallowing gone. This isn't just your ordinary obtundity or obnubilation.'

'It's torpor,' I hear Dr Wall's voice say.

'It's not just your torpor,' says the other. 'Look at that face.'

'The vegetative system is ticking over just fine.'

'That facial expression is a fossil. Here's his chart; look for yourself.'

'These things can change.'

'Look at him. He has a blank, greasy and fatuous mask for a face, indicating not only muscular immobility but emotional and intellectual bankruptcy.'

'These things never last.'

'The functions of the brain stem have been lost. Look at the chart.'

'He's sweating, though, look, there, he's sweating.'

With a new pen-squeaking clickety-click my waltz has become a samba.

'This is a coma. An apathic coma. Here comes the graph.' The EEG is monitoring my skull. 'He's got delta waves.'

'I know how to read.'

'This is an areactive apathic semitonic aperceptive coma. If anything's left it's the mind of a five, four, three-year-old child. Give me that, would you give me that?'

There is a sound of tearing and crumpling paper.

'Dr Wall, we need that, take that out if you wouldn't mind.'

As I reconstruct it, Dr Wall has rolled up my chart into a ball and stuffed it into his mouth.

* * *

Lench killed himself three times before they decided to put an end to it. Everybody's doing a number, all right, somewhere on the narrow approach to the point of diminishing returns, and this one cropped up to be his, stealing chickens and cutting them open under his bathrobe on an assortment of beds about St Mary's Peeping. They didn't even bleed that much, I know he'd have preferred live ones (who are we fooling, whose eyes are we blinding with our stricken dust?); laughing and sobbing and wrestling with a defunct Dorking soup-hen amongst the institutional pillows; but, as I'm sure he'd have said, it's any poultry in a storm, and a stirring rite was its own reward: Each time, for one split second nobody could tell him from a butchered barnfowl in all its wry glory, and even when the uncomprehending administrative cry went up 'Somebody's sacrificing a chicken in the Intensive Care Unit – !' '– in Maternity!' '– in Ear Nose and Throat!' a thrill must have run through his veins.

How could he go in for anything so apish, so empty, so pointless?

There you have it.

What?

There you have it.

Then why couldn't he — ?

You mean – the real thing? Do it all — ?

Why did he stick there? why did he boggle at that . . . . ?

Did I really – for that whisper of an instant – *feel*?

The chickens are safe. They've placed my corroded friend Lench, with the new people like him, in some species of compassionate confinement in an adapted laundry-room in the basement with the appropriate medical utensils. He converses with himself. When they want him somewhere else, for periodic servicing and maintenance, he is wheeled under surveillance through the wards mounted in a hinged and hasped enclosed vehicle inspired by the operators of Mr Austin. On these occasions, I understand, he confines his scurrilous remarks to a low running jabber. I've not personally witnessed this yet.

But I gloat with him.

It was all some kind of protest, they say, against hospital food.

* * *

Did I really feel? and move?!

'Now as to oral care,' says chief nurse, 'oral care is of the first importance.'

The discreet shuffle of feet and muffled voices draws near.

'We clean the unconscious mouth thoroughly three times a day. If we do not clean the unconscious mouth three times a day, we end up with a dry, beefy red, foul-smelling tongue coated with a thick brown sticky covering called sordes, together with swollen glands behind the ears. Nurse Slack, please? Taking a stick wrapped in a compress, you will see how Nurse Slack swabs out this particular mouth.'

So, a few more tiny incisions made – a line passed through the jugular vein down into the cockles of my heart with a pump attached, a pipe run straight into my stomach – and automation claims a few added yards of my animation's turf, and once more it's first down.

I'm going to live! After all, I'm going to live!

Everyone's so understanding. Really; let me put this thing straight. They've understood. Everything. All the needs. For attention, reason, candour, respite, amity, hope, justice, a little charity. Grief they see, and loss, and hurt and care, and even the subjective and objective bramble bush, they understand perfectly well – the illusions and delusions, the seizures of madness – nothing human is alien to them – they hold us still and pump life back into our lungs and carry on. Don't undersell humankind; where dying's concerned, *everybody understands everything.*

Who cares, you mean, if they're looking two ways?

'Tha-a-at's right. Let's see now, what'll we have going then altogether, Arkwright – stomach? yes – kidneys? right – lungs, heart, brain – ye-e-es. We'll have this chap running on all six in no time.'

'Or all fours, sir.'

'That's right. Thing is to save a life, Arkwright, save a life.'

'And have him balanced, sir.'

'Tha-a-at's right. We want his chart *balanced*. Whatever falls out.'

'Whatever falls out, sir?'

'Befalls, Arkwright. Happens.'

It doesn't matter. You won't need them now.

What do you mean 'two ways'?

It doesn't matter now, you've sworn not to need them.

What two ways?

... They go on behaving as if they don't understand.

Nonsense.

They understand what their calling can never comprehend.

But this is pap and more pap. Lever's swill – 'indispensable indifference' – I won't swallow it.

That's up to you.

It's drivel, do you read me? There are no secret orders, no grim reefs lurking beneath the surf – that's saying *I'm* paddling blithely past the truth, that's what it's saying, and I deny it. There will be no surprises.

That's for you to say. If you're happy, I'm happy.

Happy? *I'm going to live.*

My mind nailed to this pillow – my senseless body flapping, weightless. Inside, sleep comes at present with deeper ease, as if with deepening need, spreading over longer and wider spaces of time, like a fetus in the womb as it prepares for life. Lying in this progressive twilight state, preparing, gathering what forces, for what sortie, for what spectacular show?

So it's not my death we've been going on about all this while. Napping, barmy, in high-oxygen reverie I break loose and go wafting. Illumination upon illumination. It's not my death... it's something else. My case, they said, my space-filling growth, primitive tissue, new generation – classic, they said, unconventional only for my age and sex – bit of a parson's egg, they said – my nausea, dizziness, my fainting spells – their talk of my coming to term – my butterfly mask – my butterfly mask... *Not* the melanin that grows with a carcinoma .... It was the common mask of *parturition*! My neoplasm,

173

new flesh of my flesh – of course – of course, hallelujah, fuck me sweetheart — *I'm going to have a baby*!

But do you think the world is ready for this?

Between layers of earthly panic and dream, as premonitions of returning breathlessness arise and pass and arise and pass, I dwell blithesome in this rhapsody, this Immaculate Conception, day after day.

And how long is that, then, day after day? and how long has it been, anyway? Seven, eight months...nine? And – if I'm wrong as to the upshot, the outcome – of my coming to term — ?

Pregnant? at my age?

My wife will have a fit.

What have I conceived? about to give to the world?

There's something developing here, taking shape in my mind.

What have I done, so far, with my life? I've threatened the international medical establishment with a large boiled sweetie.

What a child I am.

Pregnant only with my own death? preposterous! I'm giving birth to myself.

That's it; my nativity.

Oh yes.

Oh it's the old story, isn't it? It's a question of – identity. What story is there but that? The terrific tale, the greatest story ever told, the epic for us all, the quest of quests, the mighty motive, the grand cause and ineluctable effect, the hill 69, the sunset and sunrise, the pilgrimage to our destiny – what's it all about but *finding oneself*? To thine own person be true. God bless all this travail – I'm on the way! If I'd only known then what I know now, eh? Hey?!

And if I had? So if I had? And if I had — ?

Kayak-angst. They were right. On the glassy open arctic sea in here, paddling, lying timelessly immobile, staring at nothing, sightless, vertiginously spinning, on a limitless sea, drifting, as it's said one may go drifting in the white, pulsing, motionless sound, the white rhythmic sea of...the labor room...

'My fingernails hurt,' she said.

Treeza was sitting there.

'They came collecting for a jumble sale,' she was saying, 'and I didn't have anything to give, so I gave them your shoes, darling. I knew, I could feel it in my heart that you would have wanted it that way.'

There was something about the way she looked, the depth of her neckline, the height of her hem, or the little peepholes all over her new dress.

And I realized that it was another dream.

She had made herself look all young and new again – and it wasn't long ago, it was now, and I was mute, as now, and she was herself, only decorated and revealed.

'I'd gotten this tightness in my shoulders and all up my neck, dearest,' she was saying, 'and my fingernails hurt and it hurt to shave my legs, it was awful.' It was wonderfully, frighteningly real. 'I had these pains in the back of my pelvis,' she was saying, 'and I couldn't sleep nights,' she said, 'and my whole – my fat, my fat hurt, dearest – I don't suppose you could ever have understood that, but it was so deeply important to me, dear, as a woman, knowing deep deep inside me that my very fat hurt. I don't know why I'm telling you all this,' she said, crossing her legs in my dream, the sound of the shoosh of nylon rushing up her curving thighs, 'but I must, I had to, I had to come and say it to your face, your poor dear sticky dribbly face.' She gave each of her dream-bright eyes a hanky-dab for tears. 'It was you, you see, it was you that brought it all on, you who used to go and give me such a prickly heat I couldn't stand it, and you went away and left me under the name of "Mr Wall" and had everybody to look after you and I had nothing, what was I to do?' A veil of gamboge curtains settled into a virginal aurora about her head. 'I know you would have wanted me to have what I needed, only time

175

wasn't on our side, darling, time sealed your lips, time shut your poor icky mouth, and I've had to seek through the long long nights to find my own way out of the darkness, through all the neuritis and neuralgia, to find a way that would have pleased you and pleased me too.' As she paused, I could make out where she was easing her little finger up along beneath the bottom lip of her underpants around her inner thigh. 'You do see what I'm getting at, don't you,' she said, 'darling. What's mine was yours, what was yours is mine. Dearest, this way we can be together forever.'

So, I dreamt —

So, Treeza —

A rubber plant wasn't enough for you – you had to have my brother Lloyd.

'He'll take all our worries away. He can fix everything, everything. You will always be my little prince, whatever you – however you are – and he can be my big mogul.'

You can't beat that, at the price, thought I.

'And you see – ? Together we can make another little – another you!'

You can't top that, all right.

The sac burst. Breaking over me, up from this dream, some kind of waters went flowing out.

One and two and three and four and —

Pant and pant and pant and Blow and —

– my awakening mind was twisting and swerving witlessly, sottishly backward, and there we were, Teresa and I, in the fluid morning-remembered reality, where we sat on the lady's floor and the lady taught us how to pant and pant and now Bear down and one and two and three and finally, in a white place, on a white bed not unlike this, the doctor had had to remove it, forcibly, we never got to say the one and two and three and it was full, all right, full of grapes, the whole sac had developed and swelled into not an infant but a huge bunch of grapes; a mole; he had called it a mole, and removed it, waterish, and thrown it away. Which went down in the books, down in our books as the failure of our lives.

Which it never was, but a sop to our failure, instead.

Morning; I lay awake. Marvelously awake.

If you could have – if we could only have removed all the

176

rest, the two of us, like that hytidatiform mole. Wrenched it from our minds and thrown it, thus and so, away – the stillborn words and arid grievances that the genuine unuttered griefs and needs had hatched. Made room for the world we can give life to between us now if we will.

Awake; it was only, as the phrase goes, a dream. The pleasure of forgetting the dream along with the past was deep and giddy and cool.

Speak! Speak now!

Yes – as soon as she comes.

What are you, a man or a mole? Speak!

There was no way out.

I must face it.

Months had gone by, since the night at the asylum. And then Hinkle's message arrived, with a time and an address. 'Come and see every man's dream,' it said.

It was Christmas, and I slid about in the slush up the narrow steps of the house in the grey squalid street. He was going to get back at me, trapped in the mounting rubbish of his lies; I should have quit while I was ahead. A charwoman in floppy kerchief opened the door, one of his rent-racked tenants no doubt; I followed her shambling slippers into the dank room, tentatively, subaqueously lit by a dingy lamp that was perhaps on, perhaps not; the room reeked of a smouldering coal fire in a grate. Hinkle stood with an exhausted, harrowed smile, stripped flabbily to the waist. The old woman padded out. 'I want you to see the real me,' said Hinkle, and he dropped his trousers. I'm impressed, I said. He sported no underwear. 'Wait,' he said, 'there's far more to it than that.' I shudder to think, I said. The woman padded back in, bringing a tea-tray rattling with cups and spoons. 'I ask you to promise,' he said, 'not to go until I've finished.' There was something deeply worn and intense in his features. I promise, I said. 'Good.' He locked the door. 'First you must meet the missus!' he said.

Looking at his surprise-bedmate's sagging face I bowed, and said the pleasure was mine. His thighs wobbled with laughter;

177

'I'll wager you thought,' he said, 'she could be my mother.'
Gosh no, I opined. 'Would I lie to you?' he said. It crossed
my mind, I said. 'But she was,' he said with a grim smirk,
'she *is*!' Is what?
　'My mother.'
　Go 'way! I said, and I cringed. 'From her belly – me!' Easy
come, easy go, I said, brain stumbling to keep up. Mrs Hinkle's
eyes showed signs of stress, breathless titillation, and fatigue.
'And this –' he said, reaching to a covered cot '– is our little
Brenda!' Mrs Hinkle was pouring tea with a clatter of utensils.
Hinkle held up a small pink wrinkle-plump creature, hardly
yet a child, more a species of piglet.
　'This is mother's and my Brenda, our very own wee sugarplum.'
　I stood transfixed, as it were. Intuitively I grasped that
Hinkle's creative capacity was again on the move. Sure – on
the run from the world, an expansionist in a contracting
economy, year in year out more and more alone, *Hinkle alone
would* hope to make the most of it; a principle; make or break;
it was the economy of counterfeit relations, the do-it-yourself
theme, dear to his heart; by a few sovereign thrusts in the right
place with the ingenious device he displayed at half-mast
before me, he had contrived to bring cheap to his own private
party a mother, a son, a daughter, a father, a sister, a brother,
a wife, a husband, a grandmother grandfather granddaughter
of sorts, a cousin by my implication in it, a niece, nephew,
uncle and greatuncle — 'Et cetera,' he said. What? 'Et cetera,'
he repeated. Hinkle had gone the whole hog.
　Or had he yet – was his monopoly, his autonomy complete?
　'The little rascal!' he said, snuggling his blush-bare off-
spring. A bit of a handful, is she? I mumbled, doing my best.
'A right saucy little bit,' he said delectably, twisting a section
of her skin between finger and thumb. 'What do we say to
mummy's and daddy's little girl, eh? kitchy-kitchy-koo!'
Kitchy-koo little sugarplum, I said gloomily. 'Listen, can you
blame us!' Hinkle said. 'Can you?' said Mrs Hinkle. The infant
was sucking its fingers in Hinkle's arms; why did its little
fingers seem nail-bitten to the quick? 'Look at her, *can you
blame us*?!' He held her to his naked flaccid belly, closer and
lower, bending and swaying.

A pervert, perverting the truth? and who then was I? condemn to death another's perversion, maybe, and you'll be eaten alive by your own.

'Look at her!' said Hinkle, 'she's got my ears,' he said. 'She's got my mouth, she's got my hands!' 'She's got his penis,' said Mrs Hinkle. And she had indeed. A diacritical mark alternately grave and acute, forming between her eyes, little Brenda was finding and pursing her gummy lips to her father's member. Hinkle look out, I said, she's proposing to nurse. 'This is *her* truth,' said he and he was, damn it, rising to the occasion. 'Sometimes I feel,' he said, growing red in the face – responding, curse him, responding – 'so ugly, unwanted. *Got to cut down!*' 'One sugar or two, Mr — ?' said Mrs Hinkle, setting her kettle to seethe by the fire. Hinkle, I said – his broodling slung balanced, wet pink thighs now astraddle the porklike pummel of his upright quivering schlong – Hinkle, I said, what are you doing? 'You're afraid I'll get pimples.' You've got pimples – what about that child? 'It's got pimples.' I don't care about its pimples, I said, what about its mind, its future, its prospects? 'It's love, love' he said, excited, weeping like a baby, kissing its eyes, its lips. These things happen, I said, don't cry. The kettle steamed; a light overcast rose in a haze. Hinkle was doing something appalling and dismal to his child. You're trying my patience, I said, no? you're testing my moral fibre Hinkle. Mrs Hinkle handed me a stale water-biscuit, tinged with something like soot, or mold. I can't approve, I said – (Brenda making awkward sounds) – Hinkle you know I'm unadventurous I'm a traditionalist in these things. The haze thickened to a deep squelching mist. Hinkle we can fight this thing! I said. Hinkle threw up his head. 'Fight it?' he grunted, muffled-Brenda making difficult noises; the coals in the grate hissed in the swilling heat. 'Fight it?!' He knelt into a clump on the carpet. Can I get you anything? I said. 'I've found a found a new pos – a new posture position in life,' he cried. I recognize that, I said; the world loves a family man, but —. Brenda still caught to his middle, he hunched over into a fat naked ball. I appreciate everything you're doing, I said. He began to roll about like an armadillo. But is this in the best interests of everyone? He rolled away toward a sofa, grunting 'More! – better! – *need no one* – there's *more* —' I have had just about enough, I said, Hinkle. 'Watch – !' yammered he. Why me? '– It's the Way!' 'Love's where you find it,' exclaimed Mrs Hinkle, snatching up her burbling Brenda, now spilled obliviously abandoned from Hinkle's navel, 'life's what you make it.' At the sofa, Hinkle halted. Is he finished, has he finished? I said rapidly, turning toward the door. He wheeled, and rolled again. You're trying to tell me something aren't you? I said, what are you trying to say? Hinkle was making slow progress in the direction of the door, white back-fat jiggling hotly. But it wasn't the door he was after. It was — oh hell, Hinkle: his brand – his wand – his torch, it was his wambling lurching squirming tool he hankered for, his tremulous turgid penile flute. With – craning his head – his puckering, bugling snout. Already he was rolling back at an oblique angle, thumping against chairs, rubbernecking, straining, snorting, hair of his bristling buttocks rutilant with perspiration, reaching, knees about his ears. Wang wang, he honked through snorkling lips, wang wang. See here now, I said. 'Go to it, lovie,' chirruped Mrs Hinkle, 'know thyself,' she troated. Now this I won't have – I said – this is an abuse of the term. 'To thine own self be true,' she cheered, standing on a corner table, waving amid the clouds of steam. Hinkle, rolling, came cutting toward me through the sweltering fog. The snow-sloshed windows rang with jolly lively streetside carolers' singing; the tootling kettle whistled up a hysterical wail. With a triumphant crowning Wang wang, Hinkle caught his penis between his teeth. 'Oh mummy's dolly!' squealed Mrs Hinkle, giddily diddling herself atop her table, 'it's every man's dream it is!' she crowed, her kerchief dangling from one ear. Yes well I'm just off now, I said, goodbye. 'Ulu-ulu,' said Hinkle, curling on the floor, 'ululu' he said through pouting beatific lips. Leave me out, I said, count me out, let me out now you're just being childish. In the hissing drizzle the coals of the fire turned to glass. 'Shush, he's fecundating!' keened Mrs Hinkle. What, he's what? I shrilled. 'He's conceiving himself!' she said, purring, and broke into a timely chorus of Joy to the World. Fiddling and bursting-free the clumsy lock I left them, haggard baleful Hinkle oinking, jerking, suckling, ululating, wetly snozzling back his bitter seed.

The sleet rattled down the steps.

To each his own.

Stand by him? Why did he want to make my blood run cold, demented against him?

Defend him? Never. Comic, insensate, I know, but I wished I could wash my brain in the snow, in the slush of the gutter.

What shadowy spleen made him aim to revolt me?

And why did he have to do what he did next?

Don't think about it.

But *why*?

In the night, that night, I awoke crying. For Hinkle. For *Hinkle*!

Forget him – he doesn't exist. *Hinkle doesn't exist.*

Why have his messages stopped?

Berserk it gets now.

Impossible. Impossible.

'He's having bursts.'

Mites. Midges.

'The patient is having bursts.'

Mites, midges, worms and flies settling on me, commencing to pierce and gnaw —

Yes, at last.

It's pain.

The most notorious of discomforts.

Enough to freeze the blood.

Oh help! said Pooh, I'd better go back. Oh bother, said he, I shall have to go on.

Waste. These months lying here – these months before of painless being – wasted!

Easy for you to say —

Birds, vultures, settling swarming.

Don't whet – don't taunt the clapping jaws with inklings of flight. Oh help *and* bother.

It's like to make your eyes water.

I want to get out!

Fool! It's *your* life – walk out? – why haven't you then?

They kept me!

Iron clank over the ears, skull clenching and braying —
think of things – think – what is this – is this – will it be such
– to be – bent and reamed by this great one-eyed stinking
pig-monster rutting and squealing — ?

It's on the cards.

Who says?

It's part of the deal.

Let me out!

Out? you could have turned yourself out discharged any
day you'd ever wanted, gone walking free —

Character – it was a matter of character!

– they *told* you, Pay no mind to our swerving schemes. You
get on with it! they said – and did you?

I was being a gentleman.

You *like* it here.

Hooking – fanging bills – split cartilage, bone-singing gut —

You've never proposed a single reason not to die.

Horns goring, rending viscera, exquisite, tender —

He was a gentleman and they killed him for his trouble.

Don't sentimentalize – you're not dead, you haven't seen
anything yet.

The prisoners, men and women, shivering in the cold,
hoisted and jammed into the van, bodies huddled, laid out,
spread out, jammed reeking – I'm glad for the warmth, jammed knobbled and reeking, squealing, laid about me, so long
as I can breathe – I'm not a pig, squealing, I'm not a pig —

I want to go home. It's this country, this cold winter place.

That was always a blind.

They're frigid here – detached – nothing human's here.

A duck blind – the whole thing's been a blind and you hiding
in it – you've never wanted a thing but to be alone, a stranger
and alone. A blind.

It was no blind.

Traveler in a strange land, oh so romantic, foreign body
within, foreign all around, trapped doll-within-doll-within-
blank-faced doll. Exotic were they, them, bizarre? *You* make
stick-figures of them all – wife, brother, every creature —

They do it to me – to each other — !

Does that get you off?

(– I know you,' said Hinkle —)

It's lucky for you, say I —
(– You'd come off your deathbed to save me —)
It's lucky for you I can laugh.

It's cozy for *you you can't be heard* – sprawled out in your facetious padded fairyland, pleading diminished responsibility, fussing and fuming – you've been in a coma from the day you were born.
So it's all that simple, is it?
Why do you think she's gone missing, now – why's Treeza not here?
We'll see – you'll see!
You never even *tried* – to *taste* life.
And if I did – what would I have been? Tempered – enriched – ennobled, uplifted? *And if I had?*
So if I had?
What if I had — ?
What *do* you want, then? Do you know?

Oh help, said Pooh.
The pain swims to a halt. Lights spewing within lights in torrential decay. Fireworks soaring, silent.
Oh help, said the childish fading echo.
The pain gone. Shout hallelujah once more – it can't do that to me again – it won't bear repeating.
Please sweet jesus don't let it happen again – please please don't let it.
'He's having bursts.'
'Paroxysmal bursts.'
I'm due for a revelation. *A revelation. No lie.*
I remember....
'All right, let's see.'
In the sand they found it. You must recall, it was in all the press. In the south of Iraq, in the Tigris and Euphrates plain where civilization, it's said, was born – they've discovered the site, the actual resting place of that first Mesopotamian hero, before the pyramids, before the Bible, before Babylon, the precursor of Gilgamesh the king who refused to die and set

out to seek eternal life – he was real, a flesh-and-blood man – the nameless ruler whose mudbrick palace had lain for millennia undeciphered in sun-scorched rubble at the crossroads of the ruined cities east of Ur.

And they came in their truckloads, with shovels and picks.

I'm in for a revelation, I am. The earth trembles with it.

'The bursts are going.'

'They'll be all-of-a-doo-da about this upstairs, they'll be cockahoop!'

'The bursts are gone.'

'It's a miraculous thing the human organism, it keeps coming back'

'Don't fuss, Dashwood. Look at him now.'

'Yes sir.'

'That's what you call inanimate.'

'... Perhaps if we – strike while the iron is —'

'All right Staff, see if you can rouse this man at all, eh?'

'Come Mr Wall, rouse yourself just a little.'

'Take his head, Staff, and twist it quickly. There — any doll's-eye response?'

'Not really, sir. Come on, Mr Wall, give us a sign —'

'Knickers! he's stubborn —'

'– You want your doctor to love you, don't you?'

'Ah! here comes *our* Wall! We were just thinking, Wall, what do you say to a good ice-water squirt in the ear? Think we might get some ocular movement out of your man?'

Mumbling.

'All right, let's try it.' Muttering. 'Aim for the tympanum, Staff, ready, steady, squirt!'

'Not even a groan, sir.'

'Bit hard to tell about that, with all this machinery, all this racket – did you see anything on the screen? Who's watching the screen? Would you watch the screen please? Right, another go then? Ready, steady, squirt, *there*! Anything on the screen?'

'There was something, sir.'

'What?'

'I'm not sure, sir. It might have been a bit of water, sir.'

'Blast! It's in one ear and out the other with these people.'

'Sir – excuse me, but would you want to consider the hot-knife-and-fork routine? Nurse Quigley's been heating a probe.'

'The old hot fork gambit – it's an old trick, but it may work.'
'It's sizzling, sir.'
'Let's give it a try. If you'd just hold your patient, Wall, would you, that's it, and nurse here can give him a poke. Prod when ready, nurse.'
'Aiee!'
'Who said that! was that the patient?!'
'No sir, it was Dr Wall —'
'I didn't touch the doctor, sir.'
'Don't run off, Wall — !'
'An easy mistake —'
'I didn't touch him.'
'Get a grip on yourself Wall, fear not – give him a hanky, will you George, wipe his brow – this case, driving him spare — Nurse, you simply must wait till Dr Wall's got his finger out.'
'– Yes sir.'
'He's very keen not to be confused with the patient.'
'Patient is quite peaceful, sir.'
'So I see.'
'This the real thing, then? the onset, the throes?'
'I don't know about "throes", George. But we've got *coma dépassé*.'
'A real pity, sir.'
'Who's there to pity? The intelligent adult has disappeared.'
'Of course there are tests, chemical, mechanical, electronic, we've got it all to do, we haven't *started* yet —'
'That's it.'
'If I may speak, sir?'
'Ah Madeley – didn't see you there!'
'This is not a normal case, sir.'
'Normal, Madeley?'
'Sir, a normal healthy person gets signals and sends signals. This man's not sending signals. But what if – just supposing – what if failure of function here is de-efferential only?'
'What are you trying to say, Madeley?'
'Sir, ventrally-placed lesions in the *pons* can interrupt descending corticospinal and corticobulbar pathways without impairing consciousness – subject *can* be so "locked in" by paralysis that he can't move or communicate –'

185

'Madeley —'

'– Even in advanced tetanus, sir – there's no clinical test lets us assess the state of consciousness of a curarized patient —'

'Madeley —'

'– With a damaged mesencephalic reticular formation – a numb RAS – an animal responds to no stimuli whatsoever, except olfactory – except to olfactory —'

'All right, Madeley, make a smell, then. No, go ahead, I insist, test your point, make a smell.'

Silence.

'Oh Christ, Madeley.'

'Well done Madeley!'

Ripple of applause.

'But no patient-response, Madeley.'

'That's just *it* sir – in these cases you don't get a response. In a decorticated cat, even —'

'Madeley, we are with you one-hundred percent. But it makes no odds, you can see that. Because he's not in there.'

'And if he is, just by chance? What if signals *are* going upward – just not downward?'

'In other words, you think there's something still going on on the other side of his RAS.'

'Beyond it yes sir, possibly.'

'And what feeds it, pray tell?'

'Will, maybe? Maybe he's not interested in coming out? Maybe he's *suppressing his soma*, somehow? Holding on through some species of mental constipation, cathexis, parture resistance – suffering some form of hysteria, or ecstasy? Ecstasy —'

'You're in deep water there, Madeley.'

'What about *him*, sir? Deep water – I mean, if we could only find out why he might be submersing his soma? why? To die? Or to prove he can't die? Or is he being "lived", say – by someone perverse outside himself?'

'By his "author", perhaps, the author of us all? Madeley, you wouldn't be getting religious or psychological on us, would you? You've your career to think of, you see.'

'I don't know what you mean, sir —'

'You had us worried there, old bean.'

'– What if we're just not reading him right? Just not getting adequate readings? maybe he's on his way *back*, not out.'

'It cuts no gristle with me, Madeley, the point being that he'll never make it, not now. It's one-way from here. *Sens unique.* A dead RAS – no cerebral feedback —'

'But if we've got the *directions* wrong —'

'– One dies this way.'

'But will his *author* die this way, to borrow your notion?'

'Hello? Hello?'

'And what about us – and how will we know?'

'Madeley, would you care to step outside?'

'But if he's only locked-in we can dig up *the key* – the key —'

Voices dwindle.

It's about my revelation.

How it will come.

You're asleep, dreaming softly along. And an itch wakes you out of your dream. You lie there scratching your skin – and hear sounds in the distance, some voices, a knock. And you awaken from this dream of itching and scratching and you go to the door. And all of a sudden a bell rings, an alarm crashing right by your ear – and the layers of sleep peel away, the dreaming of sleep, the dreaming of dreams, the dreams of awakenings, and in a rush – the whole world opens out around you, a hundred-eighty degrees, two hundred, three hundred and sixty degrees and you are *wide* awake, and the daylight is all around you, and all the earlier shapes lie dark and empty shells now dead behind you, and you are really alive. Will this be my revelation, when I finally come to? Awakenings within awakenings, into the light?

Have I, for centuries, for aeons, for as long as I've been, have we been living swooning in this half-light, groping our way in circles in the dim shallows of one another's torpid warmth? Will my dying be this: the thin light – emerging, searching – the thin light focuses piercingly on me, growing more and more brilliant and swarming, and you, all traces of you, dissolve backwards into the darkness and vanish, and I lie awake, alive, groping and alone in the blinding light?

Oh clever fellow, clever boy! It's one thing to have writhed well under the pin; every conceit more apt, every term more appetizing than the last.

It's another thing to live. To find the gut. The effrontery to live.

Don't think of what he did next. Think of things that are pretty; think of the girl. What of the girl, down the aisle, her lover lingering daily by her side? Does she pass sweetly over? all movement gently and finally stilled? Was it all just a nightmare? Does she awaken now?

Screaming.

In another place, an eternal scream – which we are not privileged to hear?

Hell of hells. All right, admit it – fables! Why have I gone on and on, gingerly picking my way from fantasy to fantasy and lie to lie?

The effrontery to live.

Look it full in the face. Leave all these escapes behind.

The dam had cracked. Several days before Easter, they arrested and charged Hinkle. I can think of it now, and I know why.

He believed *I* was false. Thrown by whatever personal-primordial happenstance into the simple fiction that he owed his very survival in the world to his lies – trapped in this nightmare – for him no one lived by truth, all were false, all *was* false. So he tried me, my semblance of earnestness, of constancy, of intimacy. His dragging me to watch him that winter night – Hinkle was being 'true' to himself, consistent. Indiscriminate; fevered, drunken, consumed with the principle of indifference – *calling on me to disprove* that it made no difference. Ever. Defend him, and his malignancy makes no difference. Don't defend him, and his humanity makes no difference. Light, darkness, loving, hating, familiarity, filth, living, death, everything, all the same. *Calling on me —*

In the face of his utter silence, under arrest, pending arraignment and in their righteous outrage and presentiment of public furore, he was locked up without bail. What he did next, in prison, is – as they say – a matter of record.

He mutilated himself – in a variety of dreary but important ways.

As it happened – as might have been predicted if one had

188

thought clearly – since the network of Hinkle's victims or accomplices was so entire – to the Attorney General's disappointment no one could be induced to appear for the state. And Hinkle was 'released'. Sent out, in short, to present to the world a new form-and-face not unlike that that drives Lench amuck. But the power of reversals and disguise was once again within reach, and Hinkle could be expected to make the most of his chance, to find a doctor of plastics fitting his fancies, to save his countenance and redress his losses. In principle, then, Hinkle could not be stopped. No rest for the weary. Strangling in the web of his fabrications, I now suspected, he hung by his feet, he walked on his hands, he no longer knew which end was up – yet in his place another man like him must surely find room still to move.

But then, Hinkle is Hinkle. In high style, on the next day but one, in already putrescent bandages, he presented himself of all places at the prison gate with a document in hand, itemizing with the rhapsodic aimlessness of a true visionary a range of genuine unsolved and unclaimed malfeasances about which I had long known him to make seemingly pointless but meticulous notes from pillaged police and Interpol blotters – kidnap, espionage, bombings – and for which, having accredited them to himself and without some commentary to the contrary, he could – if not here, then in a handful of other equally interested, compulsively neat and none-too-anxious-about-the-details party nations – be executed, be carried to an appointed place and hanged, gassed, burned. And what did I do when I heard? Nothing. He was now taken in with a cordial welcome. Under armed escort to the vice-warden's office, in silence he collapsed.

He can't be right, he doesn't know what he's doing. Why is he silent now?

You're wrong, do you see. It's not the law, the world that can destroy him.

Why do I abominate him – and want him to want me? *Why*?
Something's changing —
I'm changing!
'His eyes are open, doctor.'
They're getting my signals, look. They perceive my irresistible charm.

189

'His eyes keep standing open, doctor – there, do you see?'
'Yes, it's difficult, really. Corneas drying – and what are these scuff-marks and scratches on the eyeballs – is that from the pillows and such — ?'
That's not the change I mean!
'– From rotating him, doctor, when they stay open like that, it's really impossible —'
'Quite impossible to avoid it, yes. Look at him lying there.'
Yes — !
'He *has* had those bursts, though.'
'It's a puzzle, this one.'
No puzzle to me, now —
'Doctor, about the eyes – they *won't* stay shut and they *have* been causing unnecessary fright and disruption among the staff —'
'What do you think, George? Save them in case? time for a tarsorrhaphy on those eyes?'
'Looks to be, sir. Suture them up. Just in case.'
Yes – ! save my eyes!
'Look at him lying there.'
Yes look! Stop the rot! I'm going to *stop the rot*!
I've a *reason*. Hinkle's wrong – it *does* make a difference. I've turned the corner. Hinkle lying hunched in his cell, saying nil, exhausted of his lies, putting his very being out of reach, beyond his own grasp — I've found my way — *it makes a difference.*
He's nothing – he denies you – you hate him.
I hate him most in all the world but that's only the start – in denying me he's the very *banner* of my own viability —
More symbols! Abstract!
– the one who declares 'I will be myself, create myself – exist with nothing, *be*, no matter what'.
Lifeless abstractions! You call this a person? it's an empty Idea!
It's my bond, my connection with life.
These tubes – *that's* your connection with life – that's all – these plastic tubes!
No!
If he exists it's as *you* do – *in the flesh.*
If I let Hinkle go – it's an insult to my intelligence, my wit, my gut —

190

You must.

If I let him go, I let *myself* go.

You must. Look at you – helpless.

No! His silence is calling. *I will appear for him.*

'What do you reckon?'

They're talking about the unfortunate Mr Smith, placed some time in the night, it seems, next to me.

'*I* look at the screen and his line looks fairly flat to me —'

It's that distant muffling of their voices – I can always tell now, from the sound, when their backs are turned.

'How long does the law say it's got to be flat? what's the latest?'

Another of Dr Wall's patients, I gather, in this intensive-care chamber, the improbably named John Smith (an alias no doubt, and who would I be to take issue?). I picture him vividly – lean, intelligent, prone to having holes in his socks and not always easy to live with, but known for his positive expression.

'The law? The law doesn't say. What does the medical society say?'

'Which medical society?'

'Ah.'

'Right.'

'Got enough on their docket these days keeping chaps alive.'

'Quite so.'

'It would be helpful to have this decided.'

'The outside limits of reversibility.'

'Quite.'

'Something positive on death could have great practical import for medicine.'

'Indeed.'

'Would help to know when it was all right to remove things.'

'Yes.'

'Notify relatives. Bury the fellow. The lot.'

'That's it.'

'But what do you think?'

Why don't you ask *him*, you dolts?

'You know as well as I do an alive body *grades* into a dead body.'

'It's only more or less alive – correlative to being more or less dead.'

'As you say.'

Mr Smith, slightly skeptical but with a strong heart as I envisage him, and a pensive, mildly rhapsodic twinkle in his eye, perforce more sinned against than sinning at the moment — I wonder what he's thinking. And why he's changed his name. To forget what he was? to be someone new, in the anonymity of a million so-named? to lose himself, perhaps? a true loss in so charming a man, but to each his own.

'But looking at this one, just off the cuff, taking a guess, just a straw in the wind, you know, what would you say?'

'I'd like to hear what the law's saying. What's the law on this?'

'You know perfectly well what's going to happen if you ring up a lawyer and ask him to pop round and see if this man's dead – he'll be out to lunch, he doesn't want to know. Would *you* want a lawyer to decide if you've got a flat EEG? If you were a lawyer would you want to come down from chambers and try to read one of these bleeding things?'

'Well *I* don't want some family taking *me* to court for murder, it'll be panic-stations in the board room, cause an awful kerfuffle, I'm tired of being sued. What does the law *say – at all*?'

Might as well ask what the Church says!'

'What does the Church say?'

'Same as the law. You're the expert. If you say it's so, it's so.'

'What have *we* got to do with it? what can *I* say? You can see with half an eye that all I can ever say is, the man's got this symptom, that symptom.'

'You realize what we're getting into here, don't you?'

'Would you look at these machines? these machines are going along just fine, they're going a treat, there's nothing whatever wrong with these machines – you think I'm going to pronounce death when we can probably keep this laddie ticking-over forever? I'm fed up, if you'll pardon my English.'

'You're fed up.'

'If you can get some lawyer to come in here and tell me that when I say this laddie has this symptom-and-that-symptom I'm saying he's dead, then I'll say he's dead.'

'Are you sure he's got these symptoms?'

'Which symptoms?'

'You know.'

Silence.

Not a word from Mr Smith.

'He might be hibernating.'

'Is he cold?'

'A little. We might have a theoretical hibernation situation.'

'Warm him up.'

'That'll take a little time.'

'If he's irreversible, he's got time. Take the time and warm him up.'

'What about America? Any guidelines out there, of some use — ?'

'They're still arguing.'

'. . . This has really opened things up, hasn't it? It's really a whole new ball game.'

'What do you mean, opened up? It's always been open. Damn it all. One hospital has somebody who can properly interpret an EEG, another hospital hasn't – one hospital has an EEG, another hasn't – one place has a hospital, another hasn't – one doctor has a stethoscope, another place has no doctor; in one place he's a deader, in another he's not – there's only one conceivable condition in which the cleverest Charlies of us all won't still be arguing and killing chaps every day. When death no longer happens.'

'Or when it no longer matters, wot?'

'Staff, warm this man up, there's a good lass; and now Fenton – we'll have a deep brain-probes man in here, and one more independent electroencephalographer, the best, and while we're waiting I want to shoot him some dye up his carotid tree and see if anything's moving at all —'

'Right you are.'

'And then, anyway, there's always the chance of an intercurrent infection —'

'If it is him that's humming in there, and not just the hardware —'

'Maybe pneumonia.'

'To finish things off.'

'To tidy things up.'

Poor drawn, thoughtful Mr Smith, poor devil, let them send for their celebrated wires-man, let them play in their own

193

back yard, don't go under – doctor, lawyer, Indian chief, whatever you are – stretch a point, have a hope – take a page from *my* book.

I'm going to defend Hinkle.
I've felt my own skin – it's happened now once – feeling, moving – it will come again soon, like before only more.
I'm going to defend Hinkle!
Defend him?
Save him.
From the law?
No – all right – it was never the law – from *himself*. Save him from himself! We were wrong, Lench – you and I. It's not to learn something – I'm not what I 'think' – I'm what I *do*. I said Never say die – but I never said *Live*. It's do or die – it's up to *us* now, Hinkle. Stop the rot. You live for a reason, a distinguishable reason, and Hinkle is mine. My cousin, the swine, cocksucking motherfucker that he is, he sticks in my throat, he makes my flesh crawl, but I love him – because he's human, a life, because there *is* this absolute – *a life, human life* – something that won't be belied, qualified – a *life's* something *real*! All my eggs in one basket, Eustace Griffin? you bet your sweet ass!
Griffin, Lench? Hinkle? It's you that's gone lunatic.
Why do I feel Hinkle – that Hinkle's hurting? what is this impalpable untouchable thing – the pain of the others?
Lunatic —
Yes it may be – I'm breaking out. All my life I've chosen to think what was sensible and look where it's got me. I'm going to break out of this round.
You can't.
I can and I – will get up, out of this bed and walk out – now I can do it – get to him, get him out, get him healed – propel myself out, shambling, on knees and hands if you like, to a corner, a thirty-two bus, gaining force by the minute, a Circle Line train to Charing Cross, up the steps, down the Strand, to hell with the crowd, to the gothic-brick building where the

statements are made, into the halls, rise in the lift – with Treeza with me, yes – it can be done – an act of will, *will* is what failed me – it's in my hands – now it can be done!

In their cockahoop doo-da over my erstwhile 'bursts' they've sent down from upstairs for some action. Wheeling me to new rooms, foraging for the fabulous 'key', they beep my scalp with ultrasounds. Think of it man! Life! We'll start afresh, I'll feed you, give you room, give you care, let you *be*, Hinkle. They stick solid items down my bronchia to see if I'll gag. It's about being – the thing that you are, that I am — that from the time I was born I had to be born, that one's a conception devoutly to be wished. X-raying my head they inject dye up the arteries of my throat and watch for it to climb the tree of my brain. To distinguish, to make clear, to make sense of your own person. To *live*!

A delusion, your Hinkle – a *fantasy* —

No 'delusion'! – don't give me that! What fantasy – of benevolence, a beatitude of good works? purgation, redemption – of dying at last in a state of grace? No! a man that insists simply on living in likely shame and revilement – I, me – in the name of life itself – life without warrant, life for its own sake – a living execrated by prosecution and defendant alike – real life, life at all costs.

You, you think you're the first? – caught all of a sudden in the searchlight of your death — ?

My chance – make something of myself – something *real* of myself!

– he's the shadow of your own writhing self-seeking contortions.

He's not – he's solid, alive!

Irrelevant.

That's insane!

He's your shit. The shit of your life —

No!

– intimacy and your horror of it – the shit that you are – he's your *answer* to life —

There now you're wrong!

– that you smear on the face of life —

Caught you – you're wrong!

– ask Treeza —

She doesn't know, Treeza —
– the life you abhor because you're too scared to live it —
Then I must live.
– Treeza knows, Hinkle knows —
I must *live*, to purge the *sickness* of the *waste of my life*!
Aha. So you've dreamt up your cure.
More than that!
You still don't know what you want —
You're like them all —
– You've lost your chance —
– like them all – poor creatures obsessed with the wrong thing.
My cure? what's my body, to cure? It's not my body, my
body's not all – it's desire! My *desire*! My body is *easy* — *look*!
– My wrists, with chilling skin, touch the sheet.
– My elbows . . . and my heels . . . become firm: into the solid
mattress:
Pushing. I lift. I'm rising.
Look!

No one in here. In the room, for this fleeting moment gone
to fetch a thing or two – no one's here, none save the silent
Mr Smith – no one sees!
My energy – this new spring in me – it's dropped away but
it's not a dream, it's real – more – more than before. My senses
live. Too late to mend – ? it's never too late! A parting of the
rain. The streets' shine and steam and the flashing radiance of
the sky. A translucence of bud-bursting leaves, a whiff of
morning coffee, the color-flinging awnings and stalls of fruit
and fish and flowers, a sundrenched beach, her sweet beside
me, the swish and ripple of fresh sheets. Going shopping in a
crunching snow, stirring onions in the pan, working, sweating
by the fire with glancing smiles, speaking softly through the
night. Unknown dogs loping, tumbling, chasing down and
up across the park and lolling grinning in the grass. Waiting,
crystals on the windowpane, the coming thaw.
What lyricism is this? more moments of oblivion?
No! A moment of truth!

◆

'And haven't we started yet?!'

The twinkle of the eyes of the nurse whose name I can never recall is virtually audible. Obviously beaming, she stands there; and again goes away.

Ward aides are staring at Mr Smith, I hear their breathing.

'Whose is he?'

'I'm new here.'

'So am I.'

'No one claim him? what's his tag say?'

'33003.'

'Thirty-three series – new series, that.'

'You know what's coming, don't you?'

'What?'

Mr Smith. Why have I this longing to look at him?

'Well it's up to the rightful owners, i'n'it? Some people'll save anything, really, once they make up their mind to.'

They treat it as routine, the news about Madeley, that – having convulsively refused whatever the Nightingale cure is – he's swallowed fistfuls of something from the dispensary and melted. Occupational hazard, statistically, they say; doctors next after soldiers and police. Guardians of our lives; what do they see that we don't? It appears that the up-and-coming one called Arkwright's to take his place.

In here in the egg, incubating, Mr Smith sweet-mutely apparently sharing with me the slow warmth of his new sunlamp. I hear the nurses working me, sedulously cranking my members – 'Give me his foot,' 'Up with the elbow,' 'What's this?'

197

'It's his – put it back,' 'Mind the thumb.' With unexpected fondness I think of Jim Fitz and all he's taught me. The person before the law; actual persons never die. I know my rights.

They shave me. They leave me days unshorn. They shave me. Be a person for them now.

I lie here, growing stubble, like the earth, slowly growing grass.

Looks are deceiving.

My nature, and it won't come out. Hiding. My life, my death, curled up like a hibernating mole, a dormouse dreaming in me somewhere, and it doesn't come out.

Poor contortionist Hinkle – twisting, calling —

Cat and mouse? And who is the cat.

'He looks sweaty, look, the bugger,' someone whistles near me.

'Shush! you *know* they can hear, even when they're unconscious!'

'The sweaty bugger.'

I fancy I can see, can observe all that goes on around me – only things look abnormally, dismally small, tiny in a distant hospital landscape. I'm mad.

Portrait of an inpatient doing his fruit.

Having agreed, on inspection, that the blood in my retinal vessels is at a standstill, today they've stitched shut my eyelids. It didn't hurt a bit.

Nobody's perfect.

Certain riddles occur; for example: Has anybody seen my ship? Has anybody seen my wife?

Amid the sounds full upon me (shifting, warbling as though through a new, more immediate medium within me, as if the walls themselves have ears) I sense other twinges coming my way. Twinges. Not the pain, please. Not again.

I hear a moment's efficient rustling. No, don't! hell no, don't – I told you, don't —

'Don't do that, Staff!' A shuffling of nearby feet. 'He's not finished yet – take that off!'

'– I'm sorry, Matron – !'

Rustling, as they pull the sheet back down off my face.

'We've got no authority to do that.'

'She's a new girl, Matron.'

'Tsk tsk! What a bloomer!'

'Peekaboo, I see you!'

'I'll have no...bloomers like that...my ward....' Footsteps pitapat away.

Unmoved, I lie still in contracted abandon on my invisible white bed, my precious narrow lair, my raft, my floating aerie.

A new voice draws near. Someone's come to speak to me alone; the flattery of it blushes through my hidden veins; the edge of the bed creaks; he leans and commences to whisper down the channels of my ear things which the tremor of his fevered voice reveal to be things he has longed all his life to find a fitting ear to confide in:

'Balls, cunt, suck,' he says.

You surprise me, I say, sending my whispers back up the channels as best I can.

'Foreskin, boobies, wiggle wiggle, vulva, turd.'

Rough justice, I say but with little effect.

On he goes in the same idiom liberally for some minutes, incoherent, awful, ludicrous, sad, and I perceive slowly (or think I perceive) that this, in fact, was all that Jo Robinson was doing when he said, I don't want to go alone. Saying something which he had wanted to say from the moment he was born, from the instant he was an idea, a twinkle in his mother's eye. The one gentleman's vocabulary only slightly different from the other's.

Whatever the words, our mothers would never have approved.

Is this friendship, then?

Or but one of that array of dark moonless states my dream-like mother spoke of – nights one's to enter, range on serried range, eclipse upon eclipse, alone? It is not true that now here we are, so quickly, easily really, so deftly arrived at the other end of all that. There's always the morning, one can always awaken. It's a piece of cake, life. Could do it standing on my head; may have to; like falling off a log, hardly worth talking about. It's in the nature of things – one always awakens....

Half my old weight I lie coiled in my sweating fetal coma, grinding my teeth and rolling my eyes behind my stitched eyelids in ways only I can feel, making squeaky noises only I can hear.

Body in concrete, mind blowing wild on its tether, bird on a wire.

Somewhere nearby, like myself, Mr Smith is not given to conversation.

Warming up, making ready, getting set —

Holes in everything. I have this terror of a vision. I can see through everything. Things everywhere riddled with holes, holes through which I can see other things riddled also with holes, with daylight. The sponge within me is becoming the sponge without; the world is a sponge. This I take in good part, I'm easy about holes.

The blob brain grows, is swelling prodigiously, I do declare; brimming over like the poor-folks' porridge, the porridge-abounding in the three-wishes tales, bubbling, bulging, pouring out of the ears, the nose, under the door, out at the windows —

Hinkle —

We're in the clearing. I've heard the latest.

Everything's going to be fine.

They're taking up my case at higher levels. We're on our way at last. The sisters are all whispering it, though the doctors seem not to know. There's to be a hearing, for me. We're going to court. Others are to speak out, my part's to be presented, attorneys are putting my side.

Hinkle, I'm coming — !

There'll be Jim Fitz, of course. And Treeza. And Lloyd. And Wall. And Treeza. And who else? Eustace Griffin? Who? who else? *My* side, whichever that technically is, for better, for poorer – Treeza – my side. Intriguing; a real pity I cannot be there.

My jaw is somehow stuck open. So they say – my jaw, quite irrationally, keeps getting stuck expansively open.

You don't get a lot of call for that these days.

Open wide, oopsidaisy? hope to dine again for real? Sing for your supper then curse you, take down your harp from the tree, sing out – how did it go? If I forget thee – If I forget

200

thee, O – what was the bloody song?

Mist, leaking into the spaces between increasingly intolerable spells of lucidity. Lucidity registering the gradual reappearance of dolor; of a throb reasserting itself. . . .

Any messages for me?

She was to 'inquire', the ward nurse, she said she would – how my messages came. What did she learn? Hinting I made them up! what did she find? or did she bother – did she merely humor me? If I could simply ask, I could be simply told —

Me becoming faintly laced with the – you won't let it —

Laced with —

– Pain — ?

Please, if you don't mind, no —

In the rubble of the ancient city the archaeologists found the soil traps where the hero-king's palace had stood. Deep deposits of earth, sunk into the rotten sand; courses of slightly more phosphate earth in the earth of the plain; treasuries of his household's night-soil, undeniable traces, said the chemists undoing the sample bags, of royal human excreta. 'And him?' government officials and journalists excitedly pressed at interviews, 'where is he himself, then — ?' In the last days of excavation, assistants and field-workers struck the great burial-precincts. Having all hands gathered, cutting hurried cross-trenches with spades and trowels, they scoured away the crumbling sand and earth – there are photographs of leading scientists crouching, grinning, pointing – and lighted at last on the stratum, beneath the baked clay inscriptions, where he had been laid. And found – and found —

In a dream, Hinkle comes. Icily he speaks; and not looking at me, looking at no one I can see.

'I never asked to live like this,' he says.

Cerebrally, he speaks, only in the most terrible anger.

201

'I detest you all.'

I shift my place, breathless, listening.

'I am angry that you can make me cry,' he says without moving a muscle of his cankered face. 'Uncontrollably.'

Trembling I listen, inexplicably trembling.

'I am angry that I feel desire uncontrollably. That I feel need, uncontrollably. That you can snap your fingers when I go ugly and naked so, and decide my worth.'

There is a red line, seeping along the space between Hinkle's lips.

'I am angry that I cannot survive, cannot eat, cannot speak without you.'

In his cold face, the red colour is expanding between Hinkle's lips.

'And that with every living breath I must still assure you that I can, dancing and spinning on your high trapeze.'

Hinkle is in a closed room. He is clutching his anger with all his fingers.

'I will never come out.'

In the room, from the mouth of Hinkle's frozen face, bubbles of red, great shining balloons of red are issuing.

'It's me. Poole.'

The voice is the voice of Poole all right.

'I'm here now,' he says.

So you are.

'Not visiting, this time. Seems I'm here to stay. Well, until the good Lord takes me.'

Poole, thumbless Poole, sits evidently down by my bedside.

'I suppose you're wondering who's minding the shop? who's coping with all your affairs?'

Oh yes. Yes indeed.

'As you may have guessed,' he says, 'I've turned the corner.'

Where did he borrow that phrase? This terror – unholy terror that he is – that's my phrase, not his.

'I've turned the corner. The truth is, I've found my Lord,' he says. 'Dying? I'm not really dying. I'm worshipping God.

In the way that He deserves. I'll do what He wants. I'm an altered man.'

I hear his glaciating smile. Holding to stillness in my head.

'Why, I used to believe they all were mad. Always wittering-on about the human condition, and what a treat it was, and what a natural impulse it was to stay alive. But now look at me, I love life now, don't I? can you imagine? I cherish every moment. Isn't it the way, though?'

I can smell him, I do believe, in his musty fugue. Can't they approach his mouth with their swabs — ?

'I take sick, and suddenly I find I'm at one with mankind, I hear the voices of the Lord speaking down here inside me, willing my mortality upon me, ordering me to die, so that I may find the love of life. It's the voice of Man, and the Son of Man speaking you know. In spite of what I may think – you know, in spite of what I "think". Teaching me to love my life.'

Do they drop like flies as he comes near, slithering through the rooms?

'It's what I told Hinkle.'

Yes — ?!

'I'm a changed man, you can see that,' he says. 'One used to believe one was in some kind of hell – a purgatory where everything mattered – or nothing did, I forget – it made you weak to think of it. Now one doesn't have to ask, anymore. Not any more. Because one wants His will to be done. I want Him to do it to me. I want Him to do it to me *now*. I want Him to do it to me a lot. That's why I'm here.'

I hear him blowing his nose.

'He was wanting some kind of help, Hinkle.'

Yes. Yes.

'Young, playing until you dropped, you see –' he says '– that was one thing. Growing up was another. One's better-off here. One never seemed to get a grip of life. One looked deep into it, all right – but one didn't seem to get going. One never got a hold of it. A kind of hell where nothing mattered and there was no way of knowing what to do about it. People that got in the way, people, and things. One used to get tired. Growing up, one got tired, and was afraid of it. I had an awful fear of tiredness. One didn't want to do anything or see anybody that made one feel tired, and everybody made me tired. Pulled apart somehow. Shredded....

'Somebody... when I was small, someone sent me a gift in a box... it was some kind of a toad, or a frog. It came in a box with holes – for air, I guess....

'One didn't *mind* people, really. One had nothing in particular against anybody. Nothing in particular. Only their *running about*. The way people perspired. The way people *cared* so much about things, with such perspiration, and noise, and shouting things, and tittering and cackling, always laughing and crying as if they hurt, and running about, so you could almost see the steam, rising off them, out of their clothes, off their skins —. Only their *life* repels me, nothing more. It's nothing to talk about, nothing to speak of.

'I've heard of a terrible man here, somewhere in this very hospital, maybe you know him? They say they have to *force* him to let them keep him alive. Sick – I hope I never see him. He doesn't appreciate the – the ecstacy that takes possession, that exalts his fellow men, the seed placed in them by God, the magnificent obsession planted there, to seize – to save each other from their deluded egos, to save us for the Lord – to save us from caring for our personal being – one's body isn't all – to save us from ourselves.

'It's what I told your man Hinkle.

'What matters is that He does it. It's in His hands. *We* are innocent. Not that a man like Hinkle can ever care about innocence. It's not up to the likes of him, it's not up to us. We *are all* innocent, you know. It's not up to us to be "pleased". We're His creatures, great and small. What's vile, what's loathsome, it doesn't matter. We're innocent of it all – it's out of our hands. How can we be expected to "like" life? how could we have the *arrogance* to *ask* that it be to our liking? these things are in His hands. He never told us. Some He told one thing, others He told another. Some of us He never spoke to. And why should He? One hasn't the intelligence to understand, it's not in our character, our estate, we'd get it all confused and jumbled up, we are His innocents and He likes it that way, we've only to love Him and do His will and if He wills us to live we live and if He wills us to die we die, and *this* is love, and this love is *life eternal*. No one knows the size of it, that's

204

why there's despair in the world, no one perceives the size of it anymore, no one sees more than the pores on the face of God – it's the beauty beyond the loathing, it's the beauty foaming behind the stench and horror, it's the beauty larger than life, it's the beauty that spans the universe – we are only seeing the sweating, steaming, stinking pores on the face of God. It all comes to One, in God.'

He is hawking and spitting violently in his crumple-wet-sounding handkerchief.

'*This* is why I told Hinkle in that place where they kept him – It doesn't matter. Until I came, he'd really let himself go, you'd shrink to have seen him – all torn up, ugly, awful to see, hungry, I brought him some little things, some cakes – but I assured him. In prison, out of prison, right, wrong, lying or true, I told him, it doesn't matter. But maybe it does, he said, mightn't it? Whatever you do, whoever you are, I said, you'll be absolved, dissolved in God's love. It doesn't matter – and it doesn't matter that it doesn't matter. I *told* him it didn't make any difference – I don't know why he started doing it – it's a weird horrible thing, to stop, in that way. I remember, this box with the holes, that I was sent – it came from Asia Minor, somewhere. The frog, the toad-thing: it wouldn't eat either. I remember, it had a strange, ancient masklike face – but it wouldn't eat, or drink.'

The chill spreading through me.

'It stayed standing on all fours, half-crouched but erect, for days, for weeks, and wouldn't take anything I gave it, and wouldn't move – and it started to shrivel, in the body, and ooze came out of it, red – and I buried it.'

I don't want to hear —

'Was it Hinkle's? whose funeral was it I went to? and the chaplain said how joyously a man is released into the hands of the Lord? It was dreadful to see, the last time, really —'

Don't – don't tell me any more — !

'He – he stretched out his arms —'

– says Poole, hawking and spitting —

'I tried to laugh it off, believe me – I told him: if you want something done right you must do it, you know, yourself. But he only – as if to reach for me — !'

Hinkle!

205

'– you know what a repulsive – how appalling he – as if to hold – to touch me! Say, what are you — ?'

Hinkle!

'– Do you know that you are shivering?'

Hinkle – don't listen!

'Say look at your —'

Don't *hurt* so – don't leave me!

'Don't do that —'

No! No! *Poole doesn't exist.*

'– Don't – that's disgusting —'

'Sister! – another voice – 'get help – patient's blowing — '

'Get someone – what's he' – another voice – 'out! – get! – goddammit – *patient's blowing his needles —* !'

In ghastly spasms my body is throwing, expelling the needles and tubes, showering them in abomination out of their sockets, bubbling holes —

Ghoul! my delirium's ghoul you can't exist — !

Lashed manacled and wrenching to the swinging grate, writhing, thrashing, nails tearing, clawing —

Now in earnest and for real the pain starts —

Deep hammering din, mining and hauling, cleaving through the bowels of earth —

– think – into its maw – *toward* it, through it – trust nature – *the life in your blood* will carry you through – will get you out —

– cleft and riven massive glaring cracking seams coming open, bursting, clashing, splintering apart — look!

Treeza has come.

My wife's come to help – she'll see me through —

'*Help them, can we help them?*' several faces are whispering. What committee is this?

'*You can – you must!*' someone is saying – and it's – yes, it's Treeza – give it to em Treeza! lovely Treeza!

They prowl, like conventioners crowding at a bar, plastic tags on their lapels, signs printed in lunatic Latin – 'Amici Curiae', 'Amici Humani Generis' – whispering together behind the backs of their hands.

'*A child of our times,*' says one.

'*Something's got to be done!*' Treeza says.

And I perceive that this may be a dream, a pain-fainting dream.

'*Mortal man naked and frail —*'
Another of these fulsome dreams.
'*Fighting the good fight —*'
'*Please can't we start again –*' says Treeza '*– I want to start again!*'
'*– We must accompany them to the door —*'
'*It's not enough —*' Treeza says.
'*– Cheer them on their lonely way –*'
'*You don't see!*'
'*– See them properly off.*'
'*I want more!*' says Treeza.
'*These are the great simple eternal truths —*'
'*It's not enough!*' she says.
The ache comes in crescendo.
'Poor damn bloke Wall, he's become obsessed with death.'
Who says? Am I? Who's there?!
Awake.
My jaw stuck open.
Only another dream.
My jaw stuck still open. Air rushing in and out. Sere and roaring up the scorched arroyos, up the stone canyons.
Thanks and praised be – it was only another dream.
'All right-dighty,' someone is saying drily. 'I'm not suggest-ing, but let's see if we can't keep him plugged in this time.'
'Yes sir.'
'If it's not too much.'
Dream gone – bellowing in the dead-end gorges – the pain. It's just one of those things. Now without remission, more's the pity? It's just another one of those things.
Jaw jammed open, torrid, they pour sand, earth into my mouth.
I wouldn't miss it for the world.
I won't go. I'm not going at all.
This pain tells me I'm not. It's the quickening – I've lit upon *the pangs of life*!
Reaching for the vines in the cliff-face within the rock —
Question – keep up the questions – a someone named Poole – was there such a person – here?
Give me a flicker of stillness, just an instant, I'll be fine —
Could Hinkle die? Did Hinkle live?
Was he only me? Did I somewhere, far back, starving in

abyssal waters, fold him, ingest him into the very substance of myself?

– Just a grain of silence from this yawning din —

Am I alone?

'*But why* — *?*' says a voice.

Again, they're back. Treeza and those others —

Clutching hands, vines release, body tumbling away in the dream.

'*Why should any human* –' says a murmur among them '– *how can human beings* — *?*'

Standing about me, in silence, gazing.

'*Why would anyone do such a thing?*'

Something wantonly illicit is invading the phantasmic air —

'*It all comes,*' says one, '*of spontaneous impulse, passion – fruit of passion – natural freedom and pure joy* —'

'*Yes pure!*' says Treeza, '*yes of passion, yes.*'

Something inexpressibly, inexplicably vile, obscene —

'*To spread their seed, their name, their blood* —'

'*Yes, yes,*' she says.

In a spurt, I glimpse something soft, and wet.

'*A live memorial of themselves* —'

'*– Of what they'd wished – what was wanting between them* —'

'*Yes,*' says she, '*to feel alive* — *!*'

'*To hatch something to hope* —'

Flesh... hot meat in a womb, pulsating.

'*Yes – to believe* —'

Or is it a thing... lying in the road....

'*A stimulus for the – a realization of the* —'

'*Yes,*' she says, '*oh yes.*'

'*– A channel – a vessel for* —'

'*Yes yes, oh God yes.*'

'*– The pleasurable excretion of* —'

... Is it a mole.... Is it a man...?

'*– Of tenderness* —'

'*Oh it's good, it's good!*'

'*But wait* —'

... Is it a young man... a man...

'*But wait, is this recreation* —'

... An aging, an aged man, lying in the...

'*Is this by consent of the – of the* —'

'Oh it feels good, it would be so – so good —'
'– Of the created?'
Lying in the road...?
'So good it would be,' she says, *'so good having one —'*
'Having what?' someone says.
'Another one.'
'Another one?'
'Another one!'
I can't make it out —
'But for whom?'
'For me! Another one! If at first you don't succeed! If at first you
don't succeed!'
Words – blank babble – me – what's she want?

The delirious images blister and weep down the igneous walls of my dream and again I'm awake in my fashion, seething, and waiting.

Is death but the voice that asks me the questions to which I give answers whose meanings I can't understand? Collect yourself, fool.

Now through the sound of rotten sand-and-earth burning, history spreads itself before me. What if they hadn't had me? A New Improved History of Humanity, yes – collect and weigh and think: What if they hadn't had to have me at all? The world rolling by, smelting and remolding – the total thing – slumps, jubilations, plagues, restorations, passages of arms, vigils, armageddons, egg-and-spoon races, all rolling on – only: I never showed up, I never was there. A world perfectly free of me. Like a body lanced at last of a pestering boil – a feeling of great release sweeping through – a whole cosmic expression relaxes, a smile of relief spreads over the broad face of creation! He never was! He *isn't.* The doctor pulls off his plastic gloves with a benevolent, radiant smile: a false alarm – a false alarm it was, stand easy, as you were – it never happened, it was all of it – all just a dream!

Hell! what am I saying – ignore it, don't quote me —

Here now, what's this? Orifices, openings uncongenially leaking, iron flowing – I'm getting the bends.

It's still – still never about death. Even now, it's only about *pain.* Clinging to the – gulping down the gall of the —

Pain makes no difference. It can't.

But every little thing makes a difference, you said. Why do you hesitate this time, why parry and shuffle? Why this tremor, looming?

All right; I'll take pain.

As long as you're happy.

Yes that's it – this alone is how I know – this alone is my proof; the pain. Reduced, in elegant simplicity, to this. For the gutting, ruinous reason that I hear myself cry It hurts! – I know that my life is something. That I can *taste* – that I *choose*.

Molten iron coursing, bowels of rock.

I must make myself want pain. To continue to *be* – roll up my sleeves, tear open my shirt – to *be, I must want this pain*.

Think. Listen. Clutch and hear.

On some table, extended.

Phalanx of voices near, thinly, as if through walls of stone.

Don't I remember this one from way back?

Yes sir, he's post-mature.

Shareholder, wasn't he? small accounts, weekend punter, spoke at luncheons? Chap called Smith?

The very man.

Side-by-side with Mr Smith; talk about your krill, this is overcrowding with a vengeance.

Don't I know this one from before Wimbledon?

Great memory, sir. Who ever won that, anyway?

Bloody Swede.

Straight sets?

Yes.

Yes, upstairs we're looking for a new angle on this one, a fresh perspective.

Mr John Smith, reposing on his dais.

Presentation awkward. Seems to have got stuck.
You've the electrodes in place for this test?
Yes sir, cephalic and non-cephalic, all eighteen.

They're not going to make me listen to this – invading the poor joker's private trials?

Deep cranial probes for good measure?
We've drilled in four good ones.
His chemistry's balanced?
Perfect.
Arteriography?
Failed to fill the cerebral vascular tree, sir.

Playing the same games with him as they thought to do with me.

You've considered embolisms up there. There's no fat up there?
you didn't let any air in?
None at all, to speak of, sir.
What do you mean, to speak of? If there's any air, you've killed
him.
None, sir.
His dying score?
Sir?
I say, you've rated his five physiologic functions, by the book.
Certainly sir. Reflex, cerebral, respiratory, circulatory, cardiac –
each ticked with a score – two for presence, one for potential, nought
for absence. Here's his card. You'll see he's got a lot of zeros, there.
Right.
Loudspeaker ping and pong.

Why do I have to hear this – doubling up like this, squalid housing – tactless sons of bitches.

Run at standard gains, ten microvolts per millimetre, forty to five, switching pairs at each shot. Juice up – let's give him ten seconds, to see what's going on. Watch the screen.
Loudspeaker ping and pong.
Isoelectric trace, sir.
Unh-huh. Let's take it to forty seconds. Watch the tape. We can always go to seventy, seventy-five.
Ping, ping.
Nothing, sir.
All right. Seventy-five.
Ping, pong.
How is it?
Straight line, sir.
No pips, no peaks.
No, sir.
Try your noxious stimuli.
Sir?
Your noxious stimuli, Grinstead.
Yes sir.
No nocifensive reactions.
Nocifensive, sir?
No gestures, Grinstead, seeking to fend off noxious stimuli.
Ah! No nocifensive reactions! No sir – not a bit. Absolutely nothing.
Put down 'No nocifensive reactions.'
Sir, is forty microvolts enough? The Times today said Princeton delivers fifty.
All right, let's shoot him fifty.
For good measure, sir. And perhaps eighty seconds, sir?
Fifty at eighty, but that's tops.
Fifty at eighty it is.

Come on man – give them a gesture —

Ping, pong, ping.

212

Grinstead?
Absolutely nothing, sir.
Right. EEG is flat. You've got that Lovelock? Blyth?
Right.
Righty-ho.
Put down: Linear EEG, no evidence of brain activity over two microvolts between electrode pairs ten centimetres or more apart.

John, poor buzzard – have you no feelings?

He's got brain-death syndrome, all right.
I'd go so far as to say it's a notional real death, but that's for you people to say.
Not at all, sir!
Well what do you think, Lovelock? Shall we induce?

Poor lost ape, have you no pain, like mine?

Are you sure?
Dr Wall is crying again.
Who let him in here?
Dr Wall is – ahem – ah – climacteric, you know.
Brace up, Wall.
All right, now what'll it be, then, gents?
Of course, there is the Soulié case.
Yes!... Is there?
– Seventeen-year-old in Paris, patent ductus, had cardiac arrest, complete absence of electrical brain activity on EEG for six days, made total recovery and was last heard working for his baccalaureate.
Still I think we're dealing with a positive artificial survival, here.
The machine is ventilating a corpse, Arkwright.

Mr Smith is indisposed. Intriguing stuff, this, but —

– I'm not sure.
All right, a fetus, but that's tops.

– Making me ill, this talk.

– I'm not sure.
I say induce.

John – I'm not listening – John, come on —

It's the final solution.
– There'll always be Jews, sir.
What, is the man Jewish?
A touch of levity, sir, from Arkwright.
I say that this EEG puts Paid to the whole shebang.

Dizzy, nauseous —

– But that's —
A horse breaks a leg, you put it down; a dog, a bird, a fly's in
misery, you put it down.
– But then —

Sick to the stomach —

Who's got a definite reason not to put this one down, out of his
misery?
– Sir, isn't that like asking What's the definite answer?
Yes, right, certainly, everything's relative; now —
– Not relative, sir —
You're ventilating a —
– Not relative; changing.

Can't you do this somewhere else — ?

All right, now who decides?
– Aren't we always ventilating, sir – us, ourselves – ventilating,
insulating, opening windows, shutting windows —
Arkwright —

There's something going on here —

– Loosening our collars, turning up our collars, pulling up the
blankets, kicking off the blankets – drinking – pissing – eating —
Not to run amuck, Arkwright —
– Shitting —
Dr Arkwright —
– Metabolism – metabolism – not 'completion', not 'final solution'
– converting, changing's the name of the game, isn't it sir?
Quite – but he's – he's got all the symptoms of dying.
– Dying of excitement, dying of thirst, dying for attention, for
love, dying physically —

Something's going on here, something wrong —

– it's all part of it really, isn't it? – it's all part of it.
But dying physically — !
– You're right, he's in an especially tough situation, and that's
why we must really do all we can! I'm sure he is!
What do you mean 'he' is? 'He' is doing sweet fanny adams.
– Sir he may be trying to get out.

Something crazy — Smith —

'He' isn't anything, man – he's nothing, a null and void.
Still, and all, Arkwright may have a point – we could —

215

Good Lord! save a life – does that mean save a vegetable, save a carrot — ?!

Mr Smith, wake up —

A comb through your hair makes more sparks – my Lord, a leaf falling from a tree makes more air than what we're talking about here —
Still oughtn't we – we should —
Grown men standing around going on about a thing like this —
We'll have to —
Pretending 'humanity, more humanity!' this new wrinkle, that new wrinkle – what keeps us from blushing is beyond me.
We must repeat the —
Pretending 'better rules, better systems, better understanding' – red herrings.
We'll have to repeat the test.
– Repeat the test.
Yes sir – after the hearing.
Ping, pong.

Hearing — ?

Hearing. What hearing, Arkwright?
– You can test this man till you're blue in the face and it won't mean a thing, not till the appeal's heard.

Ping pong.

Mr Smith —

You mean some – there's some case —
That's it. Smith and family.

Ping pong ping.

Oh. That John Smith.
Drear name – one of a million – always dreamt of blotting, hiding, swapping it, I —

You've hauled me all the way here — ?
– yes, brother Lloyd, wife Teresa Smith —

It's me.

Blyth, what about this?

Me alone, on the table. Live and learn. Mr Smith is my live body.

– Afraid, sir, there is a bit of a legal flap, touch of a hooha going round, now that Arkwright mentions it.
– If I hadn't 'mentioned it' – you're saying — ?

Just because – got my real name – think they've got *me*?!

It is so hellish unwieldy these days, Arkwright, getting chaps together —
Och!
– things a bit drastic, moral issues, helicopters, unsavoury alternatives, a trifle shambolic – trying for a tight ship —

My flesh that they're weighing —

– at the end of the day, all comes to the same — still, as you say
– quite agree, in the interests of form —
– Wait for the verdict.
With all my heart.
Sister, close the patient's mouth.

The stark-omen mounts up like moonrise —
Live and learn —
It all comes, said Rabbit and Mr Robinson, *of eating too much.*
Plunging in the chutes and rapids
Think. Live and learn. In the wake of the crazed thought –
think —
Have I engorged myself – made a fat surfeit of me? rolling
about in the sweltering womb of my own mind, creating and
eating myself – a natural mistake – am I wrong, should I want
to die? – so engrossed upon the meat-of-my-own-being, too
swollen with ardor and purpose to pass through the narrow
way, to get on with the next business, to clamber up out of
the hole into the air and the light? Too gross to get out? *What
birth is this?*
The tunnel of molten rock debouches, opens spillingly
apart —
Of course, that's it —
The tide gates swing back and open wide
All the people – all – gorging as I have, heaped and pig-
squealing in the same rat-forsaken ark, heeling windward into
the straits —
It's Lever's reef.
No room in the ark?
Water gates gaping wide.
Every mother's son and daughter picking out that sugar-
sweet password for me, prying me open, to shove it on my
tongue: '*It all comes to the same —*'
I won't swallow, I won't say it. Everyone lies.
Run aground on Lever's reef – simply to starve? Is that what
they think? My business here on my flood-isle – to make myself
scarce? Reeling in the eddies, bitter cold. Reeds shrill singing
in the wind. To melt – slip away – to get lost? in the great All
of it all?

218

I won't – you count on it – never!
Twisting, turning
Scared. The running shits. Of what? Heavens! Of what? I
mean, honestly!
  . . . Time, squalls reaching across the waters, hours, days . . .
time blowing by . . . pain, gush of torrent in crying flood, will
wonders never cease?
Scared.
Of pain, scared?
The wail and snarling surf climbing
What then? scream?
Shall I scream my head off? the entire head in steam evap-
orating by noble stages into thin air?
All I've got to do is die, just once, and dissolve you all
forever.
Never fear, I won't, no. Pain? don't be daft. How long can
these things last? A week?
A year?
Years?
You're not going to tell me —
A lifetime — ?
On Lever's reef?
Go on – tell us another! I choose to live this living pain do
you see, that's *my* part, do you understand?
You must – you *will* meet me half way — ?
Life!
Out in the country, in a part of the country somewhere,
where we once passed brief unresolved holidays – in the sea-
sons between shifting seasons; in the valley bottoms, the boles
of the trees at night would lie in a low pool of blinding mist.
The very hand with which you held your lantern here before
you disappeared in the thickness of the fog and you stumbled
and stopped, hesitant in the vanished lane. And overhead, in
the clear black sky just above, the great moon would hang
crystal, immobile, dazzling. You could neither see what you
touched, nor touch what you saw.
The open-torn howling sky
Voices, coming my way.
It's tight. It's getting very tight.
Voices approaching. Cheerful.

The topic plain as day.
The subject, me.
The court's rendered its judgement.
In a minute I'll hear.
In a second, in a nanosecond, I'll know.

A blip on the screen.

A blip on the screen....

In a rush, I see it.
I see me.
Ever, and at best, a pulsing and spoiling froth of sensation.
Moored to the bark of the tree.
My life.
Ever, and at best.
A fleeting hiss of movement and excitation.
A crushed slight membrane – a hot coruscating spatter,
ingesting itself. Protoplasmic, a fizzle of shimmering sensation
– lying empty, then, and still, in the living grass.
One of those burst and collapsed small sacs of guts. Like a
rag, lying in stillness at the side of the road.
A slip of flesh, thinking, feeling.
Thinking? Feeling? Meaning what?
All right – a shred of throbbing matter, contemplating itself
– a mote – looking at itself.
Looking?
Doing *something* to itself. A glimmer of film *doing something*.
Doing?
Living!
Yes, living, certainly. Of course, living.
Well then?!
Living – and dying.
One of those burst and flattened small sacs of mouldering
something, lying shapeless and still, a shrinking stain by the
side of the road.

Outrageous. Not true. Absurd, not true. I'm a victim of someone else's apparitions, not my own.

I want you to know – it is not like this, of course. None of it is like this.

Is it then my only, special gift — to feel – to feel pain and the like – and never move?

Mine? Yours? Whose visions are these?

Think. Try. *Plumb deeper. Dig.*

Crouched in the dust, beneath the clay inscriptions, the directors and diggers working side-by-side uncovered the stratum of earth in which the body of the king-hero had been laid. Whispers were going round. What was it? raiment, regalia, flesh, bones, teeth? The scientists sat back on their haunches and stared. Cameras whirred. Down in the excavated pit, in the swept-smooth acid dirt there was a slight shadow. The trace of a stain, on the smooth-swept earth. The first substance, the first hint perhaps of his topmost garments? The word was passed along in a murmur: *Go down further.* With delicate camel's hair brushes they knelt closer, and slowly dusted more particles back, the faint powder of soil. And stopped, and looked again. The stain was gone.

Vividly I think and hear.

The judgement's rendered.

Clear and bright.

The court has found in my favor. Mine and the family's. There's no cause for surprise, I should have been confident of it from the start. These cases are standard now. Bright and clear. The community is sympathetic, and the patient's family wins. Keen and clear. Certainly Treeza is in no way to be blamed. As clear as day.

The court being satisfied, it directs, without prejudice, that the expert examination be conducted once again.

Good men and true.

And it rules – as a matter of principle and of common decency, in cognizance of past and present suffering and in expression of good faith and appreciation on behalf of the fellowship of humankind – that, should I as plaintiff respond in a suitable manner to this second test, I be granted the requested permission to join the swelling ranks of those who have definitively called an end to the infliction of life-sustaining measures on their own unburied corpses or near corpses at considerable needless expense to families and the many who pay rates.

O Treeza! O old friends!

O pious Primate in your gilded hat, who do you think you are?

They're sending out helicopters now in all directions to locate and book-in the wires man.

◆

The rupturous clap and cloudburst, splitting in me, the forking light, furrowed water gullying, the driving rain
   I'll beat the test. I brace myself. I'll have them now.
   Bleak the horizon of all my foreseeable days if I hold my own – my probable years, my absolute state – and So What? I say, to that. The devil may care. I spit on my hands. One could solemnize on the present occasion, no doubt; beckon and bless friends and beatify oneself with their outpouring confessions of envy, contempt, betrayal, regret, and their prayers for absolution. But not on your life. They have me all wrong. One might think to present a Testament, or Production Finale, nothing elaborate – a few acquaintances filing in review with high kicks – I want to thank my brother Lloyd, I might be expected to say, for sending me gratis to every savant, hawk and dab-hand in Europe, in the world probably; I should like to extend my special gratitude to Sister Dingle and Staff Botham for keeping scrupulously clean all catheters and instruments that entered the lung and so forth. I might be expected then to take my commencement farewells. No chance; not me; I don't whine off from a good fight, I *won't back down*, they'll hear me *speak – I will come out.*
   Seething waves, dragging in the riptide
   Let me love my life. . . .
   Clarity and chaos in overturning swells
   Oh Love, you set me waiting. . . .
   In the distance the white horses, and the break and boom of the endless combers rolling onward

223

I swear there's something more.

Damn, my mind —

As crystalline as that moon above the pooling mist —

I'm a drifting husk, my darlings, gathering my forces, forest of wires sticking out of my bald-shaven head, waste no pity on me. This pleasure I have – this everlasting impression that there is a truth to find – it breathes in my fibre somehow, bred in the bone – it's you I worry about. It's you I fear for. You next. Generations, whispering of Lever's reef.

It's *their* law. It's not mine.

Love of my life, will you come — ?

I'll give them a gesture all right – turn and face them – knees up, tongue out-thrust —

Listen – rumbling – do you hear — ?

'It's time to take the Nightingale cure.'

'Yes, it's time.'

'Repeat after me: "This isn't you." '

'This isn't you.'

' "Not the person we knew and loved." '

'Not the person we knew and loved.'

' "This isn't how you'd want me to see you." '

'This isn't how you'd want me to see you.'

' "This isn't what you would call living." '

'This isn't what you would call living.'

' "You're not here anymore." '

'You're not here anymore.'

' "I feel relieved that we've talked, what they do with your mere body doesn't matter, I feel so close to you now, you know you'll live forever in my heart —" '

'– I can't!'

'You can.'

A burbling sound, wailing —

* * *

224

I grit, I gird, I feel the room, the voices approaching not on foot but, through the pain, swimming toward me. I feel my physician's voice.

Lovely. Lucky really. My how times have changed.
Yes Dr Wall.
None of the usual gripping of the bed, twisting of the sheet with the fingers, screwing up of the face and making ungodly noises.
No, Dr Wall.
A labor of love.... We are making headway...aren't we?
Yes.
All used to think it an occasion of enormous effort and stress, universally accepted, an athletic achievement, demanding strength and persistence. In the order of things. Everyone exhausted at the end....
Yes Dr Wall.

Swept, sweeping, pain beyond the tidal bore. The crush and release, bursting waters, swell of the open heaving blizzard sea
Clean fill, I am. The wrenched dripping tap of my being. Debris falling endlessly
O Jesus.
I'm a bundle of nerves.
Damn, damn me.
But why not? It's a red–letter day.
I can't endure. Won't stay the pace.
Have to. Must muster myself —

You see —
Yes — ?
Nowadays – with lowered lights, tender loving encouragement, everyone quiet as mice – it could be lovely now.
Yes sir. Of course Dr Wall.
None of the classic mixture of grunting and groaning, eyes glazed, skin red and hot, veins standing out.
Yes sir. This one's face is smooth as a pillow – pulled smooth as a sheet.

Open your mouth wide, midwife used to say, and scream.
Sir —
Have you seen any – any contractions?
No, still quite serene, tucking in tight as a sheet.
Open your mouth, now, we'd say, and....

O Christ.
The jig is up.
This – pain – this sea of it — baying —
This is *different* —
This horror
Harrowing apart, gulfs opening
I'm taken by storm.
The jig is up. The jig is up. Not going to pull it off. Not
going to —
Must. Must. Must.
Maelstrom, orbits, spheres
Can't we pretend it never happened?
No! *this is me!* stripping to the waist —
To put on my wish-list: to die?
No – ! I didn't mean it, never – not me!
– But – *is* this me — ? Hoping, praying they get me into
the — ?
No! Never, I never said that – not ever. Stop the rot!
But – yes, I could say – simply – turn me off – and why
not, yes — Give me the strength for one second only, I could
say, to rise up and crush out my crying brain, to pull open
the chest, to rip the slithery bleeding aorta out, loose, free
with my bare hands —
Think not – think nothing of it —
Yes this pulsing froth of film that is me – this festering spot,
this abscess on the skin of existence, this tenderness wit desire
this chancre that's my life – get it off! Let me out!
No – shut your ears – blot your mind – don't listen.
Would you help me? If I needed, would you – it's me in
here —
With this beast, this monster churning, roaring
Me lying still here peaceable and quiet
Splitting, screeching

226

I *could* though, yes – ? I could if I wanted say – yes this —
blistering lesion that I am, this pustule, this pumping throbbing tumor that you call my life feeding, this memory music
laughter this pulsing cankerous blight of my being – heal it!
Yes? cure it, lance it, drain it, drain me, flush me, wash me
fresh and clean away — *Yes?* Let me out one fraction of a
second – let me slash the lines – let me out of this place, let
me go to my place in the gutter — No don't — Let me go to
my vanishing point at the side of the road —

No! Stop the rot! Stop the rot!

Well then, here we all are, aren't we?!
Yes, here we are.
I see you've got it going a treat – where can I hang my coat? –
lungs, kidneys, heart, et cetera – pumping away!
Sweet as a nut, sir.
Smashing gadgets these respirators and things. (Can somebody
take my coat?)
Topdrawer, sir. Absolutely bang on.
All these tubes and things.
Bang on, sir.
If I didn't know better I'd think it was as alive as you or me.
With knobs on, sir! Right as rain.
Well up to the usual standard, Clive.
Pity to turn em off, sir.
Well let's not put cart ahead of horse then, eh? Life's full of surprises.
That's topnotch, sir. Now as I interpret it – where's the page? –
as of the tenth, current, we have to have one of the following combi-
nations – here it is – we need the patient's consultant-in-charge plus
one other doctor, or —
Everybody's here, George. We have Blyth (that'll be me), we
have Lovelock here, we have you sir – will you hold his coat sister
please? – we even have Arkwright and we have Doctor – uh – Wall,
such as it is.
Yes indeed.
So then. The family?
Taken the Nightingale cure.
Certainly. And the Court says we know what we're doing, so we
know what we're doing, and that's it! Are there any questions?

No sir.
Arkwright?
No sir.
Right, then. Shall we give it a go?
Let's give it a fly up the merry old mast.
Right! Testing.
Testing, one two three four.
Shoot!
Ping, pong.
How does it look, then? same as last time?
Ping, pong, ping, pong.
Even less, sir.
What do you mean, Even less – ?
Dr Arkwright?
– Last time you said Absolutely nothing.
Well —
– You mean last time we might have switched him off or something, and he was more alive than today?
With due respect, Arkwright, that's why we didn't turn him off last time and we're here today.
But maybe tomorrow today will look like – what about tomorrow?
I can't make it tomorrow.
I see.
As for me, actually, I've got to catch the three-seventeen helicopter to Woking.
Fact is, sir, we could have spared you – there's been another change.
Balls.
I have it here, British Medical Report thirteen March – the brain – the EEG test – costs et cetera – 'it is now widely deemed needless'.
Balls and all – I could have been playing squash.
Still, better safe than sorry.
So you say.
Shall we try him one more time – just for the form – having you here, and such?
In for a penny in for a pound.
Right. Shoot.
Ping, pong, ping, pong.

Where is your hand?

228

What is this howl —
They think I've crossed the bourn whence no traveller
returns.

Looks to me as though he's crossed the bourn whence no traveller
returns, sir.
I'm afraid so, Clive.
It's the end of his life as we know it.
Gag reflex, nothing.
Must have got depressed.
These things tend to take hold of them when they get depressed.
Suffering from a death condition from which he has failed to make
adequate recovery.
Jelly-like.
Well and truly.
Rome wasn't built in a day.
With things as they are.
My words exactly.
There's nothing for it, I'm afraid.
Exactly.

This *shriek*!
O hell of mercy of reason hear me
Let me go — no – *clarity* – *distinguish* – *I distinguish* – hold
on – hold on –

We come to the crowning moment.
The blessed event.
Total relaxation, release, probably bliss.
Like relieving the bowels.
Exactly.
These people out there, they just don't know how simple *it can*
be to ease human misery.
Deliverance.
Well then – it's nem con, is it?
Shall we identify the body, sir?
Pull back the sheet. You have his admission form?

Yes, there's the mole, just where it should be.
What's that bump on its knee?
Picked it up in some gymnasium, sir – raw and ugly when he was
admitted. Coming along nicely now, isn't it?
Very nicely. And what's this?
His Lulu-doll.
I see. Right then – unanimous, shall we make it?
Unless – sorry about this —
Yes?
– There's no doctor receiving – where's the flaming page – no
doctor receiving organs, here — ?
I haven't the vaguest.
– Because we're not – voting members can't – sorry, sir, it's regu-
lations —
I understand.
Are you getting any organs, Clive?
I'm not, no ta very much.
You, Wall? Wall?
Wring out sponges or flannels in fresh cool water, sister —
Wall —
– And lay them on the forehead, the throat, the lips —
Wall —
– and extra blankets, sister, please – patient may get shivers you see —
Wall –! Stand him in the corner, would you, nurse? Right, then —
(– And sister a hot water bottle please if you can find one —)
Would you stand the doctor in the corner, nurse? thank you. All
right, friends! You see it lying there. Now! What'll it be? Let him
out, then, this one, shall we? Disconnect? Turn him off then, shall
we? Pull the plug? Shall we put him down?

Sure, damn you, curse you — !

No harm in trying.
As it were.

Sonofabitch bastards you'll never dare —

All things being equal.
So to speak.

My mouth! Gagging. My tongue, my mouth
Cleaving still – my tongue – to the vault of my mouth —
Why – can't *remember* – *why* — ?

Well all right, then! Now. Would someone reach me the end of
one of those, please?
Which do you fancy, sir – air? blood? urine perhaps?
As you like, Lovelock – everybody take hold of one, it all comes
to the same thing, really.
Do we actually have to – pull them out *– sir — ?*
Better safe than sorry, Arkwright.
– We do have electronics, sir – all these switches, controls and
things —
It's all right in its place, Arkwright, your fashionable contraptions,
your automation, your cold theories —
– Must we actually pull the plugs out, sir?
A little practical application, Arkwright, classic medicine, touch
of the old elbow grease, back to essentials, earn your keep, show your
stuff.
Genius ninety-nine percent perspiration, Arkwright.
– I feel very uncomfortable about this, this isn't a dog, we're
destroying a man.
Won't be noisy or anything, Arkwright – a bit of a 'pop', cork
out of a bottle, wee extra 'whoosh' and bob's your uncle.
If there is somebody in there this'll get him out, sure as shoot-
ing.
But it's —
Let's have a countdown, shall we?!
I —
I'm game.
– Sister, nurse, hold up a mirror, nurse, for patient to see —
Who's that muttering? Wall? we can dispense with the muttering,
Wall.
(– For patient to – nurse, brush his hair out of his – out of
his —)

231

Wall, would you repress the sloppy muttering.
(– Nurse, brush back his hair please gently nurse —)

In the distance, coming from some distance, nearer and nearer — Austin again. The squealing of Austin's wheels.

Pain raking, blasting, screaming apart the fissures of – of my —

Oh get me into the fire. Into the ground, into the fire, now and for all — no, wait —

In a hut of palings, amid ashes and rotting timber and polished stones, lies a woman wrapped in torn sacking and hides. Her face is blazing white with smeared clay. It is a towering island, and from its midst, streams run down to the sea. Her hair, strangely black and thick, stands on end like plumes; lying poised on the litter of shells, tin cans, and burst open pods, her skin is stained and encrusted with old dried matter, dung, the juice of fruits, cheap salves, the soils and blood of offal. Lynxes and flights of swallows on the glittering cave walls roam in swirls. Her eyes glare out of the starving white clay of her face darkly, decorative and motionless as carved polished stones, vivid, staring.

Rolling.

The roll of Austin's wheels. And... Lench's now, too?

The roll of wheels, gibbering, squealing, whistling by.

Convulsive.

Got to beat them.

Divide them – *I'm a person, a person – stripping bare —*

Between them – drive my meaning – shout – *Break out —*

Prepare to count backward from five to nought, nurse. Can you do that? can you count backward from five to nought, and then we'll all pull together.

232

Mine seems a bit slippery actually sir – could we have a sort of a dry —
A dummy run, why not — ?

One and two and three and —
Pant and pant and Blow and —
Rabbit's friends and relations and Great Primate and all, all
pulling —
Pant and pant and —
If they dared —
Would this be all?
A few streamers...? a drift of confetti, perhaps....
A single hooting horn...?
My open mouth
Tearing
Remember —
This boiling burning sea
Ah – O — !
...Jerusalem!
The *song* — !

Four, three —

The song! I remember — !
The answer? it's a chance!

Two, one and —
– Spot on, sir. Looks a beautiful rhythm.
That's it, Lovelock. Be something to remember —

Got them – at last!
– Oh drown me slaughter me dead and have done.
No – a chance to — Give it a try!

Terrific experience, really —
All ready then — ?

Everybody together in something real and basic!
Prepare to pull —
(Bear down —)
Dr Wall!
(— Now bear down, child — !)
Out of the way, Wall, bloody hell —

Racking – no more – I surrender —

Sir – I can't.
Who said that? – Arkwright?!
I won't do it.

Arkwright – my man! Together —
This roaring – we'll solve this!

Arkwright —
How can we —
Arkwright you will *go on thinking this difficulty is like all the*
other ones, won't you? 'Cure a body – life's the answer.'
But we —
Life is the problem, my friend. Life.

– yes this body – this roaring, let me out —
No – I've the answer — !

But must we – must we actually —
Don't be silly and awkward now — !

Yes oh please let me go —
– No! – turn and face them — !

Five – count Five to nought now sister – ready – steady —

(Bear down! bear down!)

Wait – listen – what —

Five —

WAIT – ! what about my – LISTEN – what about my eternal
– my perfect – what about my IMMORTAL SOUL, goddamn
you!

– Four —

Damn! it all comes of —

– Three —
Who snarled that tube? Prepare to withdraw.

– all — it all comes to —

– Two —
But Pull? *must we —*
Grip his tongue there muchacho, let's have a clear passage.
But we —
That's the trouble these days! with people these days —

– it – I, it —

– One —
– no sense of occasion —